THE
HIDING
PLACE

BOOKS BY HELEN PHIFER

DETECTIVE LUCY HARWIN SERIES
Dark House
Dying Breath

PREQUEL TO THE DETECTIVE LUCY HARWIN SERIES
Last Light

BETH ADAMS SERIES
The Girl in the Grave
The Girls in the Lake

DETECTIVE MORGAN BROOKES SERIES:
One Left Alive
The Killer's Girl

THE
HIDING
PLACE

HELEN PHIFER

bookouture

Published by Bookouture in 2021

An imprint of Storyfire Ltd.
Carmelite House
50 Victoria Embankment
London EC4Y 0DZ

www.bookouture.com

ISBN: 978-1-80019-601-8
eBook ISBN: 978-1-80019-600-1

This book is dedicated to my readers.
Thank you from the bottom of my heart for loving my stories as much as I do writing them. Xx

PROLOGUE

Nine-year-old Charlie Standish's stomach let out a growl so loud it made her giggle. She was starving. Her mum was arguing on the phone with her dad, again, so she shut the kitchen door to block out the noise. She opened the fridge door and stared at the contents with a grimace on her face. Salad: she hated it and didn't know why her mum bothered buying it, because she never ate the stuff and they ended up giving it to next door's rabbit. There was some cheese and a half-empty can of Spaghetti Hoops. She was looking for the leftover pizza; at least she could warm it up in the microwave, if her mum hadn't eaten it all when she was at school. Lifting the corner of a plate she grinned. There it was: the last two slices. She took the plate and put it in the microwave, then spent the next few minutes blowing on it to cool it down, so she didn't burn her tongue.

After eating the pizza, she decided to go outside, away from the shouting. She liked being outside and watching everyone. Her dad called it watching the world go by; her mum called it weird. She didn't care, that was what she liked to do. They could call it what they wanted. Next door kept their rabbit in the front garden. She liked the rabbit and the cat from down the street more than she liked people. Any animal was better than a person, even birds and she didn't really like their flapping wings. She had changed out of her school uniform today because she was going to her dad's and he always made her wear the new, horrid, scratchy clothes that Pippa, his girlfriend, bought for her. She hated them, the clothes, not her dad and Pippa, although she was a bit annoying. The house was too tidy and she wasn't allowed out on their front street, not that much happened because it was the strangest street she'd ever known. The houses were all in a horseshoe shape and the cars had to turn in a circle to get out of it. No one ever wandered up and down Pippa's street like they did here, and the kids that lived there were mean. They stared at her. The kids around here left her alone which was how she liked it. She could play in the front garden or walk up and down the street without worrying someone was going to be mean to her or call her names.

Letting herself out of the front door, Charlie decided to go for a walk and see if the big ginger cat was around. She liked him; he was really ugly in a cute kind of way. As she wandered down the street, she saw her mum come out of the front gate with a wine bottle in one hand – off to Julie's again. She spent more time at Julie's house than she did with her, but Charlie didn't care. Her dad would be here soon. She would see his big, loud black truck drive up and he'd take her away for the night. She spied a bushy tail disappear through the broken fencing of the front garden to the house where it lived and hurried to go see it.

'Chhchhchchhchh.'

The cat stopped, turned to look at her and stuck its nose through the fence for her to stroke. Bending down she began to rub its head and it began to purr as loud as her belly had grumbled, and Charlie laughed. Reaching further in to stroke its back, her fingers trailed along to its bushy tail and she let them brush along it. A sharp, hot pain on her forearm made her snatch her arm away from it. She looked down at the long, thin scratch which was quickly turning red with blood. She hated blood; it was icky and made her legs feel all wobbly. She began to cry. Big wet tears rolled down her cheeks as she stared at her arm.

'Hello, are you okay?'

She looked up to see who was speaking to her, nodding her head slowly.

'Did Tiddles scratch you?'

Charlie held out her bleeding arm. It was stinging so much it felt as if it was on fire.

'Oh dear, she's such a nasty thing. That looks really sore. You better go and tell your mum so she can get it cleaned up.'

'She's out.' Her voice wasn't much more than a whisper.

'Who's at home then?'

She shrugged. 'Nobody, just me.'

'When is she coming back?'

She shrugged again. 'She's gone to Julie's, could be hours. I like your trainers. They're pretty cool.'

'Thank you. Do you want to come inside so I can get that cleaned up for you? You might get poorly if we don't; cats carry all sorts of germs and it could get infected.'

'What's infected?'

'It might go green and your arm could fall off.'

Her eyes opened wide and her mouth followed suit. She didn't want her arm to fall off.

'I'm kidding. It won't fall off, but it might get red and very sore.'

She looked down at the long, deep line of blood. 'It already is.' Then she stood up. 'I don't want my arm to fall off.'

He smiled at her. 'Then you better come inside and I'll get it cleaned up for you. When your mum comes home you can tell her what happened.'

He opened the gate and pushed the wheely bin out of the way that he had dragged down the path to put on the front street.

'I'm not supposed to talk to strangers or go with them.'

'Good, I should hope not. But I'm not really a stranger, I live on the same street as you. Have you seen me before?'

She nodded.

'I guess we're not strangers then if you've seen me before and know who I am.'

She bit her bottom lip, looked up and down the street then at him again. She followed him through the gate, staring at the large, run-down house with a cracked window and the paint peeling from it.

'I'm Charlie. Is your house haunted? Because I don't like ghosts.'

He turned to look at her. 'Who told you that? It's not haunted.'

'Kids at school say it is.'

'Hmm, kids at school say a lot of things that are rubbish. I have some biscuits if you want one.'

Charlie liked the sound of biscuits. She hoped they were chocolate Hobnobs; she skipped the rest of the way along the path to the front door, which was open. He turned to her, lifting a finger to his lips.

'You have to be quiet; my mother is sleeping and we don't want to wake her.'

Charlie nodded. She wouldn't say a word. She just wanted a biscuit and her arm fixing so it wouldn't get infected.

CHAPTER ONE

Detective Constable Morgan Brookes and her sergeant, Ben Matthews, got out of the hire car that Ben had driven to the police headquarters at Carleton Hall in Penrith.

'See, we made it in time, thanks to your speedy driving, and in case you didn't know, you look very smart.'

Ben glanced down at his navy blue suit, and she couldn't miss the tinge of redness creeping along his collar line.

'What this? It's old.'

'Is it? I haven't seen it before.'

'That's because it didn't fit me before. It's been hanging in the bag inside the wardrobe since I bought it. You look very nice too; I like how you have a pair of Dr Martens for every occasion.'

'Thank you.'

'Right, now we've complimented each other are we almost good to go?'

Emily, her neighbour, who lived above in the top-floor flat, got out of the back seat of the car, and Morgan wondered how she could look this damn gorgeous so early in the morning. The three of them were here to receive commendations from the chief constable for their roles in apprehending a serial killer who had terrorised the small town Rydal Falls, where they all came from.

'It's okay, Morgan, you deserve this and I promise it won't be too painful.'

She hated how he seemed to always be able to read her mind.

'Thanks, I'm not sure I deserve a commendation for capturing Taylor Marks, though. It was more a right place at the right time kind of thing.'

Emily was smiling at Ben, and Morgan wondered if there was something going on between them. How had she missed that one? She was glad for him if there was. If anyone deserved to be happy it was Ben.

'Sorry I made you wait so long earlier by the way. My flipping hair straighteners blew up and I had to iron my hair.'

Both Morgan and Ben turned around to stare at her hair. Morgan smiled.

'You could have just borrowed mine instead of risking third-degree burns.'

'You actually used an iron on your hair, like to iron it?' Ben asked, the shock in his voice making Emily's cheeks turn a deep crimson. She nodded. Ben turned back, giving Morgan a side glance, as if to ask if Emily was nuts, which made her feel slightly better.

'Well I think this is a waste of time, not for you, Emily, you deserve it. You didn't sign up to serve your queen and country, but for me and you, Ben, it's just everyday life, isn't it?'

Ben shook his head. 'No, Morgan, it's not everyday life. That's twice now you have been in life-threatening situations, and how many lives have you saved by putting yourself at risk? You deserve a bit of praise. Me, well I'm just clinging onto your coat-tails and taking some of your glory. I've been doing this job a long time and never got into any of the messes you have.'

Morgan let out a long sigh. 'Come on then, let's get it over with.' Unsure of where they were going, she let him lead the way into the maze of buildings to receive their commendations.

*

Morgan took the certificate from the chief constable, shook her hand and forced herself to smile for the photos, then made a quick exit out of the room which was unbearably stuffy.

Ben, who hadn't been able to shake off Emily the entire time, watched her leave. He opened his mouth to speak to her, but she was out of the door before anyone else grabbed hold of her.

This was not her thing, if she was honest. Lately, people weren't her thing either, so combining the two together was bound to result in disaster. She wished she had come in her own car so she could leave, but she hadn't. She was stuck waiting for Ben to finish conversing with the top brass before she could get her ride home. If she'd had the foresight she'd have asked him for his car keys so she could have at least sat in the car. As she walked along the side of Carleton Hall, which had once been a grand residence and now housed Cumbria Constabulary's Headquarters, she shivered. There was a definite chill in the air today. The narrow road which led to the car park had a blanket of red, gold and yellow leaves lining the sides, which she purposely walked through, listening to them crunch underneath her heavy boots. She loved October; it was her favourite month of the year. Cosy candlelit evenings, jumpers, reading, pumpkin spice everything and Halloween. What more could she ask for? Maybe someone to share it with; it had been so long since she'd been out on a date she'd forgotten what it was like.

'Morgan Brookes, is that you?'

The voice called to her from the modern building next to the car park which housed the gym and occupational health department. She looked up and smiled to see Richard, who had trained her when she was a student, waving at her. Crossing towards him she nodded.

'Hello, Richard, how are you?'

'I'm good, you look great and from what I've heard you're some kind of super cop. Congratulations on the commendation by the way. It took me twelve years to get one of those.' He pointed at the certificate she was clutching.

She laughed. 'Thanks. However, I don't think it's because of my superpowers. It's more a case of being a magnet for every disaster that seems to happen.'

'Why aren't you drinking coffee and eating cake with them?' He nodded his head back in the direction of the main building she'd just escaped from.

'I hate a fuss; I'm just waiting for my ride home to tear himself away from them so I can get back to work.'

'Do you want to come and wait in here? It's a bit warmer than the car park.'

Her phone began to ring and Ben's name flashed across the screen. 'It's okay, thanks, Richard. If he takes much longer I'll come back.'

She walked off answering, 'Yes?'

'*The car is open; we won't be long.*'

'Thanks.'

'*Should I bring you some cake back? I'll wrap some up in a serviette.*'

'No, I'm good, thanks. Don't rush on my behalf. I'm okay.'

The line went dead, and she wondered how he knew her better than she knew herself. He'd expected her to bail as soon as she'd got her certificate and she hadn't even known she was going to do that herself. She didn't know if it made him even nicer or just plain annoying. It didn't matter what she thought of him anyway; it was obvious there was something going on between him and Emily. Ben deserved some happiness and Emily was lovely. She got inside the car and lay back against the headrest and closed her eyes. She had a pounding headache. Inside her pocket her phone began vibrating again and she tugged it out.

'I don't want any cake.'

'*What? I haven't got any. Morgan, are you still at HQ?*'

She opened her eyes, realising it was her colleague, Amy Smith, on the other end of the phone.

'Yes, hopefully not for long though. Sorry, Amy, I thought you were Ben, what's up?'

'*There's a missing child, Charlie Standish, and it's possible she's been missing since last night. The mother has only just realised she's not there.*'

'What? How did she not know where her kid was?'

'Exactly, response officers are with her now but she's hysterical and not making much sense. I'm going there, but you and Ben need to come. It's a possible abduction. Can you tell him to come back now? I've rung him but he didn't answer.'

'Yes, of course, we'll be there soon.'

Amy hung up, and Morgan felt a sinking sensation in her stomach at the thought of a missing girl. She was about to ring Ben when she saw him jogging down the road towards the car. Emily was some distance behind struggling to keep up. He threw open the car door and clambered inside.

'Amy.'

'I know, the control room inspector came to tell me. Christ, I hate missing kids. It's your worst nightmare, isn't it?'

He started the car and they drove to pick Emily up, who got in panting. Morgan looked over at Ben.

'They turn up though, don't they? When I was in training, some four-year-old had wandered off and was found at Morrisons by a teacher from his school.'

'Yes, they do.' He glanced in the rear-view mirror at Emily, and Morgan shut up talking, realising this might be highly sensitive information. Ben drove back to Rydal Falls even faster than he'd driven to Penrith.

CHAPTER TWO

After literally throwing Emily out at the end of the drive to her apartment, Ben drove to Cloisters Lane, where they were greeted by what seemed like utter chaos. There were police vans and cars strewn all over the narrow road, abandoned by officers and PCSOs who were now out on foot searching for Charlie. It was procedure to flood an area with staff when a child was reported missing, to help look for them, but if this was a crime scene – and God forbid it was – then they had just well and truly contaminated it. Jumping out of the car Ben surveyed the carnage. Sergeant Paul Madden, or Madds as he was affectionately referred to, was today's duty patrol sergeant. He came striding towards him. Ben held his hand out, pointing to his radio. Madds unclipped it from his body armour and passed it to him.

'This is DS Matthews, can every patrol that is currently on Cloisters Lane come to my car for a quick briefing.'

He passed it back to him. 'Any signs of her? Has the house been searched?'

'Nothing, the house has been searched from top to bottom and the dog has been inside.'

'Attic, cellar?'

'Attic has a small access to it. There are no stepladders in the house. There's no way she could have got up there.'

'Not voluntarily, no, but if someone has put her up there…' His voice trailed off.

'Shit.'

Madds shouted up for someone to find a ladder. Ben waited until everyone was gathered around; he counted six police officers and four PCSOs plus him, Morgan and Madds, and he knew Amy was inside with another officer speaking to the girl's mother.

'Thank you, but if there is no sign of Charlie then we have to do this by the book. I want a scene guard on either end of the street and I want CSI here to do a full sweep of the house. We'll coordinate a search team. I want every single street occupant spoken to and asked to check any outbuildings, garden sheds, garages. We need to narrow down a last confirmed sighting of Charlie.'

He turned to Madds. 'When did she go missing?'

'Her mum left her alone to go to her friend's yesterday teatime, said she was outside playing in the street before her dad was due to pick her up. When she came back a couple of hours later, she'd had a few too many glasses of wine and fell asleep on the sofa.'

'What, without checking on her kid? How old is Charlie?'

'Nine and no, she didn't bother checking on her, because apparently she's a very independent girl who looks after herself.'

Ben felt a white-hot rage fill his chest, and his fingers clenched into tight fists by his side.

'She left her nine-year-old unattended whilst she went to her friend's, got pissed, came home and didn't even think to see if she was tucked up in bed? Jesus Christ, what was she thinking? So much for our golden hour. That passed at least twelve hours ago.'

Madds nodded. 'In her defence, Charlie was supposed to be getting picked up by her father. So far, the dog hasn't picked up anything out of the ordinary. It traced her scent along the entire street outside everyone's house. According to neighbours, Charlie played out most days on her own and was happy to just wander up and down the street.'

Ben turned to Morgan. 'Can you go inside, speak to Amy and see what's going on, please?'

She nodded at him and walked towards the council house with an overgrown front garden full of discarded, broken toys. One half of the street was council houses, then suddenly a bit further down it was a tree-lined avenue of large semi-detached and detached houses.

A police van turned into the street and Cain, the officer driving it, jumped out and went around to the back, where he pulled out a pair of stepladders taken from the caretaker's cupboard back at the station.

'Has the house-to-house been done?'

One of the PCSOs spoke up, 'We started at that end.' She pointed to the opposite end of the street.

'For now, I want a PCSO on each end of the street. Residents can come and go but no vehicles can enter the street and only residents who live here are allowed access. The rest of you start door knocking and checking gardens. We'll take it from there. Hopefully, Charlie will turn up before we need to go back to the station for a full briefing.'

*

Morgan walked inside. It was much better than she'd imagined. It was clean for a start; the laminate flooring almost sparkled it was so smear free. The walls were all painted white: no grubby fingermarks to betray there was a nine-year-old kid living here, and it was surprisingly clutter free. She paused at the bottom of the stairs, inhaling deeply, then went into the living room, where a pale-faced woman with black circles under her eyes, who looked a little older than Morgan, was nursing a mug of tea. Her legs were tucked underneath her on a huge corner sofa. Ben, who had followed her inside carrying the stepladders, leant them against the wall. Amy stood up.

'Boss, Morgan, this is Charlie's mum, Amanda Standish.'

Ben crossed towards her, holding out his hand. She stared up at him then slowly took it. Morgan copied, reaching out to shake the woman's hand. Amanda's fingers were like blocks of ice.

'Detective Constable Morgan Brookes and this is my superior, Detective Sergeant Ben Matthews.'

She realised she didn't actually know what to say to her. What she wanted to say was *What the bloody hell were you thinking leaving your kid alone all that time?* but she couldn't. She didn't want to get off on the wrong foot; all those questions and more would be asked when she was interviewed back at the station.

'I know you've already told officers what happened, but please, can you tell me?'

Amanda looked to Amy, who nodded encouragingly at her.

'I, I had a bit of a falling out with my ex, who was supposed to pick Charlie up and take her to his. He's moved in with his posh girlfriend, so he keeps cancelling and I saw red with him. I told him he better come get her because I was going to my friend's and she was going to be here on her own if he didn't.'

She kept her head low and didn't make eye contact with her. Morgan looked at Amy. Ben had taken a back seat, letting her do the questioning.

'Have we got his details? Did he pick Charlie up?'

'Yes, Brett Mosley and he's been spoken to. He didn't pick Charlie up because he went out for a meal with his girlfriend, Phillipa Summers. Both of them have been spoken to separately and neither of them have seen Charlie since last weekend.'

'Do you believe them, Amanda? Would Brett take Charlie and not tell you, to make you feel bad?'

She shook her head. 'No, he's an idiot but he wouldn't do that.'

Morgan made a note she wanted Brett's house searched and his alibi checked out.

'So, what happened after your argument with Brett?'

'Charlie was playing outside; she loves being out there even in the rain. I was fuming because I love her so much, but it's not easy being on my own with her, and I look forward to a bit of a break when she goes to her dad's. She's a little bit slower than most kids, and she is very stubborn. She likes to wear the same things; she has a wardrobe full of lovely clothes and a brand-new school uniform, but insists on wearing her old one, which is too small and grubby; she says it doesn't scratch her like the new ones do. We argue over it; she looks as if she's a dosser with no one to care for her, but it's not true. The neighbours have phoned the social on me a few times because she's outside in all weathers, wearing those scruffy clothes and never a coat. They think I don't look after her, but I do. I try my best.'

'But you left her alone yesterday?'

'I thought he'd come and pick her up. I asked her when she came home from school if she wanted to come to Julie's with me and she said no. She doesn't like Julie much.'

'Where does Julie live?'

'Around the corner, not far away; three Bay Fell Grove. Julie could see I was upset so she opened a bottle of wine. I only meant to have one or two glasses.' Her voice broke then and she let out a sob. Amy passed her a tissue. Morgan saw movement from the corner of her eye and realised Ben had taken the ladders upstairs to check the attic.

'I'm not a bad person. I made a big mistake last night.'

'I'm not judging you, Amanda. We just need the facts right now so we can try and figure out where Charlie is and get her home safe. We also need a photo of Charlie to circulate to all officers. Have you got one?'

She nodded. Standing up she crossed to the sideboard and opened the drawer. Pulling out a plastic-wrapped packet of school photos and removing a smaller one, she passed it to Morgan, who looked down at it. Charlie looked sullen; her eyes were downcast and the small upturn of her lips looked more like a grimace than a smile; her blonde hair, freshly plaited especially for her photograph, was fraying at the ends and coming loose where it looked as if she'd been playing with it, nervous maybe about having her picture taken. Morgan felt her heart tear a little bit more for this girl.

'I ended up staying and between us we drank three bottles of cheap white wine. I was so drunk, I stumbled home. Charlie wasn't in the street and there were no lights on, so I assumed Brett had picked her up.'

'When did you realise that he hadn't?'

'When the school rang to ask why Charlie wasn't there. I told them she was at her dad's but I would ring and find out. I phoned Brett and his girlfriend answered. She said they hadn't picked her up because they'd gone out.'

'Then what did you do?'

'I panicked. I got up and ran into her bedroom but it was empty, then I checked the house and there was no sign of her. Then I rang you lot.'

Tears were flowing freely now, and Amanda was sobbing loud, hitching breaths as she struggled to control the fear inside her. Morgan glanced at Amy. She didn't get the impression that Amanda was hiding anything; she'd made a bad parenting choice that might affect the rest of her life.

'What about grandparents, friends, neighbours, are any of them likely to have taken her in?'

She shook her head. 'I don't speak to my parents; they live in Morecambe. I would think that if the neighbours took her in they would have phoned you themselves, and then social services. The only friend I have who lives around here is Julie. Oh God, where is she? What if she's hurt, or someone's taken her?'

'We'll find her, I promise you we will find her. Can I take a look around?'

'Help yourself, everyone else has.'

Morgan nodded. She went upstairs to find Ben balanced on the top of the ladder as he began to hoist himself up into the attic. His phone in one hand he turned on the torch and swept it around. Morgan grabbed hold of the ladders to keep them steady.

'Anything?'

'No, there's a couple of cardboard boxes. Hang on, I'll check them.'

His legs disappeared into the hatch and she thought about telling him to be careful, but he'd already gone. She heard him walking around and the sound of boxes being opened. He came back to the hatch and lowered himself back onto the ladders.

'Nothing, some Christmas decorations that's it.'

She whispered, 'There's nowhere to hide a body?'

'No, it's been boarded out but it's covered in dust. There's no smear marks where the dust has been disturbed.'

'Good.'

Ben stepped down onto the carpet. 'What do you think?'

'I think someone has seen Charlie playing out on her own, maybe realised that her mother wasn't in and has taken her.'

Ben nodded. 'Poor kid, she must be terrified. We need to find her.'

Morgan didn't add that she hoped she was still alive. She was praying that she was because the alternative didn't bear thinking about.

CHAPTER THREE

They went back downstairs, where Ben excused himself to go outside and speak to the dog handler. Morgan sat down across from Amanda.

'You didn't find her then?' She spat the words out.

'No, unfortunately she's not here, or hiding anywhere.'

'Why would she be hiding all this time we've been looking for her?' Another loud sob.

'We have to check, Amanda. You wouldn't want her to have somehow climbed up there and hurt herself. You know what kids are like, they get themselves into all sorts of mischief. We can't rule anything out and it's far better to be safe.' She stopped herself from saying 'than sorry,' changing the subject. 'Which school does Charlie go to?'

'Priory Grove, just round the corner.'

'Does she like it there? How does she get on with the other kids and teachers?'

Amanda shrugged. 'Not really, does any kid like school? They're pretty good with her, she can be a bit of a' – she paused as if searching for the right words to describe her daughter without sounding harsh – 'a bit of a madam; she knows her own mind and if she decides she isn't doing something, well then she isn't.'

'So, do you think she would go with a stranger then? How good is she at stranger danger? Does she understand it and the consequences if she did?'

'She's clever, she's not stupid. Just because she's stubborn and has funny quirks about her it doesn't mean she's an idiot. She did a stranger danger course the last two summer holidays on the trot with some of your lot. Keeping Safe, I think it's called. She loved it, even got certificates for it; so yes, she knows the dangers. I wouldn't let her out on her own if she didn't.'

Morgan nodded; she'd never heard of Keeping Safe and wondered who delivered it. She had a gut feeling that despite Charlie's awareness of strangers it somehow hadn't made a blind bit of difference last night. Or, perhaps it meant that whoever had her wasn't a stranger? This brought her back to the list of who she could be with.

'Can you tell me the names and addresses of anyone who visits here, who Charlie knows, even if it's just a familiar face? Do you have milk delivered; is it the same postman or woman; can you think of anyone who she would know enough to think they weren't strangers? Does she have a best friend or someone from school that she might go and see?'

Amanda sat forward, her head shaking. 'No, no, bloody no. I can't afford to have milk delivered; the post is delivered by someone different every day; and she has no best friend at school or out of it. I told you and the other woman, she likes to be on her own.'

Morgan knew she was making Amanda angry but she didn't care. Her kid, her nine-year-old kid, who she hadn't seen since teatime yesterday, was God knows where with God knows whom and she had an awful feeling that something terrible had happened to her, so it was tough: the woman was going to have to answer whether she wanted to or not.

'Is there anyone in the street she knows or speaks to? Could she have run away?'

'Christ! How many times? She barely speaks to me on a good day, and where the hell would she run away to? There's nowhere to go. Stop wasting time and go find her.'

Standing up, Morgan had to get out of there before she said something that wasn't very professional. Charlie sounded pretty similar to herself as a kid; she had been quiet and had had no real best friends until she was a teenager and spent a lot of time on her own. She wondered if this was because subconsciously she knew about her mum and what had happened to her. Had it changed her childhood on some deeper level? Whatever it had been, it had been a pretty rubbish, lonely childhood and she found herself rooting for Charlie more than ever.

Please be okay, kid. Let us find you locked in someone's shed or garage, because us strange kids grow up into pretty amazing adults and you have your whole life ahead of you. It won't always be this way. I promise you it gets better.

CHAPTER FOUR

PCSOs were deployed to knock on all the doors in the street and surrounding streets. Megan and Cathy were doing the odd numbers; Rob and Paul were doing the even. Megan started door knocking at the end of the street with the private houses, Cathy had gone to the opposite end to start with the council houses and they would meet up in the middle. The first two houses had nothing to report and both occupants checked the sheds and garages, coming back to inform her they were empty. She knocked loudly on number eleven with no reply, marking it down in her notebook to revisit. It was a long, slow job but one that needed doing and thoroughly. She carried on along the street. The next house was a little unloved, scruffy compared to the rest of the houses on this part of the street, and the front lawn was overgrown. The gate was broken and she had to squeeze through the gap between the gate and the wall to get inside. Megan figured it must belong to an older person, maybe a widow or widower. It was a shame they'd let it go so much because it was bigger than most of the other houses. She knocked loudly on the door, not really expecting to get an answer, so she was surprised to hear a voice shout, 'Won't be a moment.'

Megan stepped back, not wanting to be too close to whoever was about to open the door. She glanced up and down the street. Her stomach was a mess, churning with worry for the kid. Had someone snatched Charlie away? She had a seven-year-old son who liked to play out in the front garden and she felt sick at the thought of someone taking him away. There was the sound of a key turning in a lock, and the paint-chipped wooden door opened with a loud groan.

'Good morning, officer, how can I help you?'

She jumped, not expecting to see *him* living here in such a large house. He was an odd but friendly man who always stopped to chat whenever he saw her out on patrol. She liked him a lot despite his terrible taste in clothes. Today he was dressed in a pink and purple tracksuit with a flowery apron on top.

She shouted, 'Oh, hello, how are you?'

'Shh, my mother is asleep. She hasn't been very well. Hello, Morgan, how are you? Please excuse the state of me. I'm in the middle of baking some cakes. Mother has a bit of a sweet tooth and it's the only thing that cheers her up lately.'

Smiling at him she nodded. 'I'm Megan and God, I know that feeling. We're searching for a missing child. Do you know Charlie Standish who lives down the street?'

She pointed towards the council house where there was a lot of police activity. 'She's nine years old and has long, blonde hair. Her mum said she plays outside on her own a lot.'

He nodded. 'Does she live in one of the council houses? I know who you mean. I don't actually know her but I see her hanging around sometimes.'

'Did you see her yesterday after school?'

He shrugged. 'I might have; I don't really like kids so I don't take much notice of them.'

Megan nodded. She knew this was true. He didn't have a good time of it, especially with the local teenagers, who called him names. 'Well, if you see her, please can you let one of us know? Have you got any outbuildings, sheds, garages that kind of thing you can check for me, to make sure she isn't trapped inside?'

'There's a shed and a garage but they're both locked up; I don't use the garage. The shed is padlocked. Do you still want me to check?'

'Yes, please. You know what kids are like, they get themselves into all sorts of bother exploring.'

'Yes, I suppose they do. Hang on, I'll go and get the garage keys. You can take a look in there whilst I check the shed. Oh no.' He shrieked and ran towards the kitchen and his burning cupcakes. She heard the clatter of the oven door being slammed shut and a minute later he rushed back to the front door and passed the key to her.

'Sorry, I nearly burnt the house down but thank goodness the cakes are salvageable. Here you go, you check the garage, I'll check the shed.'

He disappeared once more leaving Megan staring after him. She peered inside his house which was not at all what she'd expected. It was very clean and smelt of warm cakes. The decorations were very floral: the walls, rugs and curtains were all a mishmash of every flower imaginable. Walking to the garage attached to the side of the house, she tried the wooden double doors, which were secure. The key didn't look as if it was going to fit this padlock. She walked a little further around and came across an old wooden door. Pushing the key inside she had to twist it with all her might to get it to turn. It finally gave way and she pushed it open. It was dark inside. Shining her torch around, all she could see were some ancient, dust-covered tools, a rusty bike.

'Anything?'

'Oh my God,' Megan yelled. She hadn't heard him come back. 'You scared the life out of me. No, nothing, what about the shed?'

He shook his head. 'Sorry, I didn't mean to scare you and no, the shed is empty apart from the lawnmower.'

'Thanks, it was worth a shot.'

She walked back around to the front of the house. 'Bye.'

'Bye, I hope you find her soon. If you need anything give me a knock. You're very welcome to come and grab a hot drink and a cake.'

With that he went inside the house and closed his front door, and she smiled to herself. He was a bit of a character but kind-hearted.

CHAPTER FIVE

Morgan walked out of the house; the atmosphere inside was awful. She was glad to be outside. Even the cold was better than suffocating inside. She stood at the gate and surveyed the street. *Where are you, Charlie?* Walking along the pavement, she began to look for the house which had been on their patrol strategy when she was a constable out with Dan Hunt, her tutor. It still smarted thinking about him and it probably always would. She tried to find it; there was definitely one around here where an RSO – registered sex offender – lived with his elderly mother who was in the early stages of dementia. The street was in close proximity to a school – too close for her liking – but he had been allowed to move back because there was no one else to care for her.

There was a loud squeal of tyres as a large black truck drove straight through the police cordon and slammed on its brakes outside of Charlie's house. Morgan watched, amazed, as a man in a paint-stained T-shirt and joggers jumped out and ran through the gate into the house. A length of blue and white police tape had wrapped itself around the front of the truck's heavy-duty chrome bumper and was flapping in the wind.

Morgan turned and ran back towards the house she'd only just left. She could hear the man's voice from outside.

'Where is she, Mandy, you tell me where she is?'

Morgan went inside to see Ben standing in between Amanda and the man who she was assuming was Charlie's dad, Brett.

'I need you to calm down, Brett, this isn't helping.'

'Who the fuck are you, her boyfriend? Was she so busy screwing you she left our kid outside on her own again?'

Morgan saw tiny flecks of red appear on Ben's cheeks and realised he was not only embarrassed but getting angry. She didn't think she'd ever seen him react this way since she'd started working with him.

'I'm Detective Sergeant Ben Matthews and I'm leading the search for your daughter. Now unless you have any information pertaining to where Charlie is, I suggest you sit down and answer any questions you're asked.'

Brett was standing in front of Ben with his chest puffed out and his arms bunched. He looked as if he was ready to start a bare-knuckle fight. Morgan slipped between them, and Brett's shoulders relaxed a little.

'I know you must be out of your mind about Charlie, but this isn't going to help find her. We need you to keep calm. Do you know where she could be?'

He shook his head as his shoulders drooped along with his head. 'No, I don't. I've phoned my parents. I have no friends around here who know Charlie.'

Morgan took his arm and walked him to the armchair furthest from Amanda. She pointed to it and he sank down onto it.

'You didn't pick her up yesterday. Did you talk to her at all?'

'No, I didn't. I told her' – he pointed towards Amanda – 'that I couldn't have Charlie last night. We had a meal booked. I bloody knew I should have come and picked her up though, instead of leaving her here.'

He was blinking back tears and suddenly was a shadow of the angry man who had rushed inside calling the shots.

'Where is she? Someone must have taken her.'

'We don't know yet, but we have everyone out looking for her, and the dog hasn't picked up on her scent leaving the street.'

'Well then she must be here still, in someone's house. Have you looked inside them all?' He jumped up again. Morgan could see he'd decided upon a course of action and was going to start demanding to search inside houses.

'We have officers door knocking as we speak,' said Ben.

'Oh, that's okay then. We won't bother going inside and actually looking then. What good is door knocking when someone might have Charlie?'

'I understand how worried and frustrated you must be, Brett, but we can't demand to go inside everyone's homes.'

'Why not? Don't tell me you wouldn't be going inside if it was your kid.' He turned to Morgan. 'I bet you haven't even got kids, you wouldn't know.'

She bit her tongue, telling herself he had a right to be this angry and upset. 'I don't have children and if I did then I probably would feel the same as you, Brett; however, we have to do things by the book. We have no power of entry unless we have evidence to suggest it's to save life and limb, to make an arrest or to prevent a breach of the peace. We don't know for sure at this stage that someone hasn't taken her away in a vehicle. We can't rule that out; it could be the reason the dog hasn't picked her scent up out of this street.'

Ben nodded at Morgan, and they both watched Brett's reaction as he changed from one of obtuse to deflated once more. He turned to stare at Mandy. Lifting his finger, he pointed at her.

'Our daughter, the one decent thing that we ever did when we were together, is missing, Mandy, and it's all your fault. If some weirdo has taken her away in a car then God knows what they've done to her.'

He turned and walked back out into the front garden strewn with a few broken toys. Morgan followed him outside, where he crouched down and picked up a doll missing an arm and wearing only a pair of socks. He pulled it to his chest and let out a cry which was half scream and half wail. She had never heard anything like it and hoped to God she'd never hear anything like it again. She did the only thing she could think of and bent down. Taking hold of his arm she helped him to his feet.

'I promise you, Brett, we won't stop looking for her, we'll find her.' She didn't add that she couldn't promise she would be the same little girl when they found her or even if she would be alive, but she knew that she wouldn't stop until she was back where she belonged.

A family liaison officer arrived at the front gate, and Morgan breathed a sigh of relief. She wanted to be out looking for Charlie not consoling her frantic, warring parents. The thought of a little girl being out there alone, scared and possibly hurt was a heavy weight inside her chest and she would do everything to bring her home.

CHAPTER SIX

Two hours later every door had been knocked on and most of the residents had been spoken to, except a few who weren't in and they were to be revisited later. Ben and Amy had returned to the station. A helicopter from the national police air service based in Lancashire had been scrambled and was currently circling the area with thermal imaging equipment to see if there was any trace of Charlie; the nearest expanse of open fields was a ten-minute walk away, but the River Rothay was only a couple of streets away, and across from the river was the Covel Woods. Morgan hoped Charlie hadn't wandered down to the river and fallen in. She could have been swept away downstream in the blink of an eye in the fast-moving current. CCTV enquiries at shops and houses along the most likely route she would have taken had she wandered out of the street had been conducted, all with negative results.

Morgan drove around to the school Charlie attended. She parked on the narrow side street where the main entrance was, careful not to block the garages of the funeral parlour that backed onto it. What a combination, a primary school and a funeral parlour in such close proximity. She supposed the kids must be used to seeing hearses coming and going but she shuddered at the thought of it. She hated funerals, hated death and the thought of dying, and wondered if this was because she'd had so many close calls with it and lost both of her parents. As she pressed her finger on the buzzer at the entrance to the school, Morgan fished her lanyard out of her coat and held it up in case there was a camera.

'Yes, can I help you?'

'Police, I'm here to speak about Charlie Standish.'

'Just a moment, come on in.'

The door clicked and she pushed it open. The secretary was sitting in a small, square glass office, which was kind of like a greenhouse. Morgan thought it must be hell in the warm weather. Was this to protect her from the kids or angry parents? It looked like something the Pope would take confession in. The secretary, an older woman with a shock of white curls, leant across the desk and slid one of the windows open. Morgan passed her badge to her. She took and inspected it then handed it back smiling.

'Have you found her?'

'No, I'm afraid we haven't.'

'Oh, the poor wee thing. Where can she be?'

Morgan smiled and thought *isn't that the million-dollar question?*

'We have search teams, a helicopter and trained sniffer dogs out looking; I'm sure we will find her soon.' She glanced down and realised that she'd crossed two of her fingers on her right hand.

'Do you see a lot of Charlie? Do you know her well?'

The secretary nodded and pointed to an old church pew with yellow and blue cushions, to match the school colours, outside a door a little further down the corridor.

'I call that Charlie's hot seat.'

'Sorry?'

'It's what the kids refer to as the naughty step. It's outside Mrs Hart's office. We have a few regulars who spend a bit of time on there, but Charlie is the main offender.'

Footsteps along the corridor behind her made her turn to face a woman who must have been almost six foot tall. She was wearing a lilac-coloured trouser suit and smelt of lavender. She held out her hand, and Morgan took it.

'Mrs Hart, head teacher and tamer of wild animals.'

Morgan smiled, and the woman, who had a long, thin face, smiled back with a grin so wide Morgan knew straight away that she liked this woman.

'Should we go into my office? Sandra, I'd die for a coffee. Would you like one?'

'Yes, please I'd love one – milk, no sugar.'

Sandra nodded and slammed the glass door shut with a little more force than was necessary. Mrs Hart led Morgan through the double doors to the office with a big smiley face on them and the words WHAT HAVE YOU DONE TODAY TO MAKE YOU SMILE? underneath it in large, yellow letters. Once they were inside Mrs Hart pointed to a chair, and Morgan sat down.

'Mrs Hart—'

She held up her hand. 'Please, call me Andrea unless you're here to tell me something terrible.'

'Andrea, no it's bad but not terrible. We can't find Charlie, or at least we haven't found her yet, but I'm confident that we will.'

Andrea sat down in the black leather office chair behind her desk and sighed.

'That poor girl, she must be so scared, but I don't understand it. I mean how did her mother not realise she wasn't in her bed? Where did she think she was? Although it doesn't surprise me, which I find more upsetting.'

'Amanda had a falling out with Brett. I take it you know both of Charlie's parents?'

'Very well, although Dad isn't on the scene so much at the moment and Mum is a bit reluctant to engage with us, despite our best attempts.'

'Tell me about Charlie.' Morgan took out her notebook and pen.

'She's a clever girl, but for someone so young she also has very set ways to do things. She won't deviate from what she thinks is the right way to do something, which causes lots of clashes with her peers and teachers. I'm trying to get her assessed. I think she's on the spectrum, but her mother doesn't agree.'

'Why doesn't she agree?'

'She doesn't want Charlie to be given a label, in case she gets bullied. What Amanda doesn't realise, though, is that Charlie's behaviour already causes quite some concern amongst her peers, and I'm afraid that she tends to get left out at playtime because of it. She's very quiet and doesn't mix well with the rest of the class, so they tend to ignore her. Not that they're mean to her, because if there is one thing I do my best to stamp down on it's bullying. In fact, it can sometimes be the opposite: Charlie is the one to upset the others, which is why she gets sent to my office a lot. I asked Mum and Dad to come in for a meeting, to see if we can get Charlie the help she needs. It's scheduled for tomorrow actually. I'd better ask Sandra to cancel until Charlie is home safely.'

'Did Charlie know about the meeting? Do you think she could have been scared and run away?'

They hadn't fully considered this angle: that she might have tried to leave of her own accord and not been snatched at all.

'I'm not sure. I phoned and left messages for both parents. I don't know whether they would have discussed it with her. I don't want to sound heartless, but I don't think she will be bothered about it even if they told her. She's just not the worrying type, which I suppose is a godsend for her.'

'Would she speak to strangers, go off with someone she didn't know?'

'I'd have to say it's unlikely, but she's a nine-year-old child, and no matter how much we think we know someone they can do the complete opposite of what we expect. That's kids in general, though, not just Charlie.'

Morgan smiled. A knock sounded on the door and a red-faced Sandra stood there looking sheepish.

'The milk hasn't arrived yet, and I've just sniffed the one in the staffroom fridge – it's gone sour.'

Andrea closed her eyes, then opened them. Pulling out the top drawer of her desk, she took out a box of lemon and ginger tea bags, holding them out to Sandra.

'Morgan, would you like a herbal tea?'

'Oh, no thank you. I only drink them before bed.'

Sandra took the box and left again. Morgan stood up, passing her a small business card.

'Thank you, if you think of anything can you let me know? Anytime, you can leave a message.'

'Yes, of course. I hope to God that you find her soon.'

'Me too, Andrea. We're doing our very best.'

'I'm sure that you are, thank you, and please pass on my thanks to everyone involved. It can't be an easy task.'

Another tap sounded on the door, and Sandra walked in carrying a mug. She placed it on the desk and then followed Morgan out into the corridor, walking her to the entrance doors.

'I do hope you find her. You know, it's not the first time a girl has gone missing around here.'

Morgan had pushed the green exit button on the wall to leave, but at this she stopped and turned to look at Sandra.

'Excuse me, what do you mean?'

Sandra looked a little too excited for Morgan's liking. 'It was a long time ago and she was a lot older than Charlie, but it's a small town, people talk.'

The tiny hairs on the back of Morgan's neck were standing on end and she felt a chill wash over her body. 'How long ago?'

'Fifteen years or so; I can't remember the exact date.'

'Who was it? Did they find her?'

'Eleanor Fleming, she was a nice girl. Came here then went to Alfred Barrow, in Kendal. She would have been around fourteen, fifteen when she disappeared.'

'Where is she now?'

'No one knows. The police never found her, and it almost killed her mother. The police thought that she'd run away, left to go somewhere a little more exciting. She was always talking about being an actress and said she would leave here as soon as she could.'

'Where does her mother live now?'

'Cloisters Lane or she used to when she attended here. I have no idea if she ever moved or not. In fact, I'm not sure if she's still alive. I haven't seen her for a long time. She became a bit of a recluse after Eleanor disappeared. I see her son though. I think he looks after her.'

Morgan felt as if the breath had just been sucked from her lungs: Charlie lived on Cloisters Lane.

'What's her son called?'

'Elliot Fleming, he was older than Eleanor so he's probably in his mid-thirties.'

Morgan knew that name – why did she know that name?

'You'll know Elliot, everyone knows him. He's a bit peculiar, a nice man, but dresses a bit flamboyant. I think he's a bit confused, if you know what I mean, but he's lovely. I'm sure he'll be able to tell you about Eleanor and if they ever heard from her again.'

'Thank you, I'll go and speak to him.'

'Do you think there's a connection – two girls going missing who live on the same street?'

Sandra was fishing for gossip that she could tell the rest of the teaching staff and probably everyone else she knew. Morgan smiled at her tightly.

'I doubt it, there are significant differences between both girls. It's probably a terrible coincidence. Rydal Falls is a small town. Thank you for the information though.'

The smile across Sandra's lips was huge. She was positively beaming. Morgan pressed the green button again.

Exiting the school, she walked across the empty playground out of the gates, just in time to see the large garage doors at the back of the funeral directors rumble into life and a hearse with a coffin inside begin to drive slowly out of them. She shivered. This was turning into the most surreal and saddest day ever. She needed to discuss the other missing girl with Ben and the team, see if he knew about it and was happy for her to investigate further. Although she didn't think it would hurt if she went and talked to Eleanor Fleming's family before she went back to the station.

CHAPTER SEVEN

Morgan drove back to Cloisters Lane. When she parked the car, she took out her all singing, all dancing Samsung work phone and opened up the quick address system. She typed in the address and the name 'Fleming': number thirteen was owned by a Gladys Fleming, and Elliot Fleming was listed as living there. Ducking under the police tape, Morgan walked down to number thirteen. This house was a bit run-down and she wondered if Gladys had lost her will to live the day her daughter disappeared. She walked up the path and knocked on the wooden door. Moments later it was opened and she realised why the name Elliot Fleming had sounded familiar when he stood there smiling at her. He was a well-known character around Rydall Falls. He seemed to attract the unkind attention of the local teenagers on a regular basis with his love of flamboyant clothes and Morgan had always felt sorry him. He was always so polite and appreciative of anything the police did, unlike a lot of people.

'Good afternoon, is it Morgan?'

She smiled. 'It certainly is. You have a very good memory, Elliot. Can I come in for a chat?'

He beamed at her. Opening the door wide, she stepped into the hallway.

'Would you like a cup of tea and a cake?'

'No, thank you. I can't stay long; I just wanted to ask a few questions.'

'Oh, I've already spoken to Megan. I'm sorry, I haven't seen the girl.'

'This isn't about Charlie. I wanted to ask about your sister, Eleanor.'

The colour drained from Elliot's face, taking his smile with it. He glanced in the direction of the stairs and whispered, 'Please speak quietly; Mother isn't very well. She's been poorly for some time now. I don't think she ever got over the shock.'

'No, I suppose she wouldn't. I'm sorry but did you ever find Eleanor? Did she ever get in touch with you to tell you where she was?'

He shook his head. 'Not a peep. We have no idea what happened to her or if she's okay. I like to think that she's happy, maybe with a family of her own somewhere. Although you would think she'd want to tell us if she had children, wouldn't you? Mother would love to know she had grandchildren to fuss over. I'm sure it would lift her out of this dark fog she seems to live in constantly if she knew that.'

Morgan felt bad for Elliot and his mum. They'd spent fifteen years worrying and never knowing if Eleanor was even alive. 'I can't imagine how hard it must be for you both. Do you remember anything about the police investigation at the time?'

He laughed then cupped a hand over his mouth. 'What investigation? They decided she'd run away to find some fame and fortune, get away from here. End of investigation, case closed.'

'Surely not?'

He shrugged. 'You could ask yourself. Although I think the detective who came around retired a few years ago. Why are you asking this now? It's been so long since anyone asked about her.'

'The secretary at Charlie's school mentioned it. I thought it needed to be looked into in case there were similar circumstances.'

'Eleanor was a teenager, a very loud, popular girl who had a boyfriend a few years older than she was, who moved away to university in London. We think she followed him. I don't think it's quite the same as a little girl disappearing off the face of the earth.'

Morgan sighed. 'No, I suppose not. I'm sorry to have bothered you. Thank you for speaking to me.'

'Anytime, just don't ask my mother. It might tip her over the edge. We don't really talk about Eleanor any more; it's just too painful for her.'

She opened the door. Walking along the path she turned to smile at him, but the door was already closed. It was hard to believe that the police never took it seriously, that a missing girl had been dismissed as a runaway. Surely there were grounds to look into it a little closer. Morgan didn't know why this had been brushed under the carpet, but she was determined to find out.

At the station, she found Ben in his office on the phone. She was about to walk in when Amy shouted, 'Better let him finish speaking to the DCI first, Morgan. How did you get on at the school?'

'How long have you worked for the police, Amy?'

'Too long, why?'

'In years, approximately.'

'Ten years in January, why?'

'Do you remember Eleanor Fleming who went missing fifteen years ago?'

'I know the name; I think it happened a few years before I joined.'

Ben walked out of his office. 'I remember Eleanor Fleming, why are you asking?'

She turned to look at him, praying it hadn't been him who had dismissed her disappearance.

'The school secretary said this wasn't the first time a girl had disappeared, and I thought it might be important.'

'I was just out of my probation period when that happened. They think she ran away, as I recall.'

'Who said that? Did you know she lived on Cloisters Lane, the opposite end to Charlie, in a large, detached house?'

'No, no I didn't. I never worked on it.'

'Who worked the case?'

'Geoff Peterson was the DS at the time. He retired years ago. He was a lazy bastard, old Peterson. The kind of detective that carried a hip flask and openly drank on the job. Where's this going, Morgan?'

'Don't you think it's a bit strange how a teenager from Cloisters Lane went missing fifteen years ago without a trace and now we have a missing nine-year-old from the same street?'

'It's a small town, and that's a popular area. It's just a coincidence.'

'Yes, but two girls have gone from it. Don't you at least think there could be some kind of connection?'

'Not really. Look at the difference in ages for a start. I know that the area was searched. I remember the flyers we put up and the newspaper articles appealing for information. We got a few of her friends that came forward and they all said the same thing: she didn't like living here and wanted to get away as soon as she could. She had a boyfriend who moved away to uni; they think she followed him. Morgan, there was nothing to suggest any foul play. Whilst I applaud your tenacity and determination one hundred per cent, we haven't got the time for you to get sidetracked with this. We need to focus on finding Charlie, not waste precious hours on a wild goose chase from fifteen years ago.'

She didn't answer him. Although she didn't agree with him, she respected him as her supervisor, and he was right: Charlie was their priority at the moment; but it didn't mean that she couldn't do some digging around to try and find Eleanor Fleming in her own time, did it?

CHAPTER EIGHT

Morgan was pacing up and down waiting for Ben's next decision. Ben was back on the phone to the duty detective, Detective Chief Inspector Claire Williams at Penrith, who was covering Rydal Falls whilst Tom, their DI, was on holiday. Morgan was hoping he was telling her about Eleanor Fleming. Amy came in carrying three mugs and placed one on Morgan's desk.

'Thanks, what are we waiting for, why aren't we out there searching?'

Amy answered. 'Because it's obvious she hasn't wandered off on her own. The dog hasn't picked her scent up. The helicopter hasn't found her yet, although I'm praying to God it does. Now, we need to start treating it seriously like a crime scene and consider that someone has taken her, or worse, hurt her and concealed her body. Sergeant Al McNulty, the PolSA lead and his team, are taking over conducting the search for her now while we look at the criminal angle.'

Morgan sat down and picked up the mug of too-hot coffee that still had black coffee grounds swirling around in the centre. She blew the hot liquid and took a sip because she didn't know what else to do. She grimaced because it burnt her tongue and tasted awful. She needed a decent coffee to keep her going, not this rubbish.

'Have you ever had to deal with anything like this before, Amy?'

She shook her head. 'No, although kids can be a right pain at times. They wander off and don't take a blind bit of notice of their parents' instructions. Yes, we've had missing kids but they normally turn up within an hour of being reported missing. I've never known one to be missing since the night before. I mean it's been what?' – she looked down at her watch – 'It's been nineteen hours since her mum last saw her, and none of the neighbours saw her yesterday or they did but didn't take any notice because she's always in the front street. No one saw anything odd or noticed a strange car or van in the area.'

Ben ended his phone call. 'Offender management have one RSO living in that street, Vincent Jackson. Do we know if he has been spoken to?'

Morgan crossed to the spare desk with the stack of clipboards on it that had the names and addresses of everyone who had been spoken to. 'What number is he at?'

'Number sixty-eight.'

She found the relevant clipboard and flipped the sheets of paper over.

'Male occupant spoken to, elderly mother asleep, has Alzheimer's; she wasn't spoken to; garden and greenhouse negative.'

'Who spoke to him?'

She looked at the collar number at the top of the sheet of paper and recognised it. 'Cain.'

'Can you get hold of him, Morgan? Amy, can you go and speak to Intel and get me his full records? I vaguely recall him but I'm sure he was arrested for having an interest in children under the age of sixteen, not under the age of thirteen.'

Morgan had to stop herself from saying Eleanor Fleming would have been the right age for him, but she didn't want to annoy Ben; however, she would bear it in mind. Amy disappeared to go to the floor above them, where the intelligence office was situated. Morgan tried ringing Cain's police radio and then his phone – both of them rang out.

'I'll go back to the scene and see if he's still there.'

Ben nodded, cupping his hand over the mouthpiece.

'Morgan, can you go and speak to Vincent anyway? See what you think of him.'

She nodded as he began talking down the phone to the Lancashire control room about the helicopter search, so Morgan left him to it.

Cloisters Lane wasn't as busy as before. The road was still sealed off at both ends and PCSOs stood in front of the police tape.

'Excuse me, Morgan, can I talk to you?'

She turned around, not recognising the male voice calling her name.

'Who are you?' she asked the man walking towards her. His smile was warm and he had a perfect set of white teeth. As he got closer, his brown eyes crinkled as he smiled. Damn he was good looking, or was it that smile that was? His head was shaved and she could see the ends of a tattoo poking out from underneath the sleeve of his white shirt, which looked as if it was far too tight the way it clung to the muscles on his chest. If Morgan had been asked to describe her ideal man, this was pretty close to what she would have said.

He held out his hand. 'Finley Palmer, I'm a reporter for the *Cumbrian News*.'

And just like that her fantasy was broken as she felt the smile on her lips turn into a sneer without even trying.

'Hey, I'm new around here. You at least have to cut me some slack on account of that.'

He was right, she supposed she should.

'What do you want, Finley? I can't discuss what's happening here. You need to contact the press office if you want an update.'

'Call me Fin, Finley is my Sunday name. I know, I have a copy of that, I just wanted to say hello and tell you I think you're awesome.'

Morgan hadn't been expecting that and she burst into laughter. 'Oh right, well thank you.'

'I mean it. I was looking into your background and what happened with the Potter case, then the killer cop and wow, I mean wow. I saw you got a commendation, congratulations.'

She felt herself becoming suspicious; he was good, very good. He'd almost thrown her off guard with the flattery, but he was a journalist so here it came.

'I wondered if we could talk; go out for a drink or some dinner.'

'Talk about what? You have the official press release.'

'About you and what happened, not necessarily for the paper. But the Taylor Marks case is going to be massive when it goes to trial; the whole story is crazy.'

She nodded. 'Crazier than you could ever imagine.'

'Right, it is. I wanted to write an article from your angle; you know, all the public and tabloids are going to focus on him. I don't think they should. I mean why should he get all the publicity? I think it's about time they focused on how amazing you are, or your team, I mean, not just you.'

His cheeks were much pinker than a few moments ago, and it struck her he was embarrassed to be asking her. Morgan realised that she actually liked him and his idea. Why should Taylor bask in the limelight for his heinous crimes? Not that she wanted any glory for doing her job, but she found the idea a little tempting.

'That's really kind of you, but I don't know if I'd be allowed to talk about any of it, especially not before it goes to court. Thank you for asking though, I really appreciate it.'

She smiled at him, turning to duck under the tape.

'Wait.'

She stopped and turned back to face him.

'How about we just go for a drink anyway? I'm new around here and don't really know anyone. We don't have to talk about any of that. You can explain to me how to fit in, and I'll buy the wine.'

'Are you always so persistent?'

He shrugged and gave her that smile again, the one he must give to every woman he tried to pick up, and she wondered how many of them were able to resist. Then she thought about the last time she'd been on a date, which was like an eternity ago. She didn't want to go home to an empty house after being reminded of how once again she'd been thrust into the limelight to stop a killer. It would be nice to have come company. Why shouldn't she go out for a drink with Fin?

'Okay.'

'Really, you will?' He sounded surprised, but not as surprised as she was at her reply.

'Really, I'll meet you at The Black Dog at eight. Do you know where it is?'

He nodded. 'On the high street. Great, thanks, Morgan, you won't regret it.'

There was that smile again and she grinned back, not sure if this was a date or if he was fishing for something; but as long as she didn't talk about work it should be okay. If he was looking for a story, he'd soon get fed up because as crazy as Morgan's working life was, her home life was the complete opposite; in fact, it was unbelievably boring.

'Bye, I'll see you at eight.' He walked across the car park as her phone began to vibrate in her pocket. She pulled it out to see Ben's name.

'Why are you not answering your radio? Who were you talking to?'

'You're too nosey for your own good. I'm about to go and speak to Vincent. I was talking to a journalist called Finley Palmer.'

'What did he want? For God's sake they're nothing but a bunch of vultures.'

'He wanted to tell me I was awesome actually, and then he asked me out on a date.'

The silence between them spoke volumes. She didn't need Ben's advice or his opinion that it was a very bad idea, but it was coming anyway.

'It's none of my business, Morgan.'

'No, it's not.' She stopped him before he could say anything else. 'I'm an adult, I'm also not stupid. No one has asked me out in ages. I could do with a bit of fun; I'm going stir-crazy working and then going home to an empty flat. Where are you anyway and why are you spying on me?'

She saw his car parked further up the street and watched him get out. He walked towards her, pushing his phone back into his pocket. He caught up to her.

'I'm not spying. I followed you out of the station, but you drove off. I was going to see if you wanted me to speak to Vincent with you and then we could have grabbed a decent cup of coffee before we head back for the briefing.'

'Oh, sorry, thanks, that's great I could do with a coffee, but when we're finished with the briefing and if there's nothing more I can do, I'll go home if that's okay. I'll be back at work tomorrow with a smile on my face.'

'And a hangover.'

'So what if I do?'

'Nothing, just be careful, Morgan, I worry about you.'

'I'm not your responsibility, Ben. You don't need to worry; I'm an adult and I'm fine.'

He held his hands up. 'Sorry, yes you are and you're right.'

As they reached the gate of number sixty-eight, she thought back to not that long ago and being terrified for her life as she ran away from Taylor Marks. Who had been the person she wanted most to come and save her, even though in the end she saved herself? It had been Ben; she'd wanted him to be the one to come along and swoop her out of harm's way. Why though? Because he's someone she trusted or because she liked him a lot more than she should? She pushed those thoughts away, back down to the depths of her mind that they'd surfaced from. She was being ridiculous; they were friends and colleagues, nothing more.

CHAPTER NINE

Morgan used her knuckles to do the honours as she rapped them against the once-white uPVC door, which looked as if it hadn't been cleaned since the day it was fitted. One loud knock, followed by two in quick succession. The door rattled in its frame at the force, and Ben nodded at her. They were on limited time to find Charlie and she felt bad for even agreeing to meet Fin later, but she needed a little time out from all of this, and if the PolSA was taking over the physical search for her then they would be focusing on interviewing everyone who last came into contact with the missing girl. The door opened the tiniest crack.

'Police.'

'Really, with a knock like that it was either going to be you lot or bailiffs. What do you want? I've already spoken to an officer.'

'Yes, you did but that was before we realised who you were, Vincent. So now my colleague and I would like to step inside for a moment and double-check what you told us.'

The door opened wide, and Morgan thought the man standing on the other side could have been a great contender for a seventies porn star. She wondered if he was joining in with Movember then realised it was still October. Ben stepped inside, and she followed him into the narrow entrance hall.

'So, Vincent, can you tell me if you know why we're here?'

He shook his head, a look of disbelief on his face.

'There's a missing kid from up the street and you want to find her.'

Ben looked at Morgan. 'He's good. Yes, we do, we need to find Charlie Standish as a matter of urgency. She has been missing a number of hours now and we're very concerned for her welfare.'

The man crossed his arms. 'She isn't here. I already told you this. How old is she?'

Morgan answered. 'Charlie is nine, and her mum and dad are beside themselves with worry.'

'I bet they are. Is this the kid who is always hanging around on the front street on her own in all weather, with no coat?'

'Yes.'

'Well, why aren't you asking her parents where she is? It's a disgrace; she's always out. Someone needs to be checking them out.'

'You're obviously well aware of the girl then?' asked Ben.

'Bloody hard not to notice her. I live near her and see her when I go in and out, so of course I'm aware of her, the same as I'm aware of the woman next door who shouts at her husband all the time and the bloke over the road who is out fixing cars all hours of the day and night.'

'You didn't take pity on her then and take her in for a bit of food and warmth, maybe offer her a safe place to stay? Although given your past record, I'm not so sure being in your company would be such a safe place to be.'

Vincent's cheeks flushed red and his nostrils widened. He was getting angry with Ben, and Morgan wondered if he was violent as well as a sex offender. Her fingers reached inside her trouser pocket for the canister of CS gas she'd pushed inside it earlier; if Vince so much as raised his hand, she'd blind the bastard.

'Look, I don't like kids.'

'Really, that's not what I heard.'

'I made a mistake. I got talking to some teenage girl online and she was the one who sent photos first. She looked as if she was eighteen or nineteen. How was I supposed to know she was fourteen? I mean how many teenagers look that old? It was an error of judgement on my part and it's ruined my bloody life, so don't you dare come in here accusing me of taking some kid off the front street. Have you got a warrant to search my home?'

'Vincent, who's there, who are you shouting at?'

'I'm coming, Mother, it's nothing to worry about.' He turned to them both and hissed, 'Please, she isn't well, don't go upsetting her. It's hard looking after her when she gets upset. You can go and search the house, then when you're finished you can get the fuck out of here and don't come back.'

'Vincent.'

Morgan looked at Ben, who said, 'Thanks, we'll take a quick look then leave you be for now. Morgan you check down here; I'll go upstairs.'

Morgan walked down the narrow hallway. She looked into the living room, where a woman who didn't look that old was sitting forward in an armchair by the fire, so engrossed in stroking a cat she didn't even notice her. There was no Charlie in there. She carried on, checking the cupboard under the stairs and then the kitchen before making her way back to the front door, where Vincent was standing with it wide open to wait for Ben. He came running downstairs and shook his head at her.

'Why is the room upstairs at the front of the house locked?'

'It's my mother's; she keeps it locked when she remembers. She thinks people come in and steal her things when she's not there. I'll ask her for the key, but if she won't give it to me you'll have to come back tomorrow.'

Ben shook his head. 'Have you got a spare?'

'I did; she lost hers so she has that one.'

'Can you try and get the key, please?'

Vincent swore under his breath. He had turned to go and speak to his mother when Ben's phone began vibrating in his pocket.

'Amy.'

'*Boss, there's a problem with the dad's alibi. I rang the restaurant and the manager said that the couple were so late for their reservation he almost turned them away. Has anyone spoken to his girlfriend without him present? He has a temper, so she might have been scared to say anything earlier.*'

'Thanks, Morgan and I will go there now.' He ended the call and walked towards the front door as Vincent came out of the living room with a key in his hand.

'It's okay, there's been a development but if things don't turn out we will be back.'

Morgan looked at Vince; he could be the right age to have taken Eleanor. 'How old are you?'

'What's that got to do with anything? I'm forty-five.'

She nodded at him then turned and followed Ben outside. Once they were away from the front door she whispered, 'What's all that about? Why didn't you check the locked room?'

'The dad lied to us. I want to speak to his girlfriend. Nine times out of ten when a child goes missing it's not a stranger abduction, and Vince was telling the truth about his conviction. It was for a teenage girl and not kiddie porn. I listened at that bedroom door and all I could hear was the sound of an old clock ticking. I called Charlie's name. If she'd been there, don't you think she would have at least tried to make some kind of sound?'

Morgan shrugged; she would have checked the room and thought he should have too.

'I'll meet you at their house or do you want to come in my car and leave yours here?'

It made sense to go in Ben's, but she didn't want to. She was annoyed with him and wanted some time to clear her head before they spoke to Brett, who was so tightly wound that one turn too far and his head would explode from his shoulders.

'I'll follow you. Where are we going?'

'Number six Cedarwood Grove; it's one of the new houses on the estate by you.'

'I know, I've heard of it.'

Getting inside her car she shivered; it was cold, but there was something more to it than a temperature drop. She had a bad feeling about Charlie and hoped it wasn't some kind of premonition.

CHAPTER TEN

Morgan parked behind Ben's car in the small cul-de-sac which was Cedarwood Grove; Brett's huge pickup dominated the drive outside the house. It was a decent-sized house for a new build; its red brick and white rendered walls with pale green windows and doors were nice, and Morgan wondered what Brett did for a living to be able to afford the mortgage on this place. Ben waited for her, and she felt conscious that they were taking up a lot of room with both their cars and that the neighbours who were home would be curtain twitching, wondering what was happening.

'Have you got cuffs on you, Ben? He's not going to take this lying down, judging by his earlier attitude. I've got my CS in my pocket. What's the plan?'

Ben nodded, pointing to his pocket from which the end of the cuffs was sticking out.

'I'm ready for him so let him kick off.'

She realised he was spoiling for a fight and wondered why he was in such a mood today: was it the fact that a little girl was missing or had her agreeing to go out for a drink with a journalist upset him? She didn't know which it was but one of them had.

'We need to know why he lied, why he was late to that restaurant reservation. If he doesn't give a reasonable excuse then we'll take him down the station.'

'What about his partner, Phillipa?'

'Try and talk to her on her own, if you can. If he won't let you then she can get brought in as well.'

She nodded, wondering how well this was going to go. There was a weird sensation in her stomach and she realised she was feeling uncomfortable about confronting Brett and Phillipa. The sound of Ben's knuckles hammering against the door brought her out of herself, and she stepped up next to him. The door opened and an older woman with long, perfectly curled hair stood there looking at them as if they were mad.

'Yes?'

'Police, is Brett here? We need to speak to him.'

Her hand clasped to her mouth as she gasped and shrank in front of their eyes. Morgan realised she thought they were here to pass a death message.

'We haven't located Charlie yet. We just have a few more questions.'

She took a moment to straighten herself up again. 'Thank God for that, this is terrible.'

There was a genuine flash of pain in her eyes, and Morgan didn't doubt her; she was genuinely upset by the girl's disappearance.

'Please come in. I'm afraid Brett isn't in the best of moods. He's blaming himself for not picking Charlie up – I mean we both are.'

They followed her into the house, which was very white. The walls, woodwork, pale wood flooring all made Morgan feel as if she'd stepped inside a giant marshmallow. She led them into an open-plan lounge-kitchen. At least the kettle and toaster were copper, otherwise how would she find them? There were no toys or books around, nothing to even suggest Charlie stayed here. Morgan couldn't help herself from commenting on it.

'Does Charlie have her own room, somewhere to play? Can we take a look at it?'

Before Phillipa could answer, Brett stormed in; his very presence upset the calmness of the house. He looked them both up and down.

'Have you found her?'

Ben shook his head.

'Then what are you doing wasting your time coming here?'

'Is there something you forgot to tell us, Brett?'

'Such as?'

The atmosphere in the room fizzed with the energy both men were giving off. Morgan had to give it to Phillipa, she looked visibly distressed by it all.

'Please would you take a seat. Can I get you both a drink? Brett, calm down, they're trying to help. I know you're upset but please stop trying to think everyone is out to get you. It's not helping find Charlie, is it?'

Brett stared at her for a second and then nodded. He sat down on one of the white leather sofas. Ben and Morgan took a chair each.

'No, thank you, Phillipa. Why don't you take a seat?'

She did, next to Brett; her hand reaching for his, she wrapped her long, elegant, perfectly manicured fingers around his.

'I'll get to the point. My colleague spoke to the restaurant who confirmed that you did go there, but they also said you were so late they almost turned you away. Would you like to tell us why you were so late and also why you didn't mention this earlier?'

It was Phillipa who spoke. 'It was my fault; I couldn't decide what to wear. I was having one of those fat days where nothing fits and I felt a mess in everything I tried on.'

Morgan looked at the slender woman in disbelief; she had the kind of athletic body she would kill for. It was obvious she worked out, ran, did yoga, probably all three. There wasn't an ounce of spare fat on her, then she realised that she shouldn't be so judgemental. She knew better than most how some days she hated what she saw staring back in the mirror at her. Brett's whole body had gone rigid as he sat straight backed next to her. Morgan couldn't tear her eyes away from their entwined hands, and she noticed Phillipa's fingers squeeze Brett's so hard they went white.

What was she telling him? What unseen communication did they think was going on between them?

'That's it, you were so late because you couldn't decide on an outfit?' Ben asked, struggling to keep the incredulity out of his voice.

Brett glared at him. 'Yes, why is that so hard to believe? It's always like this whenever we go anywhere; Phillipa struggles to believe how gorgeous she looks in anything.'

There was a real moment of tenderness between them when Brett glanced at her and smiled. Morgan felt bad, but she couldn't stop herself.

'Is it okay for me to take a look in Charlie's room?'

Brett immediately stared at her. 'Why?'

It was Ben who answered. 'Look, mate, your kid is missing and we don't know where she is. This is standard police procedure not some manhunt; the quicker we get out of here, the more time we can spend searching for Charlie. Isn't that what you want?'

'Of course, it is. I don't like the way you're blaming me.'

'No one is blaming you, Brett. Why do you have such a guilty conscience? Is there something you need to tell us?'

'Fuck you.'

He stood up and stormed out of the lounge, out of the front door and out to his pickup.

'Is he always so angry?'

Phillipa turned to Ben. 'He's angry because he's blaming himself, and you coming here accusing him isn't exactly helping anything. He wouldn't hurt Charlie; he loves her very much.'

She turned to go upstairs and Morgan followed, indicating to Ben he should wait downstairs. Phillipa led her to a doorway. Pushing open the door, Morgan released the breath she'd been holding when she saw the assortment of toys, books and dolls. She'd had an awful feeling that poor Charlie had to come here and do nothing but blend into the background.

'I know what you're thinking. I can't help it that I like my house to be minimalist and clutter free. She is allowed to make as much mess as she wants in here and, believe me, she does.'

'How do you get on with Charlie? It can be tough taking on someone else's kid, and especially if they need a little extra support.'

Phillipa crossed to the bed. Picking up a large fluffy unicorn she sat down clutching the soft toy.

'I never wanted kids, ever. I like them; I'm just not very good with them. Some people are natural parents, others aren't. I'm afraid I'm not.'

'Do you not like Charlie?'

'I wouldn't do anything to hurt her, if that's what you're asking. I wouldn't say I don't like her, it's just she doesn't like me. She won't do as she's told when it's the two of us; she hates coming here and it's awkward, but I get that Amanda needs a break and Brett is her dad.'

'How about Charlie and Brett, do they get on?'

'Yes, they do. She loves him. I know he's done nothing but be argumentative and aggressive since we found out that Charlie was missing, but he's not usually this way.'

'He was with Amanda.'

'You can hardly blame him. She left Charlie whilst she went to her friend's for a drink and didn't bother to check she was okay until the next day. What kind of mother is she to be able to do that?'

'A tired, stressed one. We all make mistakes, only some of them can be life-changing and the worst decision of your life.'

Phillipa looked at her and nodded. 'Yes, I suppose none of us is perfect.'

'You have a lovely home.'

'Thank you, I work hard to pay for it.'

'Oh, this is your house?'

She nodded. 'Of course, I love Brett but he doesn't bring in enough money to pay for the food and wine bill, let alone the mortgage. His temper gets him into a bit of trouble at work and he has to change companies frequently. He's in the process of setting up his own painting company though, which will be better for him in the long run I think.'

'Is he a violent man? You said his temper gets the better of him. Do you think he'd ever hurt Charlie?'

'God no, absolutely not.'

'What about you? Has he ever hit you?'

There was a pause this time, and it gave Morgan the answer she needed without the woman opposite her opening her mouth.

'No, I wouldn't put up with that kind of behaviour.' As she spoke, the unicorn fell to the floor and, as she bent to pick it up, the side of her shirt rose up. There was vivid blue and yellow bruise mottling the skin on her side. Phillipa saw her staring and quickly tugged it back down. She stood up, placing the soft toy on the bed and walked towards the door. Morgan followed and whispered, 'You can ask for help if you need it. I'm a phone call away.'

She passed her a card with her phone number, which Phillipa took and screwed into a ball, throwing it into a wastepaper bin by the bedroom door.

'Don't be ridiculous, I don't need help from you. I think it's time you both left. I don't expect to see you again until you call to tell me you've found Charlie and brought her home safely.'

She walked downstairs to the front door and opened it wide. Ben, who was standing in the hallway, walked towards it, and Morgan followed. The door slammed behind them, and they were out in the cold and damp, where a fine drizzle had begun to fall.

'Well that could have gone better; I'll see you back at the nick,' Ben said and got into his car, leaving Morgan staring, open-mouthed. She ran to her car, holding her hands over her head before her straightened red hair turned to a mass of frizz.

As she drove back to the police station, she replayed the last minutes of her conversation with Phillipa, trying to understand why she'd got so upset with her and realised she was out of her depth. If Brett was abusing her, there was no way she would ask for help. She was obviously a driven, successful businesswoman who wouldn't want the embarrassment of admitting she was in trouble. But if he was capable of hurting the woman who loved and supported him, what did that mean for his child?

CHAPTER ELEVEN

They met in the blue room back at Rydal Falls police station for a briefing. While the name had updated, the walls hadn't and they were still painted pink. The chief super and Claire dialled in from headquarters in Penrith; Ben, Amy, Morgan and Des filtered into the room. Al joined them; they were waiting on Wendy, who had just finished going through Charlie's house, to make sure there was nothing of forensic value which would tell them a different story to the one given to them by Charlie's mum, Amanda. Wendy rushed in, her cheeks flushed from dashing to get there. Ben smiled at her.

'Wendy, we'll start with you in case you need to leave.'

'Nothing from me. There was no sign of a struggle, no blood-stains anywhere; I didn't find anything of evidential value to suggest something had happened to Charlie inside that house.'

Ben nodded. 'So, we think Amanda is telling the truth? At this moment there isn't anything to suggest she isn't.'

'I would say so, but to be certain I would get Knotty to bring down the cadaver dog, just in case.'

'Good point. There might not have been a struggle or any violence, but she could have snapped and suffocated her in her sleep – no mess.'

Morgan shuddered at the way they were discussing Charlie as if she was already dead. Ben glanced her way, and she put her head down. Her heart felt heavy with sadness for this girl who she didn't know; if she was still alive she must be so terrified.

'We need to be aware that the head teacher from Charlie's school had called a meeting tomorrow with her parents about her behavioural issues. There's the possibility Charlie knew and maybe decided to run away; although I do think if that was the case we would have found her by now. So I think she's been abducted and we should be focusing on that.'

Everyone turned to look at her. This time she wasn't backing down regardless of the looks they cast at each other.

'We're coming to that, Morgan. Thanks for that brilliant insight.'

Everyone chuckled, and she had to stop herself from saying anything sarcastic back at Ben. Morgan continued, 'Surely if Amanda was lying, she wouldn't have admitted to us that she got drunk and left her daughter out on the street playing whilst she was at her friend's, then came home and went to bed without even checking on her. I mean, come on, who makes up lies like that? It makes her look like the shittiest parent in the entire world.'

'First of all we needed to rule out that the home address wasn't a crime scene that we're glossing over because Amanda is a convincing liar. Why not cover up one thing with something so blatantly bad that we wouldn't not believe her?'

Amy smiled at Morgan. She looked away, wondering when she would learn to keep her mouth shut and realised probably never. Someone had to ask these questions, so it might as well be her.

Ben continued, 'The area has been searched by dog and helicopter. Al, what's next?'

'It's too dark for the drone, but we'll launch it at first light. I'm going to be honest with you, Ben, if the helicopter and dog didn't pick up her trail leaving the street, then I think we need to concentrate on that immediate area. We need to physically search everywhere, attics to cellars, because I think she's still there somewhere. My team is getting ready to go back and search every garden. I know we asked the homeowners to check sheds, outhouses, etc., but we need to do it ourselves. I'm hoping that Charlie's neighbours will let us in without too much fuss. If that brings up nothing then she's been taken away in a vehicle. But from what I have now, there is nothing to suggest that Charlie has wandered off of her own accord.'

He looked over to Morgan. 'For what it's worth, I also think her mum is telling the truth and I think she's been abducted, which brings us to known sex offenders in the area.'

He nodded at her, and she wanted to reach across the oval table and high five him for agreeing with her; she smiled instead.

'We know that Vincent Jackson lives in the street with his elderly mother.' Ben paused and Morgan wondered if he was kicking himself for not checking that locked room now, because it was bothering her an awful lot that they hadn't.

'Morgan and I paid him a visit; we did a cursory check of the house but there was a locked room which he said was his mother's bedroom. Before we could check it, we got a call to say that Charlie's dad's alibi didn't work out as he'd first told us, so we left to visit Brett. Shit, Amy, you and Des go back to Vince's house now. I want the upstairs front bedroom checked and see if he has an attic or cellar.'

'Boss, we'll need a warrant.'

He shook his head.

Claire spoke up. 'No, this is on account of saving someone's life. If he has Charlie, she could be in mortal danger. If he refuses entry, which he shouldn't because his licence conditions state he has to let police in any time they visit, then cuff him and read him his rights for obstructing the course of justice. Ben, can you keep me notified of the outcome, do you need me there?'

'I think we're okay this end, Claire, thank you.'

Amy and Des both stood up, leaving the room.

Ben added, 'Brett isn't telling us the whole truth; he's hiding something, I'm convinced of it.'

The door flew open and a red-faced officer gasped, 'They've found a body, a child's body.'

Morgan felt the air leave her; they were too damn late. She wanted to scream in frustration.

'She's in a bad way, ambulance is on the way but Cain has said she's foxtrot. She has a serious head injury.'

Everyone scrambled to their feet; Morgan's hope at finding Charlie safe and well had been replaced with a sinking feeling of impending doom. Foxtrot was the police radio term for deceased.

'Wendy, I need you at the scene; Morgan, we'll go too.'

'What about Charlie's mum?'

The officer spoke, 'We need to know it's her before we let the FLO break the news.'

Ben nodded. 'Yes, maybe give them a heads-up that a body has been found, but don't say anything till we've confirmed the identity. Also, ask control to get me a pathologist to the scene. We'll get there as soon as we can.'

The blue room emptied much faster than it had filled up, and Morgan realised the churning in her stomach had been replaced with a lead fist, curled so tight it felt as if it had her insides clenched within it. It was the worst possible outcome if this was Charlie, not what she'd been praying for at all, and if it wasn't Charlie then that meant they had another dead child. It was horrendous either way. She knew Ben was waiting for her and she pushed herself to her feet, forcing her shaking legs to carry her down to the car. She had to be strong. She'd never wanted it to end like this for Charlie; now she had to focus all her attention on the monster who had committed this heinous crime and skulked away into the night to hide away, before it happened again.

CHAPTER TWELVE

Morgan didn't need directions to Piggy Lane play park. She had spent a good portion of her childhood clambering around the huge square climbing frames that doubled as a fort or castle, and sometimes a spaceship. The slide had been a quest of life and death: if you made it to the top without falling off and breaking a leg it was a miracle. There had been uproar when the council had taken it away because of the sudden health and safety regulations which had been brought in, replacing it with one less than half its size and nowhere near as much fun. She hadn't been here for years but it held nothing but happy memories for her. Ben was sitting next to her in the passenger seat talking to Cain on the radio about the crime scene. *Please don't be Charlie; let her please be okay*, was the mantra she kept repeating in her head. Cain had left his police van parked across the entrance to the small street to protect the scene, and an officer she didn't recognise was standing in front of it.

Morgan pulled up to the kerb; this was a crime scene so she went to the boot of the car to begin dressing in protective clothing. She ripped open a plastic packet containing the white paper overalls for Ben, who was still asking Cain lots of questions, before opening her own. She looked around at the fells that surrounded Rydal Falls. The dying sun cast its glow over them, and they looked magnificent steeped in the rich russet reds, golds and oranges of the changing colours of the lush greenery, signalling that autumn was in full swing and winter was drawing nearer. This was a spectacularly beautiful part of the country, and the contrast between the Lakeland beauty surrounding them and the awful scene she was about to face wasn't lost on her.

Ben ended the radio call.

'I don't understand. She's been gone almost twenty-four hours, so why keep her then dump her body out here when it's almost dark?'

Morgan felt her voice catch in the back of her throat. It was beyond shocking and utterly heartbreaking, not to mention cruel. Ben pulled the zipper up on his suit and reached out his hand, touching her arm, the warmth taking her by surprise.

'I can't even begin to get my head around it. I know this is hard but we have to switch it off, Morgan. You have to concentrate on finding out what the hell happened that resulted in Charlie, if this is Charlie, ending up a couple of miles from her home – dead. If you'd rather sit this one out, I can ask Amy to come and take over.'

'No, I don't, thank you. I want to be here to help Charlie, I'm okay.'

'Good, because I need you.'

He walked towards the officer who was clutching a crime scene log, and she whispered, 'What is that supposed to mean, Ben?' Pushing it to the back of her mind, she followed him, wrestling with the nitrile gloves that didn't want to go onto her cold fingers.

Ben rustled towards the officer. 'Where did you find her?'

She pointed to a huge oak tree; the only one along the entire road that hadn't been chopped down.

'She is directly underneath that, Sarge. We think it's Charlie. She looks like the girl in the photograph that was emailed out to everyone.' Morgan couldn't miss the look of distress etched across her face as she spoke to them.

'Any blood, visible forensics you could see?'

'Nothing, just the girl. She had a bandage around her head but it was seeping with a brownish liquid. No pools of fresh blood.'

Morgan looked at the tree then turned away. Hot tears were filling her eyes far quicker than she could blink them away, and it took everything she had to stop herself from crying out loud. Taking a deep breath, she whispered, 'This is a dump site, not the primary scene. There won't be much here, Ben.'

He nodded in agreement. 'I know, but why here? Who rang it in?'

'A woman walking her dog; she lives three doors down that street. I told her to go home and you'd speak to her there. She was looking a bit peaky.'

'Was she on the pavement or in the road?' Morgan asked so she could mentally prepare herself for what she was about to see.

'On the pavement, but very near to the road.'

Wendy arrived and began to haul the pop-up tent out of the back of the van. It was cold but thankfully it wasn't windy. As they waited for Wendy to erect the tent over the body, they stepped onto the pavement, a little bit closer.

Morgan turned and looked in Wendy's direction, her heart racing. She didn't want to look but had no choice. Ben followed her gaze and they stared at the small, lifeless shape lying on the floor, her blonde hair stuck to her head. Morgan could see something around her head; from where they were standing it looked like the kind of sports headband tennis players wore.

Ben spoke. 'He was trying to shelter her from the rain, so he put her under the tree. He also put her on the pavement so she wouldn't get run over by another vehicle. What does this tell you?'

'That he felt bad. He didn't want any more harm to come to her but wanted someone to find her. This is only a couple of miles from her home; the helicopter scanned this area repeatedly. There's a nursery that also has an after-school club a bit further up; kids come out anytime up until five, so he didn't do this very long ago.'

She stopped talking and turned around slowly, surveying the area and surrounding cars, to see if there was one with its engine running or if there was a shadowy figure sitting still in one of them.

'Ben, he could still be here, watching to make sure she was found.'

Both of them looked up and down the street. There were some cars further up but they couldn't see anyone.

'Why would he take her, hurt her, then leave her like this in the open for someone to find her? Who would do something like this?'

'Someone who cared about her and didn't want to get arrested for it. She has a head injury. What if Brett accidentally knocked her over yesterday and panicked. He could have put her in the back of his pickup and left her there; the back was covered earlier. Knowing we suspected him of something, he could have brought her here so we'd find her.'

'I like that, it makes sense. It would explain how she left the area without a trace, why he was so late for his reservation and why he wants to fight the whole world whenever we mention it. Hopefully, we'll find something that links him to this place. I want the whole area canvassed, every house, garage business along that road.' He pointed to the street opposite with a row of houses on one side. The other side was an assortment of commercial garages, lock-ups, waste land and a couple of allotments. 'We need every resident asked if they saw a pickup truck matching the description of Brett's in the area in the last hour.'

Wendy came back towards them. 'There's practically nothing of forensic value; it's a pretty clean scene. I can't say about the body, that's down to the pathologist, I'm just telling you my first impressions. Is there one on the way? The paramedics called it, but we need a forensic pathologist.'

Ben nodded. 'One was requested earlier; they should be on their way. What about oil on the road, tyre marks, could this have been a hit and run?'

She shook her head. 'This wasn't the scene of an accident. There're no fragments of broken glass, fresh blood or anything to suggest it was. She was left here by someone; the primary scene is somewhere else. As awful as it is, this was just the body dump.'

Both Ben and Morgan nodded. 'Yeah, I figured it was worth asking. And I was hoping you'd found something that was so good it would lead us straight to whoever did this.'

Wendy smiled at Ben. 'I do love your optimism and endless quest to believe that our suspects are so stupid to leave us presents that will send them directly to prison. Keep on dreaming, Ben, it's kind of cute. But you and I know that most criminals are experts on forensics now, thanks to the television.'

Morgan managed a half smile when she saw the wounded expression on his face.

'I'll go and speak to the woman who found her.' Crossing the road, she heard the sound of Ben's heavy footsteps behind her.

They knocked on her door, and Ben whispered, 'It's always the dog walkers; we wouldn't find most of our missing persons or dead bodies if it wasn't for them. Poor bastards, imagine coming home from work to take Scamp out for his teatime poopsie and you find a dead girl under a tree. It's enough to put you off ever walking the bloody dog again.'

Morgan looked at him. 'Poopsie…'

The door opened before she could finish her sentence, and both of them were surprised to see a woman standing there in a bright yellow onesie; she looked like a giant canary.

'Come in, I'm assuming you're the coppers.'

They nodded.

'Poor kid, how is she, have you heard anything back yet?'

They stepped into the narrow hallway which led straight to the staircase, and Morgan glanced at Ben, realising they were going to have to tell her she wasn't alive.

'It's not good, I'm afraid. Thank you for calling it in.'

'No worries, I couldn't have left her there. To be honest, I thought it was a dummy at first, or that kids had made a guy and were messing around.'

Morgan asked. 'A guy?'

'Penny for the guy, you know, a stuffed Guy Fawkes. We used to make one out of our dad's old clothes, stuff it with straw and drag it all over the place. The corner shop was the best place to go with it; we'd sit outside and ask everyone who went in or out, penny for the guy. Have you never heard of it?'

Ben nodded; Morgan shook her head.

'Blimey, I'm showing my age.'

Ben smiled. 'No, you're not. Morgan here is still practically a kid.'

He saw her turn to glare at him and shut up.

'Sorry, we didn't introduce ourselves. I'm Detective Constable Morgan Brookes and this is my colleague, Ben Matthews.' She purposely didn't introduce him as her superior just to piss him off. She had no idea why he was being an idiot to her today, but two could play at that game.

'Can you talk us through what happened?'

'Not much to say really. I got in from work around twenty past four and always take the dog out before I do anything. We didn't get very far before I noticed the figure lying under the tree. I'm too nosey for my own good, so I walked that way and as I got closer I realised it was an actual kid. My heart dropped so quick, I felt sick. I ran towards her whilst phoning an ambulance. It was pretty obvious there was something seriously wrong because she wasn't moving. I actually thought she was dead. It was horrible, the poor thing. I hope she's okay. I don't think I'll ever get her face out of my mind again.'

Welcome to my world. Morgan stopped herself from saying it out loud.

'That must have been an awful shock for you. Did you notice anyone in the area? Was there anyone hanging around, any cars with their engines running, that kind of thing?'

She shook her head. 'To be completely honest, I was too busy panicking about what to do with the girl. The ambulance person on the other end of the phone was amazing. He kept talking to me and told me what to do; he was so nice.'

'What did you do?'

'Not much. I bent down to see if she was breathing, and I think she was, but it was hard to tell, and I didn't actually touch her to see if she was because I was panicking. The 999 guy told me to not disturb her because I told him she was already lying on her side. It looked as if she'd been knocked down, but the weird thing was she had a bandage on her head. Who would do that if you run someone over? And don't get me wrong, it's easy to do around here. There are so many kids who play out and run across the road without giving it a second glance; I can't tell you the number of times I've nearly hit one of them. But if I did, I wouldn't bandage them up and leave them unconscious then drive away. That's cruel, isn't it?'

'Yes, it is. If when you're thinking about it all later and something comes back to you that you'd forgot about, could you give me a call? It doesn't matter what time of day or night. If I don't answer, you can leave me a message. That would be great.'

Morgan fished the last card out of her pocket and passed it to her.

'Of course I will. I hope the little girl is okay and you catch the bastard who did this to her.'

Ben spoke. 'I'm sorry to have to tell you this, but she's dead.'

'Oh, no.' The sound came out as barely a whisper and tears began to roll down the woman's cheeks.

'You did everything you possibly could have, thank you, but we think she may have been dead some time. Please keep this to yourself until the family has been notified.'

This time it was a gasp that came from her throat as her hand flew to her mouth and she nodded her head. Ben walked out of the front door before he got caught up in trying to comfort her, and Morgan followed; they simply didn't have the time – they had a killer to catch.

CHAPTER THIRTEEN

Macy Wallace knew she shouldn't be out so late, but she was hungry and she had found a quid down the side of the sofa when she'd been digging around for some money. She shouted at the small black Echo Dot on the kitchen window, 'Alexa, what time is it?'

'*It's 7.25 p.m. I hope you're having a good evening.*'

'Thank you,' Macy shouted back. She spoke more to the piece of plastic than she did her mum who was never here. Her mum worked long hours at the bingo hall in Kendal, or so she told Macy, who was sure she stayed at the bingo after she'd finished work because the wine was cheap and it meant she didn't have to look after her. Macy didn't care; she could look after herself. At almost eleven years old she was practically a teenager. She didn't need anyone to make her tea or wash her clothes; besides, her mum was a rubbish cook. She burnt toast every time, and her pizzas were so hard they could be used as a deadly weapon. After spending the last five minutes searching through the kitchen cupboards for a biscuit or piece of chocolate, she'd given up and begun hunting around for some cash. All she wanted was a bar of chocolate. She loved chocolate, it was her favourite, and she would live off it if she could. Even the cheap, smart-price chocolate would do; breaking off a piece of chocolate one square at a time and then letting it melt on your tongue was the best way to eat it. Just thinking about a bar of Galaxy was making her drool like her dog.

Grabbing her hoody off the coat rack she tugged it on. It was dark outside and Max, who was a Labrador cross, was whining at her to take him out. She might as well walk him to the shop; at least he'd get a chance to do his business and she could go to bed without him pawing her until she got dressed and took him out. Clipping the frayed rope-lead to his collar, she grabbed some poop bags and shoved them in her pocket. She hated picking up the poop, but she didn't have the money to pay the fine if she didn't and her mum said it would come out of her pocket money. Macy hadn't pointed out that she never got pocket money, but instead took it to mean that even the crappy presents she got for her birthday and Christmas would be stopped until the fine was paid.

Macy opened the front door, and Max dragged her towards the gate. She pulled the door shut but didn't bother locking it. They had nothing worth stealing, and she didn't have a key to get back in because she wasn't supposed to leave the house once it got dark. The floor was damp and the moss on the path made it like a skating rink. She skidded to the open gate and was glad to step out onto the cracked paving stones. She tutted when she saw the police tape still across Cloisters Lane; that meant she had to walk the long way around and it was raining.

At school they'd been talking about the missing kid. Macy felt bad for her. She didn't know her to speak to, but she saw her a lot. Always on her own, a bit like her really, but Macy was too shy to talk to her and besides, she was much younger than she was and she didn't want to risk the other kids being mean to her for hanging around with a Year Five. School was tough enough without that.

Macy reached the alley which ran between this street and Friars Lane, where the corner shop and her much-needed bar of chocolate were. The alley was in darkness and she wondered if she should risk walking through it. It occurred to her that someone had taken that missing kid and maybe walking down an overgrown, dark alley when she wasn't allowed out of the house might not be the best idea she'd ever had. Even though her mum wasn't around to tell her off if she found out about it, she'd be in big trouble. She sighed and carried on walking; the end of the street looked a million miles away. Max was happy to be walking; his tail was wagging. He would follow her anywhere, and she reached down to pat his head.

At the shop she tied him to the railing outside. There were a couple of boys from the year above her arguing a bit further down, and she quickly went inside before they noticed her. She didn't want to have to talk to them. She just wanted her chocolate and to get home out of this drizzling rain. The shop was quiet inside. She grabbed her bar of Galaxy and passed her quid over to Karen behind the counter.

'Hey, Macy, how's things?'

'Better when I get to eat this, Kaz.'

She laughed. 'Life's always better with chocolate.'

Macy grinned at her and slipped outside. The boys had moved a little further down the street. She untied Max and shoved her most prized possession in her pocket with the poop bags and began to run back home. Her mum would go mad if she got back and she wasn't there. The rain was getting heavier; she would be soaking wet by the time she walked all the way around. She reached the overgrown alleyway, did a quick check to see if anyone was around, then ducked into it. The street lights which usually lit it up had been smashed; her mum had said it was so the dealers didn't get seen doing their business. Macy had no idea what this meant, but she took it that whatever it was they did must be bad if they didn't want to get seen. Despite being streetwise and knowing just about everyone who lived around here, her heart was racing as she pumped her legs and ran down the narrow, rubbish-strewn path. Max's legs were galloping so he could keep up with her. As she turned the corner she could see the street lights on Cloisters in the distance. The police were still there so she was safe. What she didn't see, because it was cloaked in the shadows, was the broken slab of paving stone which was sticking up at a funny angle. Her foot hit the corner of it with force and she felt herself flying through the air. She windmilled her arms and legs to try and save herself from falling flat on her face, but only managed to propel herself forwards with even more force, and she hit the floor with a loud thud and felt painful stinging as the rough paving ripped her black leggings, grazing her legs. She hit her head and knocked herself sick. As she lay there panting, dazed and her legs feeling as if they were on fire, a voice asked, 'You okay down there, kid?'

She couldn't answer, the pain was too hot and she'd managed to wind herself, and to top it all off there was no sign of Max. She must have let go of his lead and the little traitor had carried on running, leaving her in a heap on the floor. Through the hot tears that were filling her eyes, she saw a dark figure towering over her. They were tears of pain, humiliation and fear that her mum was going to kill her for ripping her leggings and losing the stupid dog.

CHAPTER FOURTEEN

Morgan stared at the white pop-up tent and blinked; every now and again a bright flash illuminated the inside of it. A 4x4 engine roared behind them as it drove into the street, making her turn to stare, as for one awful moment she thought it might be Brett, Charlie's dad. She relaxed to see it wasn't his black pickup. It was either the chief super or even better, Declan, one of the two home office forensic pathologists who covered this area. As it got closer she was glad to recognise Declan's white Audi and felt a little better that from now on Charlie was going to be in the safest possible hands. He got out and waved at her. She waved back, heading in his direction.

'Well if it isn't Morgan Brookes. Where's that devilishly handsome but grumpy sergeant of yours?'

She pointed in the direction of Ben, who was on his phone to someone she assumed was the duty DCI, judging by the number of 'yes sirs' he'd said in the last couple of minutes.

'Is it the missing girl?'

She nodded. 'It seems so, though we haven't had a positive ID yet – but we're confident that it's Charlie Standish. Poor kid, it's so sad and horrific.'

'Kids are always tough, far tougher than anyone else. Even I get blurred vision when it's someone so young. It's hard to keep the injustice of it all from taking over everything.'

He zipped up his overalls and bent down to slip the shoe covers on.

'But you don't, you manage to keep a clear head and not let any preconceived thoughts cloud your judgement.'

He straightened up. 'Yes, I suppose I do. I have to, my role is to look for the clues, the evidence and find the answers as to why a young girl has ended up on my cold, lonely steel mortuary table. Then I hand everything over to you guys, to help you find the monster that did it. We work as a team, to bring justice to the dead, and we're a pretty good one if I do say so myself.'

Morgan nodded. She still hadn't taken a close look at Charlie's body and didn't know if she wanted to or ever would. As if reading her mind, Declan pointed in the direction of the tent.

'Should we get this done so little Charlie can be moved to a safer place than this cold, unforgiving street?'

She suddenly found it hard to swallow; a lump the size of an egg had formed in her throat and she couldn't answer him.

'It's okay, she needs us now and we are the best people to take care of her. You can do this, Morgan; I know Charlie would like you to be the one to help her. If it was me lying there, I'd want you to be the one fighting for me, because I know you wouldn't stop until you caught whoever had done it.'

He ducked under the flapping police tape then held it up for her. Ben had finished his phone call, and he watched as she led Declan to the tent. He slowly followed behind, giving them a little bit of a head start.

*

'Knock, knock.' Declan softly spoke through the closed entrance of the tent, and Morgan watched as the zipper was slowly tugged down so they could step in. Wendy's eyes looked all watery, and her normally rosy complexion was paler than Morgan had ever seen. She stepped to one side to let them in: Declan first and then Morgan. Morgan's eyes fell to the unmoving figure on the floor, and a wave of sadness for Charlie Standish – so powerful it almost sent her to her knees – washed over her. The sight of the little girl, with the bloodstained, grubby bandage wrapped around her head, with her eyes half closed, was something Morgan knew she would never be able to forget. Declan stepped forward, placing the heavy briefcase he carried on the floor.

'Well, Charlie, this is a terrible thing. I'm very sorry that you have been left here on your own like this. I'm Doctor Declan and from now on I'm going to take very good care of you, sweetheart.

'I'm going to take a little look at you now, and then I'm going to take you back to the hospital so I can take a better look and find out who did this to you. Then Morgan here is going to find the person that did and put them in prison for a very long time, aren't you, Morgan?'

She still couldn't find her voice to speak, but she nodded furiously.

Declan stood up, opened his briefcase and began to do a preliminary examination of the body.

'Look at the shape of her head; there's a significant injury there, though I can't say much until I've removed the bandage, but can you see it?'

Morgan nodded. She sensed Ben standing at the entrance to the tent but couldn't look at him. She was a wreck, and she didn't want him to think that she couldn't handle this, because she knew that she could even though the pain of it physically made her heart ache for Charlie and her mum, Amanda, who was going to have to live with this for the rest of her life. Declan worked quickly; Wendy assisted him, passing him paper bags to put around Charlie's hands, to secure any trace evidence there may be under her nails. When he was satisfied he had done everything, he stood up, turning to face them both.

'When you're ready you can have her moved to the mortuary. I'll go back now and get ready. Do you think you'll need to keep her here much longer?'

Ben shrugged and looked at Wendy, who answered. 'Like I said, this isn't the primary scene, it's a secondary one. There is very little evidence I've secured. I'm happy to have her moved if you are. We can keep the cordon on and have the entire area searched at first light.'

'That's fine by me. I don't want her here any longer than needs be. We need to get a positive ID. Even though we know it's Charlie, her mum or dad need to confirm it, and the sooner we get that done the better.'

CHAPTER FIFTEEN

The DCI arrived moments after Declan had driven away. He was on call from Barrow. Morgan left Ben to go through everything with him and began to knock on the doors of the houses nearest to the playground, but they were still some distance away. Only one person answered, and it was an elderly man who kept cupping his hand to his ear and shrugging; even when she pointed to the tent, he shook his head then shut the door. She realised that their killer had chosen this spot for precisely that reason: no overlooking properties or businesses, apart from some run-down garages. None of them looked as if they had CCTV cameras or at least there wasn't anything obvious. The nursery was quite some distance away and set back from the street, so even if the CCTV worked there was a good chance it might not have captured anything other than inside the perimeter of the car park.

Morgan reached the car and got inside, waiting for Ben; there wasn't much else she could do here. She stared at the white tent and the shadows moving around inside. She watched as the DCI, who was much taller than Ben, ducked out of the tent – a well-built man called Johnathan Lowe who used to play rugby up until his wife made him retire after one too many injuries. She wondered how he'd describe her when he thought of her: the rookie with a death wish or the miracle girl who had more lives than a cat? She'd smile if it wasn't so scary and true. The car door opened, making her jump; she hadn't even realised Ben was behind him.

'How are you holding up?'

It was a genuine question and one she would normally answer with good or fine; this time she shrugged and wondered if she'd ever be fine again.

'We're going to see Amanda Standish; the ambulance is going to take Charlie to the hospital.'

'Not the undertakers?'

He shook his head. 'No, the paramedics agreed they would take her. I don't want her to be on her own in the back of a private ambulance, zipped into a thick rubber body bag. We owe her more than that.'

'Yes, of course. That's nice of them. What about the evidence though?'

'She's been tightly wrapped in a sheet to preserve any. Wendy will supervise and sit with her and Cain in the back of the ambulance.'

'Oh, that's good.'

He got inside the car and waited for her to start the engine. She did, feeling as if she was on autopilot and not really with it.

'Ben.'

He was staring at the ambulance which had backed up to the tent, ready to take Charlie to Declan. Realising Morgan had said his name he answered, 'What?'

'Never mind.' How could she tell him she didn't want to be the one to break the news to Charlie's mum? Someone had to do it, and she couldn't let him do it alone. She wasn't a coward, but the thought of telling Charlie's mum that her daughter was never coming home filled her veins with iced water.

'What about Brett? It seems pretty convenient that he stormed out of his house earlier after we spoke to him and not long after Charlie turns up.'

'We need to process his pickup, but before we can do that we're going to have to get a warrant, and I don't know if the judge will sign it tonight. We have no real evidence to say he has anything to do with this, apart from the fact that he lied about being late and is an arsehole.'

'Maybe we should let him go see Charlie, have someone keep an eye on his movements. If he suddenly begins to power-wash the truck, bring him in?'

Ben nodded. 'I'll go to the hospital; you can go home after we've spoken to Amanda if you want.'

Morgan was aware of the time, it was way past seven and she felt bad because she'd told Fin she'd meet him for a drink at eight – but how could she go home now, she needed to see this through – maybe she could meet him later, because by the time this was over, she was going to need a stiff drink.

'I'm good, thanks. I'll come with you to the hospital.'

Ben opened his mouth, then closed it. Whatever he had been about to say stopped in its tracks. She set off driving in the direction of Charlie's house. Just a few streets before she reached it, she pulled over, slamming the brakes on and jumped out of the car. She couldn't stop the bile that had been slowly burning its way from her stomach up her oesophagus, and she leant into the bushes at the side of the road retching. Her legs wanted to fold in on themselves and she wanted to sink down on the cold, damp grass. She was finding it hard to breathe and could hear the small gasps coming out of her mouth. The passenger door opened, and she felt her cheeks burning as much as her mouth with shame and embarrassment. Tears were freely flowing down her cheeks at the horror and injustice of it all.

'It's okay, take your time.'

She couldn't even look at him. She was an emotional wreck not to mention ashamed for crying in front of him. Morgan didn't do crying in public much – this was as much as she gave.

'It's normal, everyone expects us to be hardened to it, professional, but it doesn't matter how long you've worked in the force when you come across something as bad as this.' He paused. 'Well, you wouldn't be normal if it didn't affect you in some way.'

He passed her a screwed-up piece of kitchen roll that he'd pulled from his trouser pocket, and she wrinkled her nose at it.

'It's clean; I haven't wiped my nose with it.'

Nodding her head, she took it from him, using it to blot her eyes, pat her mouth then blow her nose. Ben got back inside the car, and she leant against the side of the bonnet taking in deep breaths of cold night air. Letting it cool her burning cheeks and lungs. After a couple of minutes, she got back into the car.

'Sorry.'

'Don't be, I'm saving mine for when I get home. Should I drive?'

She shook her head and pressed the start button. The engine purred back to life and she continued the short drive to Charlie's house, where she parked outside the front. The door was opened by the family liaison officer, an older woman called Jill, in her fifties, who was coming up for retirement soon after nearly thirty years of service. She whispered, 'Is it her?'

They stepped inside, and Ben glanced at the smiling photograph of Charlie hanging on the hall wall. He nodded. 'I think so, but we need a positive ID. Does she know?'

'I told her we found a body, so she's aware.'

Amanda rushed into the hall. 'What are you whispering about? Don't tell me it's Charlie because I'm telling you now it's not her. She's not dead, you're mistaken; she's coming back any minute now, and if you lot were any good at your jobs, she'd have been home ages ago.'

The woman was wild-eyed, her hair a tangled mess of knots. Morgan couldn't look her in the eye. Ben took hold of Amanda's arm, gently leading her into the living room and guiding her to sit down on the sofa. He sat next to her and took hold of her hand. She stared at him, then at their hands, as if wondering why this man she didn't know was holding on to her. She shook her head.

'It's not her, it's not my Charlie.'

'I'm very sorry, Aman—'

The sound of the slap as the palm of her hand hit the soft flesh of his cheek echoed around the room, stunning Ben and stopping him from finishing his sentence. Morgan watched in horror as Jill leapt forward, grabbing hold of both of Amanda's hands before she launched herself at Ben again.

'Don't you come in here and tell me she's dead. How dare you because I know she isn't. I'd know if she was – I'd have felt something and I didn't – I'm her mum.'

She was standing in front of him now, her feet apart, her whole body – although Morgan could see she was visibly quivering – was defiant, daring him to say the words that no mother ever wanted to hear. He looked up at Jill who had hold of Amanda, and she nodded at him.

'The body of a young girl, aged around nine or ten, has been discovered near to Piggy Lane play park. She matches the description of Charlie; I've seen her and there is a likeness to your daughter. I need you to come to the hospital to identify her and tell us if it's her or not. I'm very sorry, this is not what we expected. Is there anyone you'd like us to contact for you? Would you like Brett to do the ID or to come along?'

She collapsed to the floor, her entire body folding in on itself, and began to sob as all the fight was sucked from her and a black hole of soul-crushing grief opened up inside her chest. Jill fell to the floor next to her, rubbing Amanda's back and nodded at Ben. 'I'll bring her to the hospital after we've tried to contact someone to be with her.'

'I'll leave you to it then. Should we go and find Brett?'

'Noo.' Amanda looked up at him. 'I want to do it. If he'd picked her up…' She left the words hanging in the air.

Morgan thought *and if you had checked she was here, at home, tucked up safe in her bed* but she never said it. She knew right at this moment it was easier to blame everyone else than yourself. At some point the blame and the guilt would come crashing down on Amanda, and Morgan wondered if she would ever recover from it all. Could you move on with your life if the most precious thing you had was brutally taken away from you? Morgan had lost her most precious thing, her mother, at such an early age but had been too young to understand and had managed to move on with her life. She didn't know if Amanda Standish would fare so well.

Morgan knew she wasn't going to be meeting Fin anytime in the next few hours and excused herself to go and sit in the car. It was only fair that she tried to pass a message on to him. Outside she looked around the quiet street. Who took Charlie from this seemingly mundane, rather ordinary street, and why? Taking out her phone, she searched for the number for The Black Dog. She rang the pub and asked Mark, the landlord, to try and find Fin, to tell him she might not make it. She'd gone to school with his son, Mattie, who was one of the few people she still spoke to from back then. Saving the phone number, she slid it back into her pocket as Ben knocked on the window, making her jump. She put the window down.

'Are we going to the mortuary?'

He blew his cheeks out and nodded. She could see the tears pooling in the corner of his eyes and wanted to jump out of the car and hug him, but it wouldn't have looked very professional. His cheek still had faint fingermarks where Amanda had slapped him hard, and she felt sorry for him. They'd tried, they really had, yet here they were about to go and see a child lying on a cold, steel table in the mortuary, and it didn't matter how hard they tried not to blame themselves, she knew they both would.

CHAPTER SIXTEEN

At the hospital, Ben approached the reception desk at A&E and showed his ID badge to the guy sitting behind the desk. He pressed a button which opened the double doors and gave them entry into the hospital, which was out of bounds to the general public this time of night. They didn't speak. The waiting room was full and every person sitting there waiting a turn to be seen was watching them. Once they were through the doors and on their way to the mortuary relatives' room, Morgan's stomach began to churn, and there was a heavy feeling in her chest. A part of her wanted to run away from here, where the clinical smell of disinfectant and suffering lingered in the air. This was a lot of responsibility for anyone never mind someone her age. She was only twenty-three. A lot of her school friends worked in the local supermarkets, blissfully unaware of how truly rubbish life could be. They could go out drinking and partying whenever they liked and still go to work hung-over, because it didn't matter if they didn't get someone's online shop right. Putting a bottle of semi-skimmed milk in the basket instead of skimmed wouldn't kill anyone; no one's life hung in the balance because of it. Unlike the responsibility her job carried. An overwhelming feeling of exhaustion and despair fell across her shoulders, weighing her down like a heavy cloak.

Cain was waiting for them on the hard plastic seats outside the mortuary. He stood up and whispered, 'Jill has just arrived with Amanda; they're waiting inside.'

Ben was staring at her, and she realised that she'd stopped dead in the middle of the corridor, lost in her thoughts. A look of concern on Ben's face made her snap out of it, and she felt a little better. She did this because she wanted to make a difference and save lives. Solve crimes and put the bad guys and girls where they belonged. Cain opened the door to the family room, stepping inside, and Ben reached out, his warm hand on the small of her back. He whispered, 'Are you okay? Can you deal with this?'

She swallowed the lump that had formed in the back of her throat and nodded.

'It's hard, but Charlie needs us more than ever. We're all she has to find out what happened and make it right.'

'I know.'

He took his hand away and the warmth dissipated. He walked into the small room, and she followed. Sitting on a low, dark brown leather sofa were Amanda and Jill.

'Why can't I see her? I want to see my little girl.'

The FLO patted her arm. 'They're making her comfortable, Mandy. You want her to be taken care of and that's what they're doing. As soon as they've done that someone will let you in to see Charlie. It won't be much longer.'

Amanda nodded. Her eyes were red and puffy from the non-stop crying, and Morgan felt bad for her. At least they had found Charlie in a reasonable state and she could be seen by her mum. Morgan couldn't begin to imagine how difficult it would be if she'd been badly decomposed.

Ben tried once more to speak to her, standing a safe distance away in case she tried to slap him again.

'Mandy, I know this is truly difficult for you. We've been to the scene where Charlie was found and there is very little evidence to tell us what happened. Whoever did this took her somewhere first and then decided to leave her there. Can you think of anyone who might take her or want to hurt her? Do you think Brett would do this?'

She shook her head. 'Brett, no way. He's an idiot and he has a wicked temper on him with a short fuse, but he wouldn't hurt Charlie then leave her on her own in the dark and the cold. I just know he wouldn't do that. He's an arse but he's not a monster.'

The door opened and Declan walked in, followed by Susie, his assistant, whose blue hair was now a magnificent shade of magenta, making the cramped room even harder to breathe in.

Declan took a seat next to Amanda. He held out his hand.

'I'm Declan, the pathologist who is going to be taking care of Charlie.'

She took hold of his hand, gripping it tight.

'You will be able to see your daughter very soon, but I have to tell you that she sustained a serious head injury and it looks a little misshapen on that side of her head. Are you on your own, Amanda? Is there anyone we can contact to be with you?'

'It's just the two of us, always has been since her dad left for another woman. I don't want anyone here; I just want my little girl.'

There wasn't a dry eye in the room. Declan blinked a couple of times and stood up.

'If you're ready, we'll open the curtains. Charlie is tucked up on the other side waiting to see you.'

'I don't want to see her through a window. I want to touch her and kiss her. I need to tell her how much I love her and I'm sorry.' Her voice trembled as she spoke, but she didn't cry.

Declan glanced at Ben, urging him to step in but he didn't, and Morgan knew why: he was afraid of upsetting her again.

'I'm sorry, at the moment we can't let you and Charlie be together because we need to check her for evidence. There could be some on her clothing or skin that could lead us to whoever did this, and we need to find out who has done this, urgently. Once this has been done and she is released to the undertaker, you can spend as much time as you need with her.'

Morgan nodded, and thought to herself, *yes we do need to find who did this before it happens again.*

Susie left the room to go and open the curtains.

Amanda was nodding and Morgan could tell that she wasn't taking much in of what they were saying.

'Can I see her now? I want to see her.'

The curtains opened, and Amanda jumped up. She placed her hands against the thick glass and pressed her face to it. Staring at the small, motionless figure on the other side, speechless. Morgan glanced up and was relieved to see they had positioned Charlie so the head injury wasn't blindingly obvious.

Ben asked softly, 'Is this your daughter, Charlie?'

She moved her head up and down. A low, keening sound came from her throat, and Morgan wanted to put her hands over her ears. She didn't want to be here and watch the woman who was rocking back and forth as her grief filled the room and whisper, 'That's my baby girl.'

Ben's shoulders slumped and he let out a sigh. He looked defeated, and Declan could see this along with Morgan and Cain. Jill had her hand on Amanda's back patting it gently. Declan nodded at Susie to close the curtains.

'Wait, what are you doing?'

It was Jill who spoke. 'They need to do their job, Mandy, like the doctor said. They have to check for trace evidence. The sooner we let them get on with that, the sooner they can release Charlie's body to the undertaker, where you will be able to sit and hold her hand, have some time together. Should we get you home?'

Amanda's shoulders slumped, her head lolled forward and she nodded. Jill linked an arm through hers, walking her to the door. Morgan opened it for them and smiled at Jill, who looked almost as exhausted as Amanda. Jill turned to Declan, 'Let me know when.'

He nodded. 'First thing in the morning. I'll be in touch.'

All three of them watched as Jill led Amanda down the dark, narrow corridor away from the mortuary.

Declan muttered, 'That was hard. I'll be in early to do the post-mortem. Can you be here by ten? I'd do it now, but it's been a long day and I want a clear head before I start. Not that I expect to get much sleep tonight after this, but a couple of hours will do.'

'We'll be here, won't we, Morgan?'

She wished she could say no but nodded. Unable to find the words to speak out loud, she needed a drink more than ever and knew she could go and find Fin. They made their way back towards A&E. 'There's nothing we can do here. Let's call it a night and get some rest. Tomorrow is going to be a long day, a very long day.'

He emphasised the last sentence, and Morgan knew what he was getting at: he was telling her not to get too drunk because he needed her with a clear head. She didn't say anything. She knew she should go home, shower and go to bed. Not bother meeting Fin for a drink, but being stubborn she knew that she would, especially because of Ben's reaction to it. She just wanted a few hours of respite from the grim reality her life had turned into.

He dropped her off at her apartment, and she wondered if he would go and see Emily. She suspected they had been seeing each other since the events a few months back, but he never switched the engine off. Instead he turned and drove away without a second glance. She pulled out her phone and dialled the number for The Black Dog, and once again she asked if Fin was there.

The voice on the other end said, '*If you mean the posh southerner with a face like a slapped arse, yes he's still here. Sitting by the fire, reading a book and feeling sorry for himself.*'

She laughed. 'Please tell him I'll be there soon and to hold on. If he has to leave, can you give him my number?' She recited her number and hung up, dashing into her apartment to freshen up and get changed into something a little less conservative that didn't smell of vomit or death.

CHAPTER SEVENTEEN

The Black Dog wasn't busy. She saw Fin sitting on his own at a table in the corner, his nose in a book, nursing an almost-empty pint, and felt guilty. Then an image of Charlie's lifeless body lying in the cold street filled her mind, it was so vivid it made her close her eyes for a moment to acknowledge the horror of the last few hours. She really didn't want to be here but she felt as if she would scream if she didn't let off a bit of steam and try to block out that tragic picture just for a little while; Fin was still here and hadn't given up on her, which was a good sign.

'Sorry I'm late, today has been, it's been awful.'

He looked up at her and smiled; it was a genuinely warm, friendly smile which reached the corners of his eyes and she instantly liked him that little bit more.

'You came. I thought you were just humouring me to get rid of me. When I got your last message, I decided to hang around just in case. It's not like I have anything else to do and I'm glad that I did.'

Morgan squeezed behind the table, sitting next to him.

'Of course I came. I had every intention of coming but my job is very unpredictable. It's not the kind of job that you can close your laptop at five and leave it all behind even though sometimes I wish that I could.'

'Oh, I know and I understand because neither is mine. I meant I'm surprised that you wanted to come and speak to me. Isn't it one of the in-house rules no fraternising with the media?'

This made her smile. 'I'm an adult. I get to decide who I fraternise with. Same again?' She needed a drink and pointed to the empty San Miguel glass. 'Let me get them; I asked you here remember. And I'm capable of going to the bar and ordering drinks.'

He didn't argue with her. 'Then, yes, please.'

She returned with a large glass of rosé filled with ice, a pint of lager and two bags of Quavers.

'I'm starving, do they do food here?'

Fin shook his head. 'I have it on good authority that Friday is burger night, but the rest of the week it's crisps and pork scratchings.'

This set her off laughing, and she pushed a bag of crisps towards him.

'No, thank you. I'm good. I couldn't deprive you of your tea. If you want we can go somewhere and grab something to eat.'

'You'll be lucky; October in Rydal Falls isn't tourist season, so there aren't a lot of places open. I'm okay, these will put me on until I can go home and make a bowl of cornflakes.'

It was Fin who laughed. 'You're joking right?'

She shrugged.

'Look, let's drink these and go back to my flat. I'm not the best cook but I can manage something a bit more substantial than a bowl of cereal.'

'We'll see, that's a bit much when we were only meeting for a drink. I don't want to put you out or anything.'

Morgan was waiting for him to ask about today, about Charlie, but he didn't and she wasn't sure whether he was purposely being polite or had some ulterior motive. His phone beeped and he took it off the table where it was face down.

'Oh brilliant, that's fantastic news. Well done, you found the missing kid. I bet you're relieved.'

'How do you know?'

'Official press release from Cumbria Constabulary.' He glanced back down and let out a loud, 'Oh, I didn't read it properly; they've found a child's body.' He turned his phone to face her, and she nodded, trying to blink away the tears that were forming.

'We did.'

'Oh that's tragic and so sad, I'm sorry. No wonder you were working so late.'

She couldn't answer him without her bottom lip quivering, so she didn't. He took a drink from his pint.

'So, what's there to do around here in October then, because if there aren't many places to eat I doubt there isn't much else to do.'

He completely threw her; she'd expected a deluge of questions about Charlie that she couldn't answer. Picking up her wine glass she took a large gulp. The icy cold wine tasted like liquid heaven as she swallowed it.

'Well we have lots of lovely walks, the Co-op is open till ten and the best place of all is the library.'

He laughed. 'That's it, seriously?'

'I'm afraid you've come to the wrong place if it was excitement you're after.'

Technically, the last twelve months for her had held more excitement than she would ever want to face in an entire lifetime, but that was the nature of her job and she didn't want to get into any of that with him. She sipped the wine, savouring the taste and the warm, tingling feeling it gave her cold, tense body. She glanced at him, he was cute. His faded jeans and checked shirt were smart yet casual and sitting this close to him he smelt really good. She wondered what he'd made of her rolled-up, ripped jeans, oversize black jumper and Dr Martens. Her copper hair hung down over her shoulders, and she'd gone for the minimal amount of make-up: mascara, winged eyeliner and nude lips. This wasn't a date, at least she hadn't taken it as a serious one. It was more of a get-to-know-each-other-and-consume-alcohol meeting of sorts. She was also aware it was a big F you to Ben and his keeping secrets by dating Emily behind her back. It really upset her that he hadn't just had the balls to say they were seeing each other. What did it matter to her? They were colleagues and she'd thought they were friends and that was why it mattered so much; friends didn't sneak around behind each other's backs.

'Actually, I'm not after excitement. I had enough of that in my last job. I wanted a bit of solitude, some peace and quiet, so Rydal Falls is pretty perfect for me.'

'You put yourself on a time out from life?'

He laughed. 'Yeah, I guess I did. What about you, why are you here? A bright, young, motivated detective like yourself, surely the world is your oyster.'

Morgan lifted the glass to her lips and was shocked to see it was almost empty; she'd drunk that fast.

'I was born and brought up around here. I don't know if I'd want to work in a busy city. Rydal Falls has been crazy enough the last year, though I can't imagine what working in a busy place would be like. Do you want another?'

'How about we go to my place? I'll make some supper and we can grab a bottle of wine at the Co-op on the way before it shuts.'

Morgan didn't know if this was wise. She didn't really know him, though she couldn't deny how attractive she found him.

'Why not? I'm starving and a bottle of wine sounds good. Do you want me to call for a taxi?'

He shook his head. 'No need, I only live a few streets away. Right in between the pub and the shop, pretty perfect really. I don't need to stumble too far in either direction.'

He stood up and she followed him, wondering if she should be quite so reckless with someone she barely knew and decided that she needed to let her hair down. Fin had come along at the right time. He didn't look like a homicidal maniac, and Ben knew who he was. She'd seen his credentials, and if he started acting all weird when they got to his flat, she'd be out of there before he could do anything and she'd never see him again.

*

They went into the shop, and Morgan picked up a bottle of rosé. She could drink a couple of bottles and still function the next day, or at least she used to be able to. Fin threw in a family size bag of salt and vinegar crisps and a huge bar of chocolate, which lifted him up to an almost godly level of appreciation in her eyes. He also insisted on paying for it all. Carrying their items, because neither of them said yes to a carrier, they walked the short distance to his flat. It was in a semi-detached house: three storey and half the size of her spacious apartment. They went inside and she followed him to the top floor. It reminded her of her dad, Stan's, flat and she felt a wave of crushing grief squeeze her heart so tight it was difficult to breathe. Fin noticed her reaction, but she couldn't stop herself from closing her eyes to blink away tears.

'Are you okay? I know it's not the nicest place in town but I promise it's clean and tidy.'

She looked at him. 'I'm fine, thanks. I was thinking about a similar flat in another time and place, sorry. I'm sure yours is perfect.'

'I guess you see some pretty distressing stuff, it can't be easy.' He opened the door and she followed him inside. It was far more spacious than Stan's flat; in fact you could have put five of Stan's inside it. It was, however, painted in a multitude of different shades of grey.

'I guess whoever lived here really liked muted greys.'

Fin chuckled. 'Yeah, you could say that. I keep imagining this is what it would be like to live on a battleship.'

This set Morgan off into fits of giggles. She followed him into the kitchen which was also grey.

'Thank God the cupboards are white, or you'd never find anything.'

He passed her a wine glass. 'Yes, I'm grateful for that small mercy.'

'Are you not having a glass?'

'I don't really drink wine. I don't mind champagne now and again.'

'Oh, me either, darling, I'm quite partial to a glass of the old champagne.'

Opening the fridge, he pulled out a bottle of beer and unscrewed the cap. Morgan poured herself a glass of wine and they turned to each other, clinking glasses.

'Cheers.'

Before she could take a sip, her phone began to ring in her pocket. No one rang her except Ben or work. She let out a sigh; Fin smiled at her.

'It's okay, you can answer.'

For the first time since she'd joined Ben's team, she found that she didn't want to, that she'd like to just have a couple of hours to herself, but she couldn't ignore it.

'Hello.'

'Sorry, I hope I'm not disturbing you.'

'Yes and no.'

'We have a problem, a huge problem, can you come back to work?'

Her heart sank as she realised by the tone of Ben's voice that something was terribly wrong.

'Yes, but what's up?'

'A call came in fifteen minutes ago, we have another missing child.'

Morgan felt every hair on the back of her neck stand on end as a cold shiver ran through her.

Fin was watching her. 'Is everything okay?'

'I'm sorry, I have to go. Thank you though, I've enjoyed myself.'

She didn't give him time to answer as she rushed out of the flat and ran down the stairs, cursing because she'd left her car at home. She rang Ben back, who answered straight away.

'I need a lift; I haven't got my car.'

'Where are you?'

She didn't want to tell him she was at Fin's flat, not that it was any of his business.

'I'm at the Co-op.'

'*On my way.*'

The line went dead, and she tried to stop the feeling of dread that had settled in the pit of her stomach. She reached the main street and huddled in the doorway of a shop. The earlier rain had subsided and there was now a cold chill in the air. What did this mean? Surely another child hadn't been taken. And if they had, did it mean they just had twenty-four hours before another body would be dumped? A car sped into the main street and stopped on the opposite side. She recognised Ben's number plate and hurried across the road. Opening the car door she was hit by a blast of warm air and slid inside. He glanced at her and nodded.

'Sorry.'

'For what?'

'Spoiling your night.'

'It was just a few drinks, well actually it was just one drink; I never got to have another.'

'Just as well, all hell has broken loose and I couldn't get hold of Amy or I wouldn't have rung you.'

Morgan sank back into the soft leather seat, glad that he had. As much as she'd wanted some time to let her hair down, she wouldn't have forgiven him if he hadn't called her out.

'So, what's happened, have we really got another missing kid?'

'It seems so. Ten-year-old Macy Wallace from Bay Fell Grove. Her mum came home from work to find the dog with its lead still attached sitting on the front doorstep and no sign of Macy.'

'Shit, that's just around the corner from Charlie's house.'

'Yes, it is.'

'What are we going to do?'

'Find her; this time she hasn't been missing long. Someone should have seen her walking the dog. Officers and PCSOs have flooded the area. We're going to pay a visit to Vincent and see what he's been up to; this is too much of a coincidence. Two girls, similar age, in the same area. The dog handler will be here shortly. Hopefully, there's more of a lead this time and we can get her back before…'

He didn't finish his sentence. Neither of them wanted to think of the outcome if they didn't find Macy. They couldn't afford to have two young girls in the mortuary. Morgan prayed that whoever had killed Charlie didn't have another girl so soon. That she would turn up any minute and be fine, because the alternative was too horrific to think about. And what had happened to Eleanor Fleming? Had she met a similar fate?

CHAPTER EIGHTEEN

Ben and Morgan rushed to Vincent's house which was all in darkness. There were two uniformed police officers waiting outside for them. Ben had told them to hang back until they arrived. He got out of the car and nodded at them. He didn't care if there was a warrant or not, he was going inside that house to search and no one was stopping him. There was a quiet fury bubbling inside his chest, making it hard to breathe, but he didn't care. Even if he had a heart attack on the doorstep he was going in – he'd drag himself inside. Before Morgan had closed the car door, he was hammering on the front door with his curled fist.

Morgan looked at the two officers and rushed up the path to where Ben was shouting through the letter box.

'You have twenty seconds to get this door open, Vincent, or we're coming in.'

He listened but there was no noise from inside. He hammered even louder, then crossed to the window and hammered on that. A light came on in the upstairs bedroom window. Morgan nudged Ben, who looked up. He opened the letter box again; no one was coming down the stairs.

'Twenty, nineteen, eighteen.' Ben stood up and beckoned to the officer holding the big, red metal battering ram. 'Seventeen, sixteen, fifteen. Put the door through.'

'Are you sure? Someone is upstairs; the light came on.'

'Yes, I'm bloody sure. They must have heard the racket. We don't know what he's doing up there. Do it.'

Ben stepped away, Morgan followed. The officer swung his arm back and with an almighty crack the wood around the door handle and lock splintered. He did this a couple more times until the door was in pieces and he was able to put his arm through and open the Yale lock on the inside. The door had come off one of its hinges and wouldn't open wide. Ben shoved it hard with his shoulder, just enough so they could get into the house. He ran inside shouting, 'Police.'

The landing light came on, and then he stopped in his tracks to see the grey-haired woman standing at the top of the stairs, her eyes wide with terror.

'Who are you? What's that noise?'

Morgan, who was standing behind Ben, heard him whisper, 'Shit.'

'It's the police. We're looking for Vincent.'

She folded her arms, crossing them over her chest. 'Christ, what has he done now?'

Ben had glanced at Morgan, hoping she'd take the job of explaining, when they heard an angry voice behind them.

'What have you done to my door, you arseholes?' Vincent squeezed himself through the gap and came rushing towards Ben.

'There's another missing girl, Vince. Care to tell us where you've been? Are you even allowed out this late? Don't you have licence conditions?'

Vince's mother came down the stairs. She was glaring at her son with so much disgust he withered in front of them, and he backed down, his anger subsiding.

'I didn't do anything, Mum, I swear.'

She reached him, slapped his face hard with the palm of her hand and whispered, 'You never bloody do. You've always been a bad lad. It was only yesterday I told your father you weren't right in the head.'

Vince glared at his mother. 'Dad's been dead twenty-five years, Mother.'

'We need to search the house.'

She nodded. 'You can search wherever you want. Don't forget to search his car.'

Ben couldn't help the smirk which appeared on his face as he motioned for the officers to search downstairs. He and Morgan went upstairs, his heart in his mouth. If they found Macy Wallace in the bedroom he hadn't bothered to check earlier, he would be devastated and beyond furious with himself. He almost didn't want to look, but knew he had little choice. That little girl could be in there. Morgan busied herself searching another bedroom, and he walked towards it, a part of him hoping to find her inside safe and not hurt. The other part was hoping she wasn't anywhere in this house and never had been, if only to save himself the guilt. He was going to blame himself over Charlie if she was. He pushed open the door, and an overpowering smell of lavender filled his nostrils. The light was on, the double bed was empty, the covers thrown back where Mrs Jackson had clearly hastily left her bed. He let out a heavy sigh, relieved that Vince had been telling the truth earlier: this was his mother's bedroom. Ben crossed to the bed. Lifting the covers he checked underneath it, then inside the wardrobes and every space he could find. The room was empty: no missing girl in here.

As he left the room, Morgan was coming out of the bathroom. 'Anything?'

She shook her head. He looked up to see if there was a hatch which would give access to the loft and spotted one at the far end of the hallway. He pointed to it, 'We need some ladders.'

'There's some in the garage.'

They turned around to see Vince flagged either side by the officers.

'I didn't take either of them. Why don't you believe me?'

'Because you live smack bang in the middle of the pair of them, and right now you're as good a suspect as anyone. No one else has recently been let out of prison for liking young girls, do I need to continue?'

Vince shook his head. 'I'll go get the ladders.'

'Go with him. Did you already check the garage?'

'Not yet.'

All three of them went downstairs. Morgan whispered, 'She's not here but we definitely need to check his car.'

Vincent came back carrying a pair of stepladders which he set under the hatch. Ben didn't want anyone else to do this, just in case.

'Have you got a torch?'

One of the officers pulled one from his body armour and passed it to him. The ladders groaned under Ben's weight, but they held as he climbed up them and pushed the piece of wood to one side. Standing on the very top step he poked his head through the hole and shone the torch around; it was empty. There weren't even any boxes filled with junk up there like everyone else's attics.

'I told you.'

'Where do you keep all your junk?'

'Until I went to prison, up there. When I was inside she got some house clearance bloke with a white van to come around and dispose of everything.'

'Why?'

'She decided she didn't need any of it. I couldn't believe it when I came back. I mean there were family photograph albums and boxes of records and stuff from when I was younger. I bet they made a small fortune off it all.'

Ben dragged the hatch across, satisfied that the girl wasn't in this house. He wasn't as satisfied with Vince though. 'Where have you been?'

'Co-op.'

'What for?'

'Milk and some bloody cat food. That greedy bastard cat never stops eating.' As if on cue there was a loud miaow from downstairs.

'Look, you've done enough damage for today, get out and leave me alone. She won't go back to sleep now and will spend the next couple of hours asking me the same questions over and over again. If you think you're shit hot at interrogating, you haven't witnessed my mother in action. She'd put you to shame any day. And who is going to sort my door out? Have you seen the state of it? I spent three quid in the shop and now it's going to cost a fortune to get a new door.'

Ben shrugged. 'Sorry, but we had no choice.'

He walked down the stairs and out of the front door. Morgan and the officers followed, leaving Vincent and his mother to face each other.

CHAPTER NINETEEN

Vincent's car was a clapped-out Ford Fiesta that had seen much better days. Morgan took the torch from the officer and shone it around the outside of the bright orange rust bucket. She tried the door handle. It was locked. Shining the light through the windows she heard Vince's voice.

'What the hell are you doing now? Don't you think you've caused enough trouble for one night?'

She shrugged. 'Needs must, Vince, where are the keys?'

He growled at her. She caught the end of it, something about shoving the keys where the sun doesn't shine. She knew they were giving him a hard time, but they needed to find Macy before anything bad happened to her – so it was tough luck. She looked at the officer standing next to her.

'Please go and get his keys whilst I arrange for recovery.'

'He's not going to like that.'

'Not my problem, I'm afraid, the welfare of a child takes precedent over what Vincent likes and dislikes. If we have to inconvenience him then so be it.'

Morgan couldn't decide if she thought Vincent was involved or not. He fit some of the criteria but not all of them. Between him and Brett though, they couldn't risk anything. Ben had gone to Macy's home address to speak to her mum. The officer came back and passed the keys to Morgan, who was in the process of photographing the exterior of the car.

'What are you doing?'

'Once I'm satisfied that Macy isn't bundled up in the boot or the back seat of the car, I'm going to request recovery to come and seize the car for a full forensic lift.'

She pressed the button on the key and there was a loud click as the door locks popped up. Morgan pulled the back door with one gloved hand and shone the torch inside. She sighed to see it was empty, well apart from the empty cola bottles and crisp packets. She checked the front of the car then the boot, which had an assortment of carrier bags stuffed into a cardboard box and nothing else. Shining the light around, she could see no evidence that a ten-year-old girl had been stuffed inside it. Then she slammed it shut so hard the officer peering over her shoulder jumped.

'Sorry.'

'Bloody hell, no kid then?'

Morgan shook her head. 'I still want it taken away and a forensic examination carried out.'

'Why? I mean there's no evidence inside to suggest it needs it.'

She glared at him. 'Sorry, I didn't catch your name earlier?'

'Oh, it's Ashley, my mates call me Ash though.'

'I can't afford to let him take the car to get valeted once we leave. I'd rather get it taken to the garage whilst we consider our options.'

He nodded. 'Good idea.'

'I think so, thanks.'

She realised that he had no idea how much he'd annoyed her and bit her tongue to stop herself from saying anything too harsh. He was new, and she wasn't that long in the job herself. They weren't that dissimilar, apart from the fact that she'd been well and truly thrown in over her head and had to learn to swim for herself. She was sick with grief over Charlie and now Macy. She wanted her to be safe more than she'd ever wanted anything. She phoned Ben, who agreed with her about seizing Vince's car. After requesting the garage to come and take it away, she passed the keys to Ashley.

'Here, I want you to wait for recovery to get here. Tell them it's a full forensic lift.'

'I will. Where are you going?'

He looked pretty annoyed that he'd just been tasked to wait an hour for the tow truck, which made her feel slightly better.

'To speak to Macy's mum. Don't let Vince anywhere near this. If he tries to get his grubby hands on it then arrest him.'

He nodded, and she headed in the direction of Bay Fell Grove, wondering if Brett could have had anything to do with either of these missing girls.

It was like déjà vu as she turned the corner: the tiny street was ablaze with police van headlights and there were officers and PCSOs everywhere. Morgan couldn't stop her stomach from churning – this was so wrong. What was wrong with the world? Who would want to take children away from their mothers? She prayed that Macy had got distracted walking the dog; hopefully, she had gone off with one of her school friends and didn't realise what time it was. That was a more plausible reason for a missing kid than the possibility that there was some real-life boogey man out there who was stealing children away from their parents. She looked down at her watch, it was almost ten. Surely she'd be home soon. It was clear which house was Macy's: it was lit up like a beacon, the warm glow from the windows filling the small, untidy front garden. This house wasn't so dissimilar to Charlie's house.

She walked through the open gate and knocked softly on the open front door before going inside. A panic-stricken woman was pacing up and down the living room. She paused to look at Morgan.

'Have you found her?'

'Not yet.'

'Where the hell is she? She knows she isn't allowed to go out when it's dark.'

Morgan glanced at Ben, waiting for him to introduce her, but he was too busy looking around. He seemed distracted, which wasn't like him, and she wondered if it was because he'd picked her up from Fin's. She held out her hand.

'I'm Detective Constable Morgan Brookes.'

The woman didn't take it. She looked at her then carried on pacing up and down, pausing to get a cigarette packet from the sideboard drawer.

'Carol, I'm Macy's mum.'

'Is Macy's dad around?'

She let out a high-pitched, bitter cackle and lit her cigarette with a trembling hand, then she took a deep drag, closing her eyes. When she turned to Morgan they were still closed.

'I keep thinking if I close my eyes this might all go away, but it won't. You're still in my house and I still don't know where my daughter is.'

Morgan's heart felt heavy. 'I'm sorry, I can't even begin to imagine how you feel.'

'Do you have kids?'

She shook her head, that question again.

'Then no, you can't. Macy's dad isn't around. To be honest, he never was even before I got pregnant. He's a long-distance lorry driver from Glasgow.'

'Is there any chance he could have picked her up, taken her with him?'

'God, none whatsoever. He hasn't been here since we moved in 2016, and I don't think he even knows where we live. I never told him.'

'But we can't rule that out. We'll need his contact details so we can get in touch. Can you get them, please?'

'I don't know where he lives. He has another family in Glasgow that he does live with – a wife and three sons. We were his dirty little secret. I don't think he would bother his arse to come here and take his daughter away, when he made it quite clear he wanted nothing to do with either of us after she was born.'

Ben was finally paying attention. 'All the same, we need his name and last address that you have for him. We can ask Police Scotland to go and visit him, to make sure he hasn't been and taken Macy.'

'I can give you his last address, but he hasn't got her. Where's that kid Charlie that went missing? She only lives around the corner. Some fucking weirdo is out there taking kids, and you want to fanny around contacting Macy's dad who hasn't even sent her a birthday card since the day she was born.'

'I'm sorry, Carol, it's what we have to do. We have to rule out every possibility.' Morgan could feel the heat from Carol's eyes as she glared at her. 'Do you have a friend we can contact to come and sit with you, or a family member?'

'No, I don't. I go to work at the bingo, then I come home. It's just Macy and me, it always has been. I'm not a drunk like that Charlie's mum, and I don't let her play outside with no warm coat on. I do my best for her. I have to work or we wouldn't get any money. I wasn't supposed to be working tonight, but someone was off and I said I'd do the overtime; it's coming up to Christmas – do you know how expensive it is? I love Macy more than anything but Christ she thinks money grows on trees; she has no idea how much everything costs. Like that bloody dog; she begged and begged for a dog but it's just an extra mouth to feed.'

Morgan asked, 'Do you know Charlie's dad, Brett?'

Carol shrugged. 'Yes, well more than I know her mum. Why?'

'How do you know him? Have you seen him around lately or spoken to him? Would Macy know who he was?'

'Christ, no she wouldn't have a clue. I know Brett more than Mandy though.'

'How?'

'We went out with each other for a couple of months back when we were at school, but he dumped me for Mandy. I met Macy's dad on the rebound. I was sixteen, had a drunken one-night stand and ended up pregnant to an older married man who lived a million miles away and couldn't care less. Anything else you need to know?'

Morgan glanced at Ben, this put Brett into a whole new light. He knew Carol, so he probably did know who her kid was.

Two uniformed officers knocked at the door. 'Boss, we've searched the area. The dog handler is on his way but he's coming from Carlisle. No one has seen her. Everyone said the same thing: it's dark, they shut the curtains and have the television on so have no idea what's going on outside.'

Ben nodded. 'CCTV?'

'PCSOs are on with that.'

Morgan turned to Carol. 'Why would Macy go out when she isn't supposed to? Does she normally walk the dog so late?'

'She might have found some money in a coat pocket and gone to the corner shop. We have no biscuits or chocolate in and she has a right sweet tooth. That's the only time she ever does what she shouldn't, either that or the bloody dog was whining to go out.'

Morgan looked at the sandy-coloured dog, cowering in the corner, and wished it could talk. But at least there was another potential lead here. She knew where the shop was, and she knew it had CCTV; she'd gone to a shoplifting there when doing her training.

'I'll go speak to them,' she told Ben and left, needing to get out of the smoke-filled house.

*

She walked back towards the street where both Charlie and Vince lived. Ashley was still waiting for a recovery truck to come seize Vince's car. She paused. *Which way did you go, Macy? What's the quickest way to get to the shop?* There was an alley a bit further down from Vince's house; it wasn't lit up but Morgan headed towards it. What if she was in there, maybe she'd fallen over and hurt herself. This thought spurred her on and she began to run towards the darkened cut through. She reached the entrance. 'Macy, Macy are you here?' Silence greeted her and she felt deflated. She walked through the alley barely able to see where she was going. Turning on the torch on her phone to illuminate the dog crap and rubbish, within a minute she was out onto the brightly lit main road, where the shop was a little further down. The shop was busy, but there were two women working and she went to the front of the counter and showed her badge.

'Do you know a little girl called Macy? Has she been in tonight?'

The blonde-haired woman passed the change over to the customer she was serving and turned to Morgan.

'Yes, she was in about an hour ago. She bought a bar of chocolate, then left.'

Morgan felt a spark of hope. 'Did anyone follow her? Did you see where she went when she left?'

'Is she okay? She's a lovely little girl.'

'I'm afraid she's missing.'

Both women gasped. 'Oh God, no.'

'What chocolate did she buy?'

'Galaxy, it's on offer for a quid.'

'Thank you, I'm going to need the CCTV footage from before she entered until after she left, please, so I know where she went.'

'She went back to the cutting but I didn't see anyone following her. I was going to shout after her to go the long way around, but then I got a customer and figured she wouldn't hear me shouting anyway. Bloody hell, I wish I had now, poor kid. Is there anything we can do? Should we help to look for her?'

Morgan shook her head. 'No, we have a team of officers out looking and a dog handler is on the way.'

Karen looked at her. 'I feel sick. I wish there was something I could do.'

'Do you know her mum?'

'Sort of, she comes in here and is always friendly.'

'Maybe you could check in on her at some point. Do you know where they live?'

She nodded. 'My brother lives a few doors down from them. I can't believe this.'

Morgan left them to it and raced back towards the cutting. She needed to see if it led onto any back gardens or if there were any garages or buildings that faced it. Turning the torch back on her phone, she slowly retraced her steps from minutes ago, shining her torch all over the floor. She was almost at the end of the alley when she spied a bar of Galaxy lying discarded in the weeds which were growing along the fencing. She stopped and stared at it. A shudder ran the full length of her spine. Christ, this was terrible. The poor kid had almost made it to the end of the dark alleyway and onto the brightly lit street. Afraid to trample the scene or contaminate it, she rang Ben.

'*Where did you run off to?*'

'Macy was at the corner shop. I think I found where she was taken from. I need patrols to the alleyway which runs from Cloisters through to Friars Lane.'

'*How do you know this?*'

'She bought a bar of chocolate at the shop with a pound coin. The shop assistant saw Macy enter the cutting, and I've just retraced my steps and found a bar of chocolate that's been dropped in the weeds. It's not soggy so it hasn't been here long. We need CSI here now, Ben. She's only been gone an hour or just over.'

'*Excellent work, Morgan. Wait there. I'll get someone.*'

Morgan heard footsteps behind her. She turned and held out her hands.

'Sorry, you can't come this way. I'm going to need you to go back the other way.'

'What? Says who?'

'Police, that's who.'

'Hurry, Ben, get me some patrols now.'

She hung up, hoping that she wasn't going to have to fight every person who wanted to take the short cut. She wasn't dressed like a copper; it was far easier to order people around when you were wearing a uniform. The man tutted but turned and began walking back in the direction he'd come, and she sighed.

*

When the alleyway was sealed off with police tape at both ends, and also the street directly in front of the entrance and exits, Morgan walked back to where Ben was now standing having a discussion with the dog handler, who had finally arrived. This whole thing was a logistical nightmare: because it was a missing child, officers had trampled all over the streets in the surrounding area looking for her. Which didn't give great hope for the dog picking anything up, but it was worth a try. Morgan stifled a yawn; she was tired and cold. She wanted Macy home, Charlie to be alive and a hot shower with a large glass of vodka to soak away the pain and help her sleep. Ben waved her over, and she walked towards them.

'We're going back to the station; I want to bring in Brett and Vincent for questioning. PolSA is taking over here. He's just assembling a search team.'

Morgan nodded. She was glad to be getting out of the cold; the temperature had dropped and she could barely feel the tips of her fingers they were so numb. As for her feet, she wanted to pull the boots off, along with her socks, and stick them on the first radiator she found, to bring them back to life. She followed Ben to his car. 'Who's with Macy's mum?'

'Family liaison officer turned up ten minutes ago.'

'I bet they've never been so busy. It's shit.'

He nodded. 'Yep.'

They got into his car and drove back to the station in silence. Morgan was ticking off a checklist of everything that she needed to do to find Macy – they had to find her because the alternative was unthinkable.

CHAPTER TWENTY

Morgan walked out of the station and blinked – it was morning, and she hadn't even realised. They hadn't been able to bring Brett in, as they still couldn't find him, but they did have Vincent in the cells, and he was proclaiming his innocence to everyone, loudly. His solicitor would have him out of there in the next couple of hours because they had nothing concrete to tie him to both girls, despite him being their best lead. Her head was a mess. Morgan was used to insomnia but she had begun slurring her words an hour ago, and Ben had insisted she go home, saying he would be doing the same for a couple of hours, so they were ready to be at the post-mortem in Lancaster for ten. Knowing she was no good to anyone when her head was so messed up, she had listened to him for once and said goodbye.

'Morgan.'

She looked to see who was shouting and saw Fin waiting by his car. He waved at her and she wondered what he was doing here. She looked around; there were no other journalists here – he was the only one. Crossing towards him she found herself slightly irritated that he was here, outside her place of work waiting for her.

'What are you doing here?'

His smile disappeared and he looked as if she'd just insulted him. She tried to shake the grumpiness out of her voice.

'I meant who are you going to see?'

'No one, I came to pick you up.'

She was tired, beyond tired, and couldn't think straight but she knew that this didn't make sense.

'How would you know I'd need picking up? How long have you been here, Fin?'

His cheeks turned pink. 'A little while.'

'Have you nothing better to do than hang around outside police stations?' It occurred to her that maybe he didn't, and this was what journalists did. She'd never really spent time with a reporter before and had no idea how their working life panned out.

'Is that all the thanks I get? I woke up then couldn't get back to sleep and called you, then I messaged you and got no reply. I figured that something bad had happened and you'd pulled an all-nighter, so I came here. I was waiting for the front desk to open so I could give you these.'

He bent inside the car to retrieve a large takeaway coffee cup and a paper bag which he held out to her, and she felt awful; in fact she felt like the most ungrateful cow ever.

'Oh, I'm sorry. I didn't mean to bite your head off; it's been a long night. You shouldn't have but thank you.'

He shrugged. 'Would you like a lift home?'

She had left before Ben; he was still on the phone. She'd needed fresh air and hadn't even considered how she was getting home.

'Yes, please, I would.'

She got into his car, and he passed the coffee over. Opening the bag she peered inside at the still-warm croissant.

'Thank you, Fin, this is really kind of you.'

He grinned once more, and she felt better. 'It's only from the twenty-four-hour garage, but it's the thought that counts. Did you have a rough night?'

'Yes, it's been awful.'

'You didn't find the girl then?'

She looked at him, raising one eyebrow, wondering how he knew so much about everything. How well did she know him?

'Press release: a missing child report went out early hours. I got a text message; I get alerts whenever something newsworthy is released.'

'Oh, of course you do. Sorry, I can't tell you anything if you're looking for an exclusive.'

'I know you can't and I wouldn't expect you to. I'm not here to fish for details so I can go and write a story, Morgan. I'm here because I wanted to see you and make sure you were okay. I was gutted you had to leave early last night, but I'm also aware you had good reason to and that your work is the most important thing in your life.'

She sipped the warm coffee, savouring the aroma and sighed. She couldn't be bothered getting into any arguments. He was trying to be nice and she was in a horrible mood.

'I'm tired and not very pleasant to be around when I'm like this.' She wondered if her insomnia would kick in. Since she'd found out who she was it hadn't been quite so debilitating. She still woke at 4.25 most mornings, but she'd been able to roll over and drift back off if she didn't give in and get out of bed.

She gave Fin directions to Singleton Park Road. He drove the rest of the way in silence and she could have kissed him for it. When he pulled up in front of her apartment, she watched Emily come out of the front door, the perfect vision of beauty in her smart two-piece trouser suit, her long blonde hair in a high ponytail. Emily stared into the car, realised it was her and waved frantically. Morgan waved back, wishing she didn't always look as if she was homeless whenever she bumped into Emily. She got out of the car.

'Thank you, Fin. I'd ask you in but I really need to grab a shower and a couple of hours' sleep.'

'Of course you do. I'll maybe see you later if you're not too busy?'

She nodded, closing the car door softly and walking towards the front door, not turning around to wave. She didn't know what was going on with Fin. He was lovely and very handsome, which kind of made her wonder what he saw in her. It occurred to her then that she could ask him to dig into Eleanor Fleming's disappearance. He had more time than she did, and he could do some research into it on her behalf. Reporters were supposed to be good at that sort of stuff; plus it would keep him busy and maybe stop him hanging around waiting for her. She realised that this might be overstepping the mark, she could do this without Fin's help. Once she was inside her apartment, Morgan took the croissant out of the bag and ate it in three huge bites not even tasting the buttery pastry but leaving a trail of flaking crumbs along the floor to the bathroom as she headed to the shower.

She closed her eyes and let the hot spray soak into her back and shoulders, which were aching, her mind alternating between images of Charlie and Macy. Both cute kids, both lived with their single mothers, both had been left to fend for themselves a lot of the time. Did that make them streetwise, or targets for whoever was out there stealing children? She couldn't stem the flow of tears that began to pour down her cheeks. It was heartbreaking. She couldn't bear the thought of some monster taking these kids away from their parents. Even if they weren't the most perfect mothers, they still did their best and she wanted nothing more than to bring them both home safely. Charlie was dead; nine years old was far too young to have your life taken from you in this nightmarish way. Once the conditioner had been rinsed away, she stepped out and towel-dried herself. Pulling on a pair of cosy, soft pyjamas she towel-dried her hair. She'd deal with that mess when she'd had some sleep.

She climbed into bed and began to breathe deeply through her nose and out through her mouth, trying her best to block out the image of Charlie's pale, dead face. She lifted her pillow and took out the chunk of smoky quartz that her aunt Ettie had given her. She clutched it in her left hand, hoping that it would help ground her in some way, for at least a couple of hours, to take away the sadness and pain tearing her insides apart; in less than a minute she stopped counting her breaths and her eyes closed.

CHAPTER TWENTY-ONE

Macy opened her eyes and stared at the flamingo-pink ceiling above her head; this wasn't her bedroom ceiling. Hers was a dirty white, with a large patch of black mould in the corner to the left of the light. She went to sit up and realised that she couldn't move her arms or legs. Opening her mouth to scream, she sucked in the piece of material wrapped around it and began to choke on dry air and cloth. Her heart was racing, and she had never felt so scared in all her life. Where was she? Her mum was going to kill her, and she hadn't even got to eat the flipping bar of chocolate that caused her to be in this situation. She shut her eyes and tried to calm her breathing down; she was okay. At least she was breathing. And then a dull throbbing pain in her knee reminded her of the spectacular fall in the rubbish-strewn alleyway she'd gone through last night when she knew she should have walked around. Tears filled her eyes, and she felt the big, wet drops roll down her cheek. She didn't cry, ever, not even when her mum was being mean to her and made her put the bins out or wash all the pots and pans when she made a Sunday roast. Lifting her arm to brush them away before anyone saw them, she let out a muffled scream of anger that she couldn't even wipe her own eyes. She blinked furiously instead. She wasn't some scared kid. She wouldn't let the man who had brought her here see that. How had he got her here? The last thing she knew she was lying amongst the empty beer cans and crisp packets with her knees on fire. Lifting her head to try and look around, a wave of sickness washed over her. Her head hurt really bad. Had she knocked herself out when she fell, or passed out?

There were footsteps outside the room, heavy footsteps that were walking up and down. She shut her eyes. Whoever it was she didn't want to see them. Until she knew where she was or what was happening, it was better to pretend to still be asleep. A woman's voice in the house somewhere was shouting at someone else, but she couldn't hear them properly because it sounded faraway. Whoever it was sounded mean and she wondered if she was going to come in here and shout at her.

Her body tensed as a key began to slowly turn in the lock of the bedroom door. She squeezed her eyes tight shut. *Please God, don't let them hurt me. I want to go home and see my dog.* Whoever it was never came into the room. The door didn't open wide. She stole a glance through her almost-closed eyelids but couldn't see them clearly without giving it away that she was awake. Then she felt the cool air as it opened and whoever it was stepped inside. They walked quickly towards the bed, and she heard the clanking sound of metal against a plate or something like that. She realised it was a tray and felt a spark of hope; maybe she was in some weird hospital where they kept you tied up for your own good. She'd watched a film on Netflix about a girl in a hospital where they kept everyone tied to beds. This made her feel a little better, but she was still too afraid to open her eyes in case it wasn't a nurse standing there. What if it was some crazy man with a knife? Was it the man who took Charlie? Her mind was overflowing with thoughts.

She heard a faint voice whisper, 'I'm going to remove the gag and untie one hand so you can eat something. If you scream, make any noise or try to escape, my mother will hear you. She's not a very nice woman. I don't think you would like to meet her, so eat your breakfast quietly and we'll take it from there. If you make so much as a sound that she can hear, she will kill you, I can promise you that much.'

Coldness seeped through her body. She didn't move although she guessed he knew she was faking being asleep because her body was so stiff and scared. He turned and walked out of the room, closing the door behind him and turning the key.

Macy opened her eyes and turned to look at what he'd brought. To her surprise there was a stack of pancakes covered in chocolate and sweets; fresh cream was melting off them, pooling at the sides with the chocolate sauce, and she felt her stomach let out a groan. There was a glass of orange juice. She was so thirsty that she leant over and grabbed the glass. She couldn't move much, just enough to reach the tray, and when she did her head felt as if it was going to explode but she focused on the glass. Her fingers grasped the cold, small glass and she lifted it to her lips, almost downing it. The sweetness was tinged with a bitter taste, but she didn't care – she was too thirsty. After she'd finished that she picked up the spoon and began to scoop the cream and chocolate sauce onto it. Licking it, she smiled at how good it tasted. The pancakes were good, the nicest ones she'd ever had. Much better than the ones her mum made that were always burnt and stuck to the pan. She ate every bit and wished she could reach enough to pick up the plate and lick that clean. Her sweet tooth satisfied she turned back on the bed. Whoever it was couldn't be that mean if they were going to feed her nice things. She looked around the room. It was very pink, disgustingly pink, and there were posters on the wall of some boy band she didn't recognise. Her eyes began to feel heavy. She tried to untie her other hand, but her fingers were too clumsy and the room was beginning to spin. Closing her eyes, she lay her head down. She would just sleep for a little while and then she'd escape. She could make a run for it if she untied her hand and legs. Macy let the darkness take her away from this strange room and the feeling of pure terror which had seeded itself in her stomach.

CHAPTER TWENTY-TWO

Ben had done everything he possibly could: Al and his search team were scouring the area; the PCSOs had been out in force door knocking; CSI had processed the alleyway where Morgan thought Macy had been abducted from; Vincent had been sent home back to his mother. The only person he hadn't spoken to yet was Charlie's dad, Brett, who seemed to have done a disappearing act. When the FLO had gone to break the news it was only his partner at home. He needed a couple of hours' sleep and then he'd be back at it. He needed to shower, shave and put on fresh clothes. He hated the thought that his crumpled suit might have the lingering aroma of stale sweat clinging to it. He wished he still smoked; he'd given up years ago but when he was at this level of stress a sneaky cigarette out the back of the old station had usually done the trick. He made it to his car without his phone ringing, which was pretty good, and then it began vibrating in his pocket. He recognised Declan's number.

'*Good morning, have you been home?*'

'Not yet.'

'*Really? I have had the worst night's sleep in a long time and was going to say I can go in earlier if you wanted to get a head start on the PM, but you better grab a couple of hours first.*'

'There's another missing girl.'

'*Shit, for real?*'

'Unfortunately; we can't find her, and she lived very near to Charlie Standish.'

Declan let out a long whistle.

'*We have a huge problem then, my friend.*'

'We do indeed. I'll get there as soon as I can.'

'*No, get yourself home. Charlie will wait a little longer.*'

Declan hung up.

Ben was no longer tired; he was exhausted beyond exhausted, but he wanted to get this over with. What was that saying, 'sleep when you're dead'? At this rate he might just keel over with the sadness and stress. He would go and wake Morgan up.

He began to drive in the direction of their favourite coffee shop, Rydal Falls Coffee Co. Hopefully, a decent coffee would be enough to bring them both back to life and able to concentrate on what to do to find the sick bastard who was stealing kids and killing them.

Ben ordered two large coffees and an espresso, to give his brain a shot of pure caffeine to wake him up. As he drove into the entrance of the beautiful detached Georgian house where Morgan had the ground floor apartment, he wondered who the Porsche 911 belonged to. Maybe someone had rented the middle apartment; it had been the last to be refurbished. It had occurred to him at one point that he might be better downsizing and moving here. At least he could be near to Morgan and keep an eye on her. Then he'd realised that was plain weird – it made him sound like a cross between a parent and a stalker not her friend and boss. Parking next to the Porsche he got out and walked around it, admiring it. He'd always wanted an Aston Martin DBS but this was pretty nice too, and both of them were way out of his league. Coffees in one hand, he rang the doorbell and wondered if she was fast asleep; he felt bad for disturbing her. Her voice crackled through the video doorbell.

'*What are you doing? You should be at home getting some rest. Have you found Macy?*'

He peered into the camera. 'No, unfortunately. Why are you awake? So should you.'

From inside the large entrance hall, he heard the sound of her front door opening and then she pulled back the door and he caught a faint scent of her perfume; she always wore Coco Mademoiselle. Her burnt copper hair was piled on top of her head in a messy bun, and she was wearing her pyjamas. Her face had been scrubbed clean of make-up and he could see the smattering of freckles across the bridge of her nose. He stepped inside, and she closed the door behind her.

'We need to talk.'

She led him into the open-plan lounge-kitchen area, where he saw that bloody journalist standing pouring boiling water into a cafetière of fresh coffee, and he felt a spark of something so power-ful inside his chest he wasn't sure if it was anger or jealously. He realised the car he'd been admiring outside probably belonged to him, which annoyed him even more.

Morgan smiled at Ben. 'Do you know Fin Palmer? Fin, this is Ben, my sergeant.'

Fin held out his hand, and Ben reluctantly clasped hold of it, repulsed by the feel of his too-soft skin. He glanced down and noticed his nails were perfectly manicured, wondering what kind of guy bothered getting a manicure. When he let go it took all of his might not to wipe his hand against his trouser leg. He didn't like the guy standing in front of him, grinning with his perfect, too-white smile; his teeth looked far too big for his mouth. Ben wondered how old he was. On first glimpse, he'd looked around the same age as Morgan, but close up he had telltale signs of wrinkles around his eyes, although his forehead was far too smooth for a bloke. He wondered if he'd had Botox or whatever it was they pumped into your skin to iron out the signs of ageing.

Fin spoke. 'We haven't been formally introduced. It's a pleasure to meet you. Morgan speaks highly of you considering you're her boss.'

Morgan looked at Fin, arching an eyebrow, which made Ben feel better. She didn't look amused at his introduction. She took the coffee cup from his hand, and he noticed the flicker of irritation cross Fin's face; it looked like he was drinking the pot of coffee himself.

'So, what have you come to tell me if you haven't found Macy?'

Ben couldn't stop himself. He glared at Fin, who had the good grace to turn away. He realised that he'd rather talk to Vincent Jackson any day over this smarmy bastard. Fin walked towards Morgan, where he began rubbing the palm of his hand across her shoulder blades. She shrugged him off.

'There's no news on Macy, and Declan said he's ready to start the post-mortem earlier if we're okay with it. He couldn't sleep either so has gone to the hospital.'

'Poor kid, it's not looking good for her, is it?' Fin stated.

Morgan glanced at Fin. 'He has good contacts; he seems to find out everything before we do, don't you, Fin? I'm waiting for him to tell me he's found our missing girl.'

Ben took great pleasure in watching Fin's cheeks turn a bright shade of scarlet.

'I'll leave you to it; obviously, you have things to discuss you can't in front of me. Morgan, I'm around if you need anything, give me a call.' He bent down towards her face. Ben couldn't believe it – he was actually going to kiss her on the lips in front of him. Morgan realised what he was about to do and turned her cheek, so they brushed the skin above her cheekbone instead. Fin straightened up. He looked annoyed, which gave Ben a degree of satisfaction.

'Thanks, Fin, I appreciate you coming. I'll see you later maybe.'

He nodded but was already opening the front door. He shut it behind him a little too loudly.

They looked at each other then grinned.

'I think you've upset your new boyfriend.'

She tutted. 'He's not my boyfriend, and I don't know why he started acting like he did. I barely know him.'

'Do you like him though?' The question came out of his mouth before he had time to censor it.

She shrugged. 'I do; he's handsome and charming. He seems to know an awful lot about everything and he drives a nice car, but…'

'But?'

'I don't know, I'm not really looking for anything other than a bit of fun. I'm too busy for a start, working for you all hours of the day and night.'

'Oh, sorry. I thought you liked being on my team.'

Morgan put her coffee on the marble counter and walked around to Ben. She wrapped her arms around his shoulders, hugging him.

'I'm joking, I love working for you. I even like you, mainly because you bring me coffee but also because you're probably the best friend I have.'

He laughed and pulled away.

'Crikey, Brookes, if I'm the closest thing to a best friend you have, you need to get out more.'

She slapped his arm, then sat down opposite him.

'So, what are we going to do?'

She shrugged. 'I'm going to get ready then we're going to attend Charlie's post-mortem, after that we are going to search hell or high water for Macy.'

'Yes, ma'am.'

Morgan rolled her eyes at him.

'You'll make a pretty good DS one day, probably even DCI if you keep at it.'

'What about you, why haven't you gone for your inspector's board exam?'

'I wanted to a few years ago, but then after Cindy I realised that work wasn't everything and who did I need to impress. I don't need a bigger house; the one I'm in is far too big for me to rattle around in. I have no family to provide for. I figured that what I was doing was enough to keep me sane; I didn't want any more. I wanted a bit of work-life balance, to spend more time going for walks along the fells, reading, you know, that kind of stuff.'

'And do you?'

'Do I what?'

'Read more, go out walking, that kind of stuff.'

Ben laughed, shaking his head. 'Erm, not since you arrived on my team, Morgan. Ever since you joined us, Rydal Falls seems to have catapulted itself from a sleepy, Lake District town into the murder capital of the northwest.'

'Oh, Ben, I don't know what to say.'

'Morgan, I'm not blaming you. I'm grateful we ever met. That day when you were fresh out of training at the Potters' house seems so far away, like years away, but in reality it's not even twelve months. You are a huge asset to my team. You are also the cause of a substantial amount of grey hair – why do you think I shaved my head? – and a fair few more worry lines on my forehead, but they are a small price to pay to have such a brilliant detective on my team. I'm going to go home and shower because I need to change, then should I pick you up or are you driving?'

'I'll come for you, in an hour. That should give us more than enough time to get to the hospital.'

He nodded as he walked to his car. He felt guiltily relieved that Emily's blue Mini Cooper was nowhere to be seen and neither was the Porsche. Emily was lovely and good company, but she was a little forward and he didn't know if it was his age, the fact that he still felt guilty over Cindy's death or the small spark of fire he kept having to extinguish inside his chest when he thought too much about Morgan. Whatever it was, he was happy to keep their relationship as light and uncomplicated as possible, but he had the feeling that Emily wanted much more than he could give her at this time.

CHAPTER TWENTY-THREE

This time there was no need to walk through the busy A&E department to get to the mortuary; they went to the side door and rang the bell. It was opened by Susie, who was dressed in blue scrubs. Her magenta hair was in a high ponytail, showing a beautiful large, newly acquired, lifelike black and grey rose tattooed on the left side of her neck; a pair of earbuds were pushed firmly in her ears. She grinned to see them both.

'Morning, the boss is just getting ready.'

They stepped inside, and she closed the door behind them, locking it.

'Your hair looks amazing and that tattoo is gorgeous, Susie. Who did it?'

Morgan felt Ben's eyes boring into her and she knew he was thinking WTF, but he was a bit old-fashioned and Morgan loved tattoos.

Susie removed an ear bud. 'What?'

'I love your hair and that tattoo. Where did you get that done?'

'Aurora Tattoo. It's only around the corner, on Brock Street. They have the most amazing artists working in there. If you want one ask for either Emma, Sammi or Kerryn. It's so cool, it's in the basement of an old church, you'd love it, Morgan. I always wanted to be a tattooist but I'm not very good at drawing, then this job came up and I thought working with dead people was probably the next best thing.'

'Thanks, I'll take a look.'

Ben was staring at Susie, wide-eyed, as if she was from a different planet, and Morgan glared at him.

Declan appeared at the doorway and smiled. 'Is Susie telling you about her fantasies again? She can't draw a line straight on a dead body that isn't moving; God forbid she ever tried to tattoo anyone who was alive.'

Susie stuck her tongue out at Declan, and Morgan was happy to see the pair of them were getting along much better than the last time she'd been here, when Declan had done nothing but complain about his new assistant.

He rolled up his sleeve to show them his latest tattoo: a black and grey lion with the greenest eyes Morgan had ever seen.

'She's right though, they are amazing; Sammi did mine. Come on, Morgan, show us yours. I know you have a few.'

Ben spoke before Morgan began rolling up her trouser leg.

'They're all very nice but can we get this over with, please?'

Declan nodded at Morgan. 'Yes, of course we can. Just a bit of banter, Ben, to ease us into the next couple of hours. Which are going to be horrific, by the way.'

Declan addressed Morgan, 'He's jealous because he's boring and isn't one of the cool club, aren't you, Ben? Hey, maybe you and Morgan can get matching bestie tattoos and go together.'

Morgan stifled the laughter that was threatening to explode from her mouth because Ben looked as if he was about to burst into flames, his face was so red.

'Sorry, sorry, I'm getting carried away. I blame these two kids, such a bad influence. I don't know how you stay on the straight and narrow, Ben, working with this one.' He winked at Ben, who finally cracked a smile and his shoulders dropped a little.

'Me either, it's tough.'

Declan clapped his hands together. 'Right then, down to business it is. Would you both like to get suited up. Wendy and her very quiet colleague are already here. She's an early bird that one; they were waiting by the door when I got here.'

Morgan went into the changing room first, followed by Ben. They both began to wash their hands, and then put plastic aprons and gloves on. There was a narrow door which led into the mortuary. Morgan stared at it for a few moments wishing that something nicer was waiting behind it. Sighing she opened it, stepping inside and shivering at the difference in the temperature, as cold air was being blasted around the large, brightly lit, sterile room. Wendy and Isla, the new CSI, looked at them and nodded.

Wendy said, 'I'm photographing; Isla is bagging up. Isla, this is Morgan and that's Ben, both of them are from CID.'

Isla smiled at them. Along the back wall was the bank of fridges where the bodies were kept. Morgan glanced at them then back at the empty steel table in the middle of the room. The radio was playing Smooth FM. Declan walked in and went straight to the radio, turning the station over to Radio 1.

'I don't think Charlie will want to listen to the sixties golden hour.'

Morgan felt her heart tear a little and a lump form in her throat. God this was going to be the hardest thing she'd ever done, but she was glad to be here for Charlie; they hadn't managed to help her when she was alive but they could do whatever they could to find her killer.

As Susie went over to the fridges, Morgan felt her whole body tense. The heavy clang of scraping metal as she opened a door echoed around the room, setting Morgan's nerves on edge. Susie pulled out the drawer with the small body in the middle of it. Both Susie and Declan wheeled it over to the table and lifted her effortlessly onto it; her shrouded body looked far too small to be lying on the huge cold table that could quite easily accommodate heavy adults. No one spoke, but all of them stared, until Wendy's voice broke the silence.

'This is so shit.'

Declan answered. 'It is, but we are here to take care of her the best possible way. Charlie might not have stood a chance in life, but we will make certain that between us all, we catch whoever did this to her.'

Everyone nodded in agreement. Declan and Susie began to gently unwrap Charlie's body. Morgan had to force herself to keep looking at the table when her pale, cold face was visible. She blinked a couple of times.

'Well hello again, Charlie, it's me, Declan, we met yesterday and I told you I was going to take care of you. You've been a very brave girl. I hope you understand that what we do today is out of necessity; we have to find out what happened to you, sweetheart.'

Wendy was openly crying, and it took Morgan every piece of strength not to join in with her. Ben was looking away. Susie carried a box of tissues over to Wendy and patted her back as she offered her one.

'Sorry, I just… I have a niece the same age and—'

Declan gave her a couple of minutes to wipe her eyes and blow her nose.

She held her head up high and nodded. 'Right, I'm ready.'

No one judged her; they all felt the same way.

Declan smiled at her. 'We'll let you photograph her before we remove the clothes and the bandage. Let's hope that whoever bandaged her head left us some nice DNA evidence behind, so that we can catch the bastard as soon as possible.'

Morgan was praying that wrapped inside that bloodstained crepe bandage was a hair with a follicle to extract DNA from. It would be a miracle and save them lots of wasted time. At the back of her mind was an image of Macy, who had snuck out of the house when she shouldn't, to go and buy a bar of chocolate. How many kids had done the same without a second thought? She used to sneak out of Stan's house to go and meet her friends. You didn't think of the consequences such a small action could have. Macy had got herself a bar of chocolate and gone straight home to eat it. She hadn't expected to be abducted by a child-killing monster, neither had Charlie.

'Well the X-ray was right.' Declan pointed to the left side of the skull. 'Death was caused by blunt-force trauma, which looks to me like it happened perimortem.' He looked around at everyone, took in their confused expressions. 'It means this injury, which is catastrophic by the way, was caused around the time of death and was the cause of death. If it didn't kill her immediately, it wouldn't have taken long. See the fractures in the skull; they were caused by the velocity of the blow. The cranium is a complex structure of bones that protects the brain and is made up of three layers: the outer table, which is the hard outer layer of bone; the inner table, which is the inner layer of hard bone; and the spongy layer between the two is called the diploe. Whatever caused this blow has caused the outer, inner and the diploe to shatter; radiating fractures have spread outward from the site of impact.'

Ben, who was trying to look everywhere but at Charlie's fractured skull, asked, 'So, what do you think caused it?'

'Hard to say. There are many objects that could have been used but there are no distinguishing marks which can be identified. Sorry, I'm not being very helpful, am I? It was definitely a heavy blunt object. I've seen similar injuries in the past. She's either been hit by a heavy object or—'

'Or?' Morgan asked.

'Or she could have been hit by a car or a van, something with those big metal bull bars or a heavy-duty bumper would have had sufficient force behind it to cause that kind of injury. Although there doesn't look like there are any other injuries except for that linear abrasion on her right arm.'

He picked up her arm to examine the long, thin scratch.

'This was caused by the relative movement of a pointed object on the skin. Something like a nail, a thorn maybe; it could even be an animal scratch. Susie, get this swabbed, please, just in case our killer accidentally scratched her and left us some nice DNA behind. It's definitely not from a high-impact collision, there would have been a lot more abrasions and cuts if it had, I'd also expect to see lots of bruising if that had been the case. The head injury would have to have been more of a slow-motion impact.'

Morgan instantly thought about Brett's pickup; it had a big chrome bumper running around the front of it, she was sure it did. Had he gone to see Charlie and somehow accidentally ran over her head then panicked?

Ben asked, 'What about time of death?'

Declan glanced up. 'Well rigor mortis was in full swing when we brought her here last night, so she had been dead for anything up to thirty hours. I suppose if you take it from the time of the log that was called in reporting her missing, you'll have a good estimation. The lividity, or purplish discolouration on her back to you and me, tells us she was lying on a flat surface for at least six hours.'

'How?'

'Well it begins within thirty minutes after the heart has stopped beating. It can only be altered if the body is moved in the first six hours; after that it's fixed because the blood vessels begin to break down. Hopefully, when we examine her stomach contents there may be something in there that will give us an indication and a better time frame. The digestive system stops working after death, creating a time capsule of a victim's last moments. It varies, but typically it takes around six hours, depending on the food consumed after eating, for the stomach to be completely emptied of digested food. If there's nothing in there then she didn't die as soon as she was taken.'

Morgan shuddered at the thought; poor Charlie. She was scribing and wrote everything down that Declan said, so they could go back to the station and work out a timeline and any clues that needed following up on.

When Declan finally stood up straight with a groan, Morgan felt a sigh of relief. The bandage hadn't given away anything other than what they were assuming was Charlie's own blood, but it had been bagged up ready to be sent off for analysis. Declan took the small metal bowl containing the contents from Charlie's stomach to the long workbench, to take a look at it.

'Ah, I think we're in luck. There are some chunks of undigested pineapple and what I think is ham.'

Morgan looked at Ben. 'Pizza, we need to find out what Charlie ate before she went out.'

He nodded.

Declan added. 'Pizza normally digests in a couple of hours, so if she did eat it before she left her house then she died within two to three hours of eating it. Does this help narrow your time frame?'

'Yes, it does. Thanks, Declan.'

'You're very welcome, Ben. Now at least we know that, thankfully, nothing of a sexual nature happened to her. The only injuries Charlie sustained were the fatal head injury, and that single scratch on her arm.'

'If it was an accident, and whoever had done this had got her to the hospital, would she still be alive?'

Declan turned to look at Morgan.

'That is a very good question, but the answer is no. The impact caused such catastrophic fractures to her skull, which would have resulted in Charlie dying even if they'd rushed her to the hospital. There wasn't anything they could have done to fix it. Now, if you want to leave the rest of this to us, we can fix Charlie up a little better. Can't we, Susie?'

Susie nodded and smiled at Morgan. 'Yes, I'll sew everything back together neatly. Her mum will never know any different.'

This made her feel better. Ben turned to leave, and she followed. Behind her were Wendy and Isla, carrying the brown paper sacks containing Charlie's clothes.

CHAPTER TWENTY-FOUR

Detective Constable Amy Smith was filing her nails, the heating blasting hot air around the small Ford Focus whilst she waited near the entrance to Cedarwood Grove for Brett Mosely to put in an appearance. She'd been relieved not to have to go to the kid's post-mortem – as tough and experienced as she was she still hated having to deal with murdered kids. Thankfully, it didn't happen very often in this part of Cumbria. She'd sent Des to get coffee and something to eat. She really fancied a nice, big, gooey slice of cake but knowing Des he'd come back with two goat's cheese salads and a bag of veggie crisps. He had a newish girlfriend he was trying to impress with his vast culinary knowledge and healthy eating, which was fine. God knows she was always trying to make better choices when it came down to her food, but there were certain limits and if he turned up with anything that contained goat's cheese or tofu she didn't think she'd be responsible for her actions. As if to confirm it, her stomach let out a huge growl. She saw a flash of silver in the rear-view mirror as he parked the car and waited for Des to bring her food to her. They were in separate cars so they could go for toilet breaks and coffee breaks but still be keeping watch. As the passenger window slid down, she saw a large paper coffee cup come through it along with a brown paper bag.

She stared him in the eyes and asked, 'What's in the cup and the bag?'

'Jesus, Amy, how about thank you so much Des for going and getting lunch, I really appreciate it.'

'No thanks until I know what it contains and it better not be a soya decaff latte.'

He shook his head. 'It's a large fully caffeinated latte with cow's milk, and the bag contains a tuna mayo baguette with cheese and no salad. Good enough, your majesty?'

She grinned at him. 'Much better than I thought, thank you. What did you get?'

She expected him to tell her some disgusting concoction, when he said, 'Same as you.'

'What? No way. I don't believe it. Are you having a cheat day, Des?'

'She left me for the guy who owns the new gym that's just opened on Salter Road, so what's the point?'

It wasn't often that Amy was lost for words but she felt sorry for Des; he looked crushed.

'Gertha is a fool then.'

'Birgitta, not Gertha and not really. She's a lot younger than me and we work such crap hours. I just really liked her.'

What unfolded next happened so fast that neither of them saw it coming. They didn't see the man striding towards them, his face a mask of contorted pain and anger. Des, who was leaning in the passenger window talking to Amy, felt an arm like a vice clamp around his neck as he was dragged backwards.

Amy screeched, 'Oh shit', and managed to knock her coffee all over herself and the driver's seat as she clambered out. Grabbing her radio off the front seat she shouted down it, 'Urgent assistance Cedarwood Grove, now.' She hit the orange emergency button on the top of it for good measure, because she didn't have time to pass an update to the control room whilst Des got a good kicking off Brett Mosely. Des's head was tucked under Brett's arm and his face was going purple. Amy ran towards the two men. Pulling the canister of CS gas out of her pocket she held it up to Brett's eyes.

'Let him go now. I'm sorry for your loss but this is the wrong fight.'

There was a steady stream of tears flowing from Des's eyes they were watering so much.

Brett looked at her, his eyes black with fury and pain, and Amy knew he'd lost it; he wasn't going to listen to her. She flicked the cap off the small black canister, aimed for his eyes and pushed her finger down on the red button, releasing a stream of liquid into his face. It took a couple of seconds before he yelled in pain and anger, but he released his grip on Des's neck, who fell to his hands and knees, coughing and spluttering, taking in gulps of air. Sirens turned into the street and before she could do anything else the sound of heavy boots pounding towards the three of them filled her ears. Two uniformed coppers grabbed hold of Brett, who fought them every step of the way as they tried to drag him towards the van, fighting despite being temporarily incapacitated. Des had his eyes squeezed tight shut.

'Jesus, Amy, did you aim for me or him? I can't fucking see; my eyeballs are on fire.'

Amy laughed – too loud – but it was funny in a terrible way. 'Well, I have third-degree burns on my fanny from that coffee. I spilt it all over myself trying to get out of the car. What did you tell them to do, heat it enough so it would burn my tongue off?'

Des let out a groan. Despite the pain there was a hint of a smile at the corners of his mouth. More footsteps as another van arrived. Madds, the duty sergeant, got out along with two more officers.

'What have we got here then, Keystone Cops? You had one job, the pair of you, and look at the mess you've made. Have you wet yourself, Amy?'

Amy grinned at him, tempted to tell him to get lost but she couldn't. He was right, and although he wasn't smiling, there was a twinkle in his eye she recognised from her days on section. He'd be telling this tale for weeks to anyone who'd listen.

'I suppose at least you have him in custody and we know where he is now.'

'Is that some kind of well done, Sergeant? And no, I'm not incontinent: I dropped my coffee everywhere.'

'Well done. It's a disaster, Amy. Do you know how much of a shitstorm this is going to cause? Pepper spraying the grieving dad of a dead child on the front street in full public view? The press is going to love this. It will be on Granada *Reports* tonight. You and Desmond are going to be famous.'

'If he hadn't attacked Des, then none of this would have happened.'

Madds shrugged. 'That may be, but no one will care about the first part of the story; no one cares if a copper gets a kicking. Get yourself back to the station and get cleaned up. Where's Ben anyway? Did he think letting you two loose on your own was a good idea?'

'He's at the post-mortem and yes, actually, he knows that we are quite capable, thank you very much.'

This time Madds did laugh as he walked back to the van he'd arrived in, shaking his head.

'Do you two want a lift back; you can get in the cage?'

Amy shook her head. 'No, we're fine.'

Madds walked away, and Des muttered, 'Blind and a broken neck, is that your definition of fine, Amy?'

'Do you want to listen to him making fun of us all the way back to the station? I don't; we'll go back in your car. I'm not sitting in wet coffee either.'

She helped him to his feet, linking an arm through his and led him towards his car, where the keys were still in the ignition. After guiding him into the passenger seat, she retrieved her tuna baguette and the keys from the other car and locked it. She sent a text to Ben.

Brett Mosely is in custody, ring me when you can.

Then she drove them back to the station to get cleaned up and to face the barrage of questions that were about to come their way, and the multitude of forms that needed to be completed. At least their DI was back from his holidays. She'd rather explain it all to Tom and get her bollocking from him than have to face whatever duty inspector was covering for him.

CHAPTER TWENTY-FIVE

The station was buzzing; there was a lot of loud, raucous laughter coming from the briefing room where the next shift were being given their orders for the next ten hours. Ben glanced at Morgan as they walked past and muttered, 'Nice to know they're so happy. You wouldn't think there was a dead girl and another missing, would you, listening to that lot.'

Morgan didn't say anything. Sometimes dark humour was the only thing to get you through a shift. This job could be a mixture of exhilarating, terrifying and heartbreak all rolled into one. They went upstairs to the CID office. Halfway up, Madds shouted, 'Ben, a word.'

Ben looked down at him, and Morgan could tell he wasn't in the mood for whatever was coming his way. He went back downstairs into the sergeant's office, and she carried on to their office. Inside was Amy, who was sitting at her desk with her head in her hands, and a very red-eyed Des. Morgan didn't know whether he'd been crying and she'd just intruded on something very personal between the two, but then Amy glanced up at her and grimaced.

'Are you okay, Des?'

He shook his head. 'No, I'm blind in one eye thanks to Amy.'

'For Christ's sake, if I hadn't gassed him, you might be dead and then it wouldn't bloody matter if you were blind or not, would it, you moron.'

Morgan felt her mouth open wide as she looked at Amy, then Des, wondering what had happened. Before she could ask, Ben stormed through the door, slamming it behind him. He looked at Amy, then Des, and shook his head.

'Christ, what a mess. Are you okay, Des? Do you need to go to the hospital?'

Des shook his head. 'No, my throat's a bit sore but not as bad as my eyes.'

Amy threw her arms up in exasperation. 'Ungrateful. Next time I'll let you get strangled and save giving myself third-degree burns.'

Morgan glanced at Ben, hoping he was about to throw some light on what was happening.

'Talk me through it.'

Amy stood up, and Morgan stared at the dark patch on her trousers.

'Des went for lunch; he was talking to me through the car window and next thing Brett Mosely had him in a headlock, strangling him, I mean he was choking the life out of him. I jumped out, burnt myself in the process then pressed the emergency button for help. I asked him nicely to let him go, but you could tell he'd lost it, boss; his eyes were black. So I gassed him, accidentally getting Des the drama queen in the process. Patrols arrived, took him into custody and he's waiting in the cells ready to be interviewed.'

Ben ran a hand over his head and nodded. 'Well at least he's here so we can talk to him. Well done, both of you, you did what you had to do and don't worry about it. I'm gutted about Charlie and I didn't know her, so I can't imagine how he's feeling, but he can't go around trying to kill my officers because he's enraged, and where's he been for the last twenty-odd hours anyway? What's he hiding? He hasn't been honest or frank with us from the start, so he can forget any bloody lawsuit if that's what he's threatening. We'll give him a bit more time to calm down and then I'll go and speak to him, see how I get on with him.'

Tom, who had followed Ben in, nodded in agreement. 'You both did what you had to in difficult circumstances. No one wanted this outcome, and the sooner Mr Mosely realises we're on his side the better things will be. I'm so glad I came back off my cruise today. You know I don't even feel as if I've been away.' He winked at Amy, who smiled.

'Glad to have you back, sir.'

'So, have we found the other missing girl yet?'

He was met with silence. 'I see, what exactly is being done to locate her? And this is not some dig at anyone, it's merely a question and I need bringing up to speed with what has and hasn't been done so far.'

Ben walked over to the large whiteboard where 'Charlie' and 'Macy' were written in black marker pen. 'Macy has an absent father who lives in Scotland. Police Scotland are on with visiting him to see if he picked her up at all. PolSA has taken over the search for her; task force is out; so is the dog handler again. PCSOs are door knocking again, and the area is sealed off until we decide if we've finished collecting anything and everything of forensic value. Macy's home address has been searched from attic to garden and there is no sign of her there. All family and friends have been spoken to. The last confirmed sighting we have of her is when she visited the corner shop last night to buy herself a bar of chocolate. She slipped into the cutting between Friars Lane and Cloisters Lane with her dog, but somehow, she never made it home. Morgan found the bar of chocolate in the weeds just before the exit onto Cloisters. She was so near a place of safety, and it seems she was plucked from the alleyway and taken. The dog turned up at the home address and was whining in the front garden when mum arrived home from work.'

Tom was shaking his head. 'Unbelievable, how near is this cutting to where Charlie was taken from?'

'Two hundred yards give or take.'

'Who is our prime suspect? Do we have one?'

'Well, we have Vincent Jackson living smack bang in the middle of Charlie's address and the cutting; he's a registered sex offender.'

'I know who he is.'

'He lives with his elderly mother. We've brought him in for questioning and taken his car away to be examined, but we have nothing other than his previous record tying him to both girls.'

'Why do we have Charlie's dad in custody? Apart from the assault on Des, what's the full story?'

'He was very evasive when asked where he was when she went missing. He was supposed to pick her up and have her for the night, but he told her mum he couldn't. Instead he went out for a meal with his new girlfriend, and they were so late for the reservation they almost never got seated. He omitted to tell us any of this when questioned the first time.

'We've just come back from Charlie's post-mortem, and the cause of death was blunt-force trauma to the head. The pathologist thinks it could have been caused by a 4x4 or a pickup truck with a heavy-duty bumper, which is the kind of car he drives.'

Morgan added, 'There's also the fact that he went out with Macy's mum, Carol, years ago; he left her for Amanda, Charlie's mum. Boss, I found out that another girl went missing fifteen years ago.'

Tom nodded. 'Eleanor Fleming, certainly did. She ran away to the bright lights. So, he's good for it if we were going off circumstantial evidence, but is there any motive, anything that ties him to it more than what we have forensically?'

'No.'

'Then I'm afraid you need to speak to him and get a full account of his whereabouts then he's going to have to be released.'

Des looked at Tom. 'What about assaulting me? He can't just walk around trying to strangle people because he's having a bad day.'

'No, he can't, you're right. But, right now, at this very moment, his solicitor is going to say he was acting out of character because of his grief and that it's not in the public interest to prosecute him. We need to focus on finding the other missing girl before it's too late. Maybe we could watch him discreetly.

'Amy, you can do some digging into his background. Does he have a lock-up, garage or anywhere he could hide a child without the fear of getting caught? Does he have any previous for violence? That kind of thing.'

Morgan spoke up, 'When we visited him at home and Philippa showed me Charlie's bedroom she bent down and I couldn't help notice she had a large area of bruising on her side. She got very defensive when I asked her about it, so it's possible Brett is violent towards her.'

Tom nodded. 'Thanks, we'll bear this in mind.'

Ben walked into his office and came out clutching a handful of printouts. 'We can make a start with every RSO in Rydal Falls, then extend out to Kendal. I want all of the registration numbers of any vehicles they own or have access to running through the ANPR cameras, to see if they flag up as being in the Rydal area around the time frames that Charlie and Macy went missing. Amy, you and Morgan can go together; Des are you okay to join me once I've spoken to Brett? It will give you time to grab a coffee.'

Des nodded. He looked deflated, and Morgan glanced at Amy, who mouthed, 'Woman trouble.' Morgan nodded. She didn't care who she was with or what she was doing as long as they were doing something productive to try and find Macy.

'Are there many in Rydal? I mean this town isn't huge like Kendal or Barrow.'

Amy, who was looking at the computer screen, said, 'Six here; Kendal is much worse. I think there are seventy in the whole of south Cumbria, but that includes Barrow which is a big town.'

'Sir, what about Eleanor?'

He fixed his brown eyes on Morgan. 'What about her?'

'I think she might have been the first victim, that maybe whoever took her killed her. You don't disappear without a trace at that age without someone knowing something in a small place like this. What if the killer got caught for another crime, a serious one, and has spent time in prison and only just been released? That would explain the huge gap from Eleanor to Charlie. Maybe both girls were in the right place at the wrong time.'

Tom smiled. 'Very good, Morgan, I like it, but at the moment we have to focus on finding Macy, then we can see if it all links back to Eleanor Fleming.'

She felt deflated, but not entirely surprised by his reaction. He was right; of course Macy was their priority. But it bothered her that everyone in Rydal Falls had given up on Eleanor without so much as a second thought. She would make it her mission to discover what happened to her.

'Oh okay, I guess we should make a start then.'

They walked out of the office and Amy whispered, 'I'm going to need to nip home and change my trousers.'

'Of course, should I drive then you can jump out at your house?'

She nodded, and they went out into the rear yard of the small station, where the wind was whipping the fallen autumn leaves from the trees which surrounded it into a frenzy.

'It's bloody freezing. I think I'm going to put my thermal long johns on. Are you warm enough, Morgan?'

Morgan looked down at the trouser suit she was wearing and realised that she wasn't going to be warm enough at all, but she didn't want to waste time. 'I'll be okay, thanks.' She made a mental note to change into something more suitable for tomorrow.

*

Outside Amy's house there was nowhere to park, so she double-parked with the engine running and the hazard lights flashing. Her phone began to ring.

'Hello.'

'*Good afternoon, gorgeous.*'

She smiled at Fin's soft, well-spoken southern voice.

'*I just wanted to make sure you were okay.*'

'I'm good, thanks, cold, stressed but okay. How about you?'

'Me, I'm great. Are you busy later? I was wondering if you wanted to get a bite to eat, have a couple of glasses of wine and basically let your hair down after our disastrous date last night.'

'I'd love to, but.'

'Ah, there's always a but with you.'

He laughed but Morgan detected a hint of annoyance in his tone.

'But I have no idea what time I'll finish.'

'How about you phone me when you get home. I could pick up a takeaway and a couple of bottles of wine.'

She saw Amy dashing towards the car with a spare coat draped over her arm.

'Sorry, I have to go and yes, that sounds fab. Any news on Macy?' She had promised herself she wouldn't ask him about it, but the words slipped out before she'd had time to think about them, and she hoped he wouldn't want information back in exchange for anything he told her, because she couldn't and wouldn't do that.

'Not at the moment, sorry.'

'Oh, right. Thank you, I was hoping you might have heard something through the grapevine.'

Amy, who was now inside the car, looked at her. 'I'll speak to you later, Fin, bye.' She hung up.

'Fin, is that your new boyfriend, the reporter who has Ben's knickers in a twist? I hear he's really good looking and drives a Porsche, so I guess he's loaded too.'

Morgan stared at Amy. 'How do you know this stuff? You know everything.'

Amy shrugged. 'I have my sources and I love to know what's going on. I can't help it if I find stuff out. I'm a detective; I'm supposed to know what's happening. Do you like him then?'

'Are you just nosey?'

Amy laughed. 'C'mon, you can tell your Aunty Amy. I won't blabber to everyone.'

'Yes, but it's complicated. So where are we going first?'

Amy grabbed the sheet of names and addresses from the back seat and looked at them.

'We'll go to the flats on Sun Street first. There's a bloke there who used to be a security guard, who has a fondness for indecent images of children under the age of thirteen.'

Morgan shuddered; the world was full of monsters wearing many different disguises.

'What about this Fin guy though?'

'What about him? He's a nice distraction from all of this heartache. I don't know him that well; it's really just a bit of fun. I don't want anything serious. I just want to be able to let my hair down and enjoy some conversation which doesn't involve work.'

Amy nodded. 'I bet Ben's not too happy.'

'Why wouldn't he be? He's my boss; what I do in my own time is my business.'

'For a start he's a reporter. He might not seem sneaky but I bet he's fishing around for something, and I thought, you know, that you and Ben might.'

'Might what?'

Amy glanced at her. 'Nothing, I thought you were friends.'

'We are friends, but that's it.'

'Would you like to be more than friends though? I think you'd make a good couple.'

'Jesus, Amy.'

'Sorry, I'll shut up now.'

'Ben's got a girlfriend or at least he's seeing someone.'

'Nooo.' The words came out as a shocked cry. 'Who?'

'Emily, who lives in the flat above me. I've seen his car outside and she's mentioned him a few times.'

'Bloody hell, well the little sneak. It's true, the quiet ones are the worst.'

Morgan didn't have anything to say to that and they drove the rest of the way to Sun Street in silence, Morgan wondering if she could do some more digging into Eleanor's disappearance without getting herself into trouble.

CHAPTER TWENTY-SIX

Three hours later they had visited all six names on their list: five men and one woman, who had moved here from Doncaster. All of them had let them inside their houses, flats or bedsits to have a look around. They had met little resistance if not a little shock that they were there asking about the two girls. It was well after teatime and Morgan was tired not to mention hungry. She phoned Ben.

'Everyone on the list has been spoken to and their addresses checked; nothing to report I'm afraid.'

'It was worth trying I suppose, thank you. I really hoped that one of them might have had Macy.'

'So were we. What next?'

'Nothing, I have plain-clothes officers sitting in cars around Piggy Lane, just in case they decide to leave her there like Charlie. I don't know what else we can do, right now. There's been no contact from anyone, so she hasn't been taken for ransom. Police Scotland have spoken to her father, who hasn't been out driving for three weeks; he has a broken ankle.'

'Oh, bugger.'

'Yes, quite. There are officers posted all around Rydal Falls in plain clothes; I drafted some in from other parts of the county. Apart from knocking on every single door in Rydal, and there isn't enough manpower for that, I literally have nothing left at the moment. Brett cried like a baby. He had nothing to do with Charlie's disappearance. He's been seeing another woman which is why he was late for his anniversary meal. He's a despicable, lying, cheating bastard but I don't think he's a killer. He admitted to going out with Carol and then asked what it had to do with anything – it was ten years ago and it's a small town; they were all in the same year at school. I have to say I believe him, and his other girlfriend was spoken to and confirmed his alibi.'

She could hear the bitter sound of blame and disappointment in his voice and it made her want to squeeze him tight. He was taking it hard, as if this was his fault.

'Ben, you're doing everything you possibly can, this isn't on you. Are you going home for a break? When was the last time you actually slept?'

'I don't know what to do. Headquarters has drafted in DCI Claire Williams as a full-time advisor from the Murder Investigation Team, to go over everything we have or haven't done. A fresh pair of eyes might give us some new perspective; I've emailed her the files we have so she can read through it all tonight.'

'What should we do?'

'Go home, you especially are running off empty, Morgan. Get some rest, eat, sleep if you can, and if anything crops up I've been assured we'll be the first to be called out.'

He hung up, and she knew that by 'crops up' he was thinking of Macy's body turning up. Amy was watching her.

'He said to call it a day. There isn't much we can do.'

Amy shrugged. 'This is rubbish. Have you not got any bright ideas? I mean you're like the super detective of Rydal Falls who swoops in to save the day.'

Morgan felt a flush of anger that Amy was being so sarcastic, but the look on Amy's face was one of hope and she realised she was being serious and not rude.

'Knock on every door, park up on Charlie's street, but Ben said he already has plain-clothes officers dotted around, so it's already being done. I don't know what else to do. It makes me feel sick and so flipping useless. Can you drop me off at home? I need to do something to release the tension. I wish I had a punching bag, I've never felt so frustrated.'

'Get yourself to the boxing gym on Dalkeith Street. Paul Ryan was a copper before he left to become a personal trainer. He's been a boxing coach for years. It will do you a world of good and it might help you if you actually learn how to punch properly, with all the scrapes you get yourself into.'

'Thanks, I might just do that but not tonight. I'm going home to try and relax.'

*

When Amy reached the drive of Morgan's apartment she let out a whistle.

'He is keen; how long do you think he's been sitting in that Porsche waiting for you then?'

Morgan felt a shudder of annoyance at the sight of Fin's car. He was always hanging around waiting for her and it was beginning to grate on her nerves. She got out of the car and waved bye as she strode towards the car where Fin was sitting in the front seat typing on a MacBook. She knocked on his window a lot harder than she meant to, and he jumped, realised it was her and gave her that wide, perfect smile. He pressed a button and the window glided down effortlessly.

'Jesus, you scared me.'

'What are you doing here, Fin? This is getting a bit weird.'

His face went from joyous to wounded, and she felt bad. 'Oh, sorry, I just wanted to make sure you got home safe. Is it weird? I was just using the car as a mobile office and thought I'd park up here and surprise you.'

'Yes, it's very weird but that's also kind of you. I could have been at work until the early hours though. You could only sit and wait here for so long. Would you have gone home?'

He shrugged. 'Eventually.'

She realised if she was going to have to put an end to this relationship before it got going now was the time, but she couldn't do it. She needed company, someone to talk to and to take her mind off the last couple of shitty days. Why not let Fin be that person if he was willing?

'Come on, I'm starving. Didn't you offer to get a takeaway and supply the alcohol?'

He grinned at her. 'I did, I'm hungry too and will eat anything that you want. I'll even go and collect it.'

'Well like I told you before we have little choice in the autumn months when the tourists are few and far between. There's a Chinese, Italian or the chippy – take your pick, because I will literally eat anything I'm so hungry.'

'Italian?'

'Yes, Gino's does the best pasta. Let's go inside and I'll ring it in, then you can go collect it whilst I have a shower.'

Fin was out of the car, locking the door before she could say another word.

'Hey, you better move your laptop.'

He shrugged. 'Why? We are literally out in the middle of nowhere. Who is going to walk down this long, deserted country road to reach this place and steal it?'

He had a point, it was very unlikely. They went into her apartment and she took a menu for Gino's out of the kitchen drawer, passing it to Fin. He studied it then told her what he wanted, and she rang the order in.

'Should I pick up a couple of bottles of wine?'

'If that's okay, I need a drink after today.'

He didn't say anything but crossed to where she was standing and pulled her close to him. Then his lips were on hers and this time she didn't stop him. The warmth from his body felt good and for a moment she was tempted to tell him to forget about the food and to carry on, but her stomach let out the world's loudest groan, breaking the moment and they pulled apart. Fin laughed, and she blushed.

'I think you need something to eat, that was mighty impressive.'

'Haha, thank you.'

He left the apartment, and she locked the door behind him.

By the time the doorbell alerted her someone was at the door, she'd had a shower and was dressed in her nicest, only pair of black silk pyjamas that she'd bought for a special occasion. She figured this was as special an occasion as she was likely to have. As she looked at her phone to check who was standing outside the front door, she saw it was Fin. His hands full with pizza boxes and a carrier bag that clanked when he moved his hand. She opened the door and he came inside. They sat squashed on the oversized chair in the lounge and ate the pizza straight from the boxes, not bothering with plates or cutlery. In between sipping ice-cold rosé and mouthfuls of pizza, Morgan began to feel human again. She pushed all thoughts of Charlie and Macy out of her mind just for a few hours. They talked about the latest films, books and who should have won the Booker Prize for Fiction, and the best new series on Netflix. When there was nothing but pizza crusts left and empty wine glasses, she let out a yawn and grabbed Fin's hand.

'Let's go to bed.'

He took it and let her lead him into her bedroom.

CHAPTER TWENTY-SEVEN

This time when Macy opened her eyes it was dark. The small lamp on the bedside table was on and the tray with the empty plates had been replaced with a sandwich and a can of cola. She had a pain in her tummy and realised that she needed to wee, badly. If she didn't go to the toilet soon she would wet the bed and she hadn't done that since she was a baby. The door opened a little way and she saw his face, hiding in the shadows. This time she didn't pretend to be asleep. She began to wriggle and make a mewling sound. He rushed into the room, closing the door behind him, lifting his finger to his lips.

'Shhh, what's the matter?'

He tugged the gag out of her mouth and she whispered, 'I need to pee.'

He grimaced. A look of disgust flashed across his face but he nodded.

'Yes, of course you do. How silly of me. You can use the bathroom but no funny business or any noise. If you do as you're told you can go home tomorrow, but only if you keep quiet. We can't let my mother know you're here. Do you understand?'

She nodded. He untied her hands and feet, but before he let her stand up, he quickly checked outside to make sure the hallway was empty. He kept hold of the back of her T-shirt and marched her to the bathroom. Opening the door and practically throwing her inside, he hissed, 'Hurry up.'

Macy rushed to sit on the toilet and felt a sigh of relief she hadn't peed in her pants. She looked around another room of pink and purple flowers. There were bottles of shampoo, perfume and a dish full of old-fashioned fuzzy hair curlers on the side. She looked around for something she could use to help her escape and spied a small pair of scissors on the shelf above the sink. Flushing the toilet, she grabbed them and tucked them into the waistband of her leggings. Then she opened the door, and he stared at her and she realised that she knew him. Her head was thudding, and her brain felt as if a thick fog was inside it; she couldn't think straight. Why was she here? What did he want with her? As she stepped outside, he grabbed the back of her T-shirt again and led her back to her prison cell. Once they were inside, he whispered, 'Hold out your hands.'

She held them out, turning them over for him to see and hoping he wouldn't decide to pat her down. He motioned for her to get on the bed and she did. She didn't feel as if she could think straight enough to fight him, but if he tried to hurt her then she was ready. She would stab him in the eye with the scissors and make a run for it, and if his mother tried to stop her she'd stab her too. She shivered but got on the bed.

'Are you cold? I'll get you a blanket. We don't have duvets because Mother doesn't like them. No, in this house we use flannelette sheets and woollen blankets in the winter, cotton and polyester in the summer. Duvets are for lazy people and we are not lazy; we make our beds.'

Macy looked at him and thought that perhaps he was crazy; he talked as if he was. She didn't know what he was on about. He went to the wardrobe. Opening it slightly, he pulled a thick blanket out of it and carried it to the bed.

'Sorry, I need to tie your hands up first, but we don't need to tie your feet if you don't make a fuss.'

Nodding, she let him tie her wrists once more, although they didn't feel quite as tight this time. He left her feet which was good: she could wriggle around at least. She lay still and he threw a heavy woollen blanket on top of her.

'Do I need to gag you or will you be a good girl? My last friend wasn't a very good girl. She was too noisy and cried a lot; I had to stop her crying. You can understand that, can't you? So it's very important that you don't make any noise, because I like you and I wouldn't want to have to make you be quiet like I did with her.'

She nodded furiously.

'If you make a noise, you know what will happen, don't you?'

'Yes.'

'Okay, I'm trusting you not to mess this up. I'll be back after to check on you.'

He scurried towards the door then paused. Turning around, he rushed back over and shrugged as he began to tie the material around her mouth once more, although not as tight as the first time.

'I'm sorry, I want to trust you I really do, but you need to earn my trust. If you don't do anything stupid I'll remove it later.'

Then he was out of the door. She hoped that he might forget to lock it, but the key turned once more and she felt a sense of sadness wash over her. She wanted to see her mum. She lay there, her eyes glistening with tears and heard a voice shout from downstairs, 'Have you been eating in your bedroom again?'

The hairs on the back of her neck prickled at the sound of her voice. She sounded strange and scary, no wonder he didn't want her to know he had her hidden away. The man sounded terrified of his mother.

'Sorry.'

And then the house was silent once more, apart from the loud ticking of a clock somewhere. Macy lay there and tried to imagine how she could escape. She knew that she could; she wasn't going to end up staying here forever, and what about that Charlie kid, was she here too? Was she the friend he'd had to hurt to keep her quiet? And if she was, where was she now?

CHAPTER TWENTY-EIGHT

Emily had invited Ben over for supper. He had been very late and had phoned her to explain why. She had insisted he still come because she'd made enough food to feed a small army and it was a shame to throw it away. So he had and had seen the arrogant bastard's car parked on the shared drive. It annoyed the hell out of him that he'd just wormed his way into Morgan's life the way he had, and now it was gone eleven and he was still there. There were no lights on in Morgan's apartment, and it irritated him way more than it should, considering he'd just been to see her neighbour for supper. A kiss and a cuddle were all he could commit to at the moment, and Emily seemed happy enough with this arrangement, which made him feel bad for her. He didn't know if it was because he still felt like the worst husband in the world over Cindy, or whether it was because he was feeling so guilty about not finding Macy yet. As he walked to his car, he had the overwhelming urge to pick up one of the rockery stones and launch it through the back window of the Porsche. He didn't, he wouldn't, he was supposed to be on the right side of the law, which sometimes was tougher than he'd ever imagined. There had been a few times over the years he'd wanted to punch someone, though he never did, despite how wronged he'd been. Instead, he got in his car and reversed out. He was going home for a large glass of something strong to help him sleep. If he wasn't thinking about Charlie or where the hell Macy was, he was thinking about Morgan and it was almost getting torturous – so many questions with very few, if any, answers and they were all circling inside his mind like a tornado picking up speed.

When his alarm went off he groaned. Checking his phone, he had no missed calls, so they hadn't located Macy whilst he'd been off duty. After tossing and turning most of the night, he had not long gone into a deep slumber but he forced himself to get up and shower. He arrived at work before anyone else and collected the assortment of discarded mugs from desks and took them to the small kitchen area, to wash them all before filling the kettle. He wanted solid production today, he wanted Macy located and returned to her mother, and he wanted to know that Morgan had decided that Fin wasn't the right person for her, that he was a leech. Ben was pretty sure he was after something else, more than just her company. How many journalists drove cars like his? None that he knew of, even if they did come from London. He would have to be pretty amazing to afford that kind of motor. Taking the large mug of coffee he made himself, he went into the cramped office that was his and shut the door. He didn't spend much time in here; he preferred being out in the main office unless Amy was on one and making fun of everyone, or Des was trying to convert them all to be vegans, which was never going to happen because they all ate far too much crap. He put it down to the stresses of their job, the long hours and the stuff they dealt with day in and day out. Rydal wasn't a huge town, but it was big enough to have its fair share of problems. Granted the winter months were a lot quieter than the summer; winter was more domestics between the local residents. Summer was a barrage of lost property, shoplifting, sheep chasing and a lot of drunken antisocial behaviour around the pubs and one nightclub, which was sort of a slightly bigger pub that stayed open later than the rest. Logging on to his computer, he didn't go straight onto the police intranet which he usually did; instead he opened Google and typed 'Fin Palmer' into the search bar. As the page loaded, there were links to Facebook, Instagram, something from YouTube. He clicked his way through them and didn't see anything or anyone who remotely looked like Fin. Perturbed, he tried 'Finlay', 'Finley' and every other variation of his name but came up with nothing about a journalist from down south who was now working in Rydal Falls. He heard voices and looked up to see both Amy and Morgan filing through the door into the office and he quickly closed the page on his screen. He felt bad sneaking around, but surely someone like Fin had a social media presence? Where were his articles or links to them at least, if he was who he said he was?

Morgan knocked on his door and opened it a little.

'Morning. Would you like a brew?'

He raised his mug in her direction. 'I'm good, thanks.'

She smiled and closed his door. A voice in his head whispered: *What are you doing? This is way too far and it's none of your business. She's your friend; it is your business. You're only looking out for her best interests.*

His phone rang and he picked it up.

'Matthews.'

'*Oh, you sound grumpy today.*'

He smiled.

'Morning, Declan.'

'*That's better. The undigested stomach contents were confirmed as the remains of ham and pineapple pizza. Did you find out what Charlie's last meal was?*'

'Yes, Mum confirmed she ate pizza when she got in from school: ham and pineapple was the only kind she would eat.'

'*So, that means whoever killed her did so within two hours of her consuming it.*'

'Mum left the house to go to her friend's around fifty minutes after Charlie came home, and said she wasn't in the street and she thought that Dad had changed his mind and picked her up. So that means Charlie was with the killer at this point then, and either she died straight away or within the next hour.'

'*Did you ask her about the scratch on Charlie's arm? We've had nothing come back from it, unfortunately there was no DNA that could have led to our killer.*'

'She couldn't remember seeing it when she came home from school.'

'*Interesting, she might have got it from overgrown brambles maybe or a cat? It's very fine and you know how temperamental cats can be, we used to have one that would let you stroke it then out of the blue claw your hand to pieces. Have you checked all the gardens? What are they like? Are they well-kept or messy? I don't know the area where she lives. I don't think she was that far from home, Ben.*'

'Declan, you are a bloody genius. Thank you.'

'*Just doing my job. I want you to catch the bastard and find the other missing girl alive. We owe it to Charlie to do our best. I have to go, someone is calling on the office phone. If Susie is ringing in sick, I will probably cry.*'

He hung up, leaving Ben smiling. At least they had something to focus on. He went into the office where Morgan, Des and Amy were waiting for him to brief them. The door opened and in walked a windblown, flustered-looking Claire Williams. Everyone stared at her, even Ben; he had expected a phone call, maybe even a Teams meeting but not her to come in person.

'Morning, sorry I'm late. It was a bastard driving over Shap in this weather; I thought the wind was going to blow the hire car over the side. How are you all? Am I interrupting?'

Ben was still staring at her as if she'd walked in with three heads and not the one. Morgan stood up.

'Would you like a coffee, ma'am, warm you up a bit?'

She nodded. 'Yes, please, Morgan. That would be amazing.'

Morgan stood up and exited the room to go and make the coffee, and Ben found his voice.

'No, sorry, you're not. Interrupting I mean. Thank you for coming; it's very much appreciated. I have the policy book in my office for you to go through.'

He wasn't sure if it was. Did he want her sticking her nose in and telling him what a crap job he'd done up to now? Not really, but he also wasn't selfish enough not to accept her help; if it meant they had an extra pair of hands to bring Macy home safe that was all that mattered.

CHAPTER TWENTY-NINE

Morgan searched the kitchen cupboard for a mug that wasn't chipped or tea-stained and found one at the back. She gave it a scrub, rinsed it and took the coffee back to Claire, who was now at the back of the room leaning against a radiator. She was wearing a two-piece trouser suit similar to what Morgan had on yesterday and had almost frozen to death in. She hoped she wasn't going to be leaving the office much or she was going to freeze. The wind and rain had been cold enough yesterday; today it was much worse. The rain as it began to fall against the glass was thick with sleet. Morgan was glad she'd put on a thermal vest, thick black polo neck jumper and fur-lined leggings to keep her warm. She'd bought them in the sale at Primark last summer and wondered if she'd ever find a use for them. After a long night with Fin, she'd finally fallen into a deep sleep, expecting to wake up and find him sitting there at the end of her bed, but he'd left early and for that she'd been grateful. She'd been a little too drunk last night and it had shown. She wouldn't normally invite someone into her bed who she barely knew and felt more than a little embarrassed that she had. Not that she was complaining; the company and warmth had been nice, which was more than she could say about the sex. She didn't have the luxury of a string of lovers to compare Fin to, but it hadn't been at all what she'd expected; in fact, if anything, it had been quite dull.

'Morgan, if you could go with Amy and do that.'

She looked across at Ben, not even realising he'd been talking to her, and she felt her cheeks redden. A sharp kick under the desk from Amy and she nodded emphatically, no idea what she was nodding for but it seemed the right thing to do. Claire smiled at her, and she smiled back. Morgan liked Claire. She was nice, but very thorough and determined. Amy stood up, and Morgan followed her. Grabbing her thick waterproof coat from the back of her chair, she followed Amy out into the corridor.

'Earth to Morgan, Christ, where did you go? I thought your brain had been stolen out of your mind.'

'I was thinking.'

'About?'

'About last night.'

'Oh, what about last night? Please give me something to keep me going, some nice piece of gossip that will see me through for the next couple of days. Did you and Fin…?'

'It's none of your business what I get up to.'

'Tell me you didn't sleep with the journo? Not that I'd say no, because he's good looking and that car is enough to make me throw myself at him without a second thought.'

She shrugged. 'That's really shallow, you know, it's only a car.'

'Only a car? That car means he has plenty of cash.' She rubbed her fingers together. 'Cash means you get nice presents, go to nice restaurants, do nice things.'

'I'd rather have a picnic by the side of a lake with someone who wasn't as dull as dishwater, than all the money in the world.'

Amy laughed. 'God, he must have been crap in the bedroom then if the money means nothing.'

'Of course, money is nice, you'd have to be a fool not to think that. But there's more to life than that. I'd rather spend time with someone who—' She stopped talking. Who was she going to say? She had thought that Fin would be a distraction, take her mind off everything, but in fact she wasn't sure if it had made it worse.

*

The street where Charlie lived was no longer sealed off, but there were PCSOs parked in cars either end keeping an eye on it. Morgan waved to them as they drove past and parked a little further down. The ground was covered in big wet puddles, and she was glad to have a pair of boots on and extra thick socks. They got out of the car and both looked across at Charlie's house, which looked like a florists had opened in the scruffy front garden. There were flowers, teddy bears and balloons covering the grass.

Amy muttered, 'That's nice, not sure if I'd want everyone traipsing in my front garden, though, to lay a tribute. I couldn't be arsed.'

'It's sad. From what I can gather, no one bothered with Charlie when she was alive and out all weather, alone.'

'Guilty conscience, maybe the neighbours didn't know what else to do.'

'I'll take this side, you do Charlie's side. We're looking for what?'

Amy smiled. 'God, you weren't listening at all, were you? We are looking for anything sharp that could have caused a scratch on Charlie's arm that's within walking distance of her house. An overgrown garden with brambles, wild roses maybe.' Morgan nodded. 'Declan mentioned it could have been caused by a cat so we're looking for a neighbourhood cat as well.' Amy was staring at Charlie's front garden. 'It's a bit of a long shot, I know, but we've got to try.'

'Yes, we do, what else is there?'

'Exactly.'

Morgan began to walk along studying the front gardens, to see if there were any that were messy. Along this side they were all perfectly landscaped, apart from one: Eleanor Fleming's house. Clipped hedges, mowed lawns, paved paths with neat flower beds and not a bramble in sight. Morgan squeezed through the gate and began to look closely for anything that could have caused the scratch. There were no roses or brambles. The door opened a crack, and she turned at the sound of the voice.

'Have you lost something? Can I help you?'

She glanced across the road. Amy was strolling along the opposite side doing the same. Staring into the front gardens from the pavement, she realised she might have gone a little too far.

'Morning, sorry, I was looking for a piece of paper which blew out of my hand.'

'Oh, let me help you. It gets really windy along this part of the street for some strange reason. Hang on, I'll put my shoes on.'

She felt bad, she was crap at lying, but she didn't want him to think she'd singled out his garden because it wasn't as tidy as the others. Smiling at him and carried on looking around, and he joined her. After a minute he stopped.

'Sorry, Morgan, it's not here. Have you tried next door?'

'Yes, no worries. Thanks for helping.'

He smiled at her and went back into the house, about to shut the door.

'Can I just ask a little more about Eleanor?'

He froze on the spot, and she realised that he didn't like to talk about it. Even after all this time, it was still painful for him.

'What about her?'

'Oh, you know: who her friends were, the name of the officers who were dealing with it, did she have a boyfriend? Oh, actually, sorry, I forgot she had a boyfriend who moved away, didn't she? Do you think she followed him? Was there a chance she was glad to escape? Did she have any reason to leave the family home?'

'That's an awful lot of questions.'

It was and she realised this, but it was bothering her and she was itching to dig out all the files on her as soon as she got a minute.

'I know, I'm sorry to keep dragging it up and upsetting you. I just don't like how no one bothered too much that she'd gone.'

'You don't think she ran away?'

Morgan shook her head. 'I'm not fully convinced. Truthfully, are you?'

He shrugged. 'I'm not a detective, I'm not anything or anyone with knowledge of such things.' He stepped back outside, closing the door, and lowered his voice.

'My mother didn't think so, but she didn't want to think anything bad had happened either, so she went along with it, with what the police told her. It broke her. She was always such a strong woman. She brought us up on her own, in this house, and took very good care of us. She was strict with us, but no more than we deserved I suppose. After Eleanor left she turned to God, devoting her time to Him. I was old enough to look after myself, so it didn't matter to me what she did. I wanted to move away too, but I couldn't leave her in the end. She stopped eating properly and the only time she left the house was to go to church. It left her, both of us, a mess, but we believed what we were told. Who were we to question the police? Now, she's not well at all and spends most of her days in bed. Eleanor's running off might have given her the life she wanted, but it ruined ours and for that I can't forgive her.'

'I'd really like to speak to your mother. Could you ask her if I can come back at a time that suits her?'

A look of pain – or was it annoyance – flashed across his face. 'I'll ask her, but I can't promise you she will be interested. How can I get in touch? She's sleeping now and I can't disturb her; we had a very unsettled night.'

'Of course, thank you.' She tugged a card out of her pocket. 'This is my work number; if it goes to voicemail then you can ring my personal number. Hang on.' Taking a pen she wrote her phone number down and her house phone, just in case he didn't like to phone mobiles. He was a bit old-fashioned, not that there was anything wrong with that, she just wanted him to be able to get hold of her if his mother decided to talk to her.

He took it from her. 'Thank you, I'll ask. Oh, the detective who dealt with it was a Mr Peterson. I don't think he'll still be working now: he was getting on when he took it on.'

'Was he good?'

'Compared to you, Morgan, probably not. He liked to drink, I think; his breath always smelt of stale alcohol.'

'Thank you for your help.'

He smiled at her. This time he did go inside and shut the heavy wooden front door behind him.

Amy was walking towards her on this side of the street, and Morgan went out of the garden to meet her.

'Now what?' asked Amy.

'We carry on. Let's head in the direction of Macy's house. It's not that far away. What was Vince's garden like?'

Amy shook her head. 'Neat and tidy, not an overgrown bramble in sight.'

'Hmm, that's a shame. Imagine if he'd had a huge tangle of them spilling onto the road – it could have been case closed, bye Vince, enjoy the rest of your life inside.'

'If only it were that simple. It would have been on *Luther* or *Vera*; they seem to get nice clues handed to them on a plate.'

Morgan smiled. 'I wouldn't mind being handed to Luther on a plate.'

Amy sighed. 'Me either, now I would understand you fawning over the boss if he looked like him.'

Morgan knew then that she had to snap out of it. If it was so obvious to Amy that she liked Ben then the whole station might know. She decided to make more of an effort with Fin. They'd consumed two bottles of wine and eaten a huge amount of pizza before going to bed. It would hamper anyone's passion.

'Right then, let's find us an overgrown garden. We haven't got all day. The clock might be ticking for Macy.'

'God, I hope that kid is safe. I couldn't sleep last night thinking about her.'

This took Morgan by surprise. She hadn't realised that Amy had a soft heart underneath her tough exterior. 'Yes, let's hope so.'

*

As they began walking along Bay Fell Grove, they were too immersed in looking into people's front gardens to notice the man watching them from a distance. She had got out of a white Ford Focus, which had been left unlocked, along with a much taller woman. For coppers they weren't very security conscious. He peered through the window and spotted a small, black handbag on the passenger seat floor. Opening the door just enough to reach inside, he grabbed the bag and felt inside it; there was a small purse, a notebook and a letter inside it. He wasn't interested in anything except the letter. Tugging it out of the bag, he stuffed it into his pocket, put the bag back on the floor and closed the door. He looked around, no one seemed to be paying him any attention, so he continued his slow stroll. Obviously, the investigation was still focused around this area, which was a bit of a worry for him. He walked past the house with a sea of fresh flowers outside, along with balloons and teddy bears, a wave of sadness washing over him. A woman wearing police uniform got out of a car at the end of the street and he almost had a heart attack: had she watched him steal from the handbag in the car he'd just been looking inside? Picking up his pace, he carried on walking towards her. She glanced his way but then began to cross the road. As he got near, he called out, 'Morning, officer.'

She turned to him and smiled. 'Morning.' Then turned away as her radio began to ring like a phone. He didn't stay to see anything else. He needed to get away from here. That had been close, too close for his liking.

CHAPTER THIRTY

Ben, Claire and Tom were in the small office which had been turned into an incident room to deal with Charlie's murder and Macy's disappearance. A Gold command meeting had been called with the chiefs at headquarters, and Ben had the policy book in which he'd written down everything the team had done since the initial call came in; every procedure and investigation was there ready for anyone who needed to see what had been done so far. Initially, Tom had decided not to use the HOLMES 2 computer system, but now he had drafted in some staff from the Intel unit and had them frantically inputting everything into the system. The only problem for Ben with HOLMES was that it wasn't as fast as he'd have liked it to be; he much preferred to do the thinking himself. They'd only ever had to use it once before and that was for the Riverside Rapist enquiry. Claire finished going through the book and passed it back to him.

'I can't see that there is anything different I would have suggested. This is all as it should be.'

He nodded. His shoulders, which had been tight, relaxed a little. He didn't care about getting in trouble, but he cared deeply if he'd made bad decisions that could have cost Charlie her life, and Macy's too.

'So what are we doing now? Is there anything that needs to be done that we haven't already?'

'How long has Macy been missing?'

'Approximately thirty-eight hours.'

'How long was Charlie missing before her body turned up?'

'We think she went missing around six p.m. and was discovered approximately twenty-three hours later, around five p.m. the following day.'

'Then why do you think Macy hasn't turned up?'

'It's possible that the offender tried to help Charlie, and that maybe somehow the injury was accidental, which was why he left her in such a public place.'

'Then why take another girl? If he felt bad about hurting Charlie, why take another so soon?'

'It didn't work out how he'd imagined and a chance encounter with Macy was too good an opportunity to miss. It's likely that Macy ran straight into him in the dark alleyway, and if that's so then he must live locally to both Charlie and Macy. If that's true, he can watch the investigation from the window of his house.'

'This Vincent Jackson, he also lives in the same area and has previous?'

'Yes, we took his car away to be forensically examined, but nothing has come back from that yet. Vince has also been questioned twice, and his solicitor said unless we had some concrete evidence other than circumstantial, he did not want to see him brought in a third time.'

'But he's the only substantial suspect that we have?'

'At one point, I did think that Charlie's dad might have somehow accidentally hurt her when he was supposed to have picked her up and panicked, but after he almost strangled Des in broad daylight yesterday, and we brought him in, he admitted he'd been evasive with our questions because he's having an affair and cheating on the woman he left Charlie's mum for.'

Claire nodded. 'Sounds like a great guy, does Brett.'

Ben smiled. 'Charlie had a scratch on her arm that her mum said she didn't have before she left the house. I've sent Amy and Morgan out to scour the area for overgrown gardens, anything that could explain how she got that injury. Claire, I don't know what else to do. I know we're sitting on a ticking time bomb and every second is another threat to Macy's life.'

Tom stood up, and he began pacing up and down the small room. 'Let's bring Vincent in again. This time we'll get CSI to go over his house with a fine-tooth comb. Does he have access to any lock-ups, garages, buildings that we may have overlooked?'

'I don't think so, sir. What will we do with his mum? She's elderly and has dementia.'

'Grab a PCSO to come and sit with her whilst we search. Is she allowed to be home alone, or does she need full care?'

'I think she's okay for a little while. She was okay whilst we had him in custody yesterday.'

'If not get on to adult social care, see if someone can arrange for her to go to a safe place.'

Ben nodded. As much as he wanted it to be Vincent – he fit what they were looking for – he had a feeling that Vince was purely in the wrong place at the wrong time. There was no way he could hide two young girls in a house with his mother and not get caught. He didn't want to waste time following a lead that was futile and not going to help them find Macy, but he also knew they had to prove to the public that they were doing everything they could, and by targeting Vince it looked like they were.

Claire looked from Ben to Tom. 'I'm happy with that if you are. What about the riverside? There's lots of fields and the woods on the opposite side, could he have a hidey-hole in them where she may be hidden? I think we need to extend the search from the immediate area and spread outwards. We can ask Mountain Rescue to help with the woods and the riverside. We have to expand. If we've tried everything locally and are getting nowhere then we have to face the possibility that whoever has her has access to somewhere out of the public view, enough to hide a child without anyone hearing and seeing. Is that okay, Ben?'

An uneasy feeling in the pit of his stomach told him that no, it wasn't okay. They were moving the search way out of the area, the area, which he hoped was the right thing to do. What else could they do, though? There had been no evidence to say that either girl had been hidden away in plain sight.

'So, we'll get an arrest team in place and bring Vince in again and rip his house apart from top to bottom. At the same time, we'll have dedicated search teams scouring the riverbanks and woods. Is there any chance that Macy could have wandered off herself? I mean it's rare, but sometimes the most obvious reasons are overlooked. Charlie's killer might not have taken Macy. This could genuinely be a missing girl who has wandered too far and injured herself.'

'Yes, that's a possibility, Claire. We have to take it into consideration.'

She smiled at him. 'Now, I'll get the coffees in whilst you get the cogs moving, Tom, and arrange the search teams.'

She grabbed her jacket off the back of the chair and her purse from her bag, then walked out of the room and the station.

Ben went back into the office where Des was watching her from the window.

'She had enough of you already, boss?'

'No, she's gone in search of coffee.'

'Can't say I blame her. Morgan's brews are pretty awful. So, what's happening then?'

'I don't know, Des; I think I've just been sideswiped. They're getting Mountain Rescue in to search the woods and the riverside.'

'We did that when Charlie went missing, pulled out all the stops, helicopter and the lot.'

'I suppose it's the next step; we don't seem to be getting anywhere fast.'

'Is she bringing coffee back for you and me, or should we get out of here and go find our own? Hadn't you better break the news to Morgan and Amy? They're still out hunting for overgrown gardens.'

'Come on, we'll go find them.'

Ben didn't know what the niggling feeling in the pit of his stomach was and whether it was purely down to the fact that they still hadn't located Macy, or the fact that his investigation had just been taken over by someone else.

CHAPTER THIRTY-ONE

The sound of the key turning in the locked door startled Macy. She hadn't even realised she had drifted off to sleep again. Why was she so sleepy? She wasn't normally. The door opened and he stood there for a few moments in the shadows; this room was so gloomy and dark. Her mouth went dry and her heart was pounding in her chest as she wondered if this was it: had he decided it was time to do something horrible to her? Well if he did she was ready. The small scissors were still tucked down the back of her pants; somehow she would get free and use them on him if she had to.

Opening the door, he walked inside and flicked on the light, causing a muffled screech of panic from Macy as she scrabbled around trying to escape.

'It's such a shame. You are like a caged bird, so delicate and beautiful. Your hair is the loveliest golden colour. I would have liked hair as soft and silky as yours.' He lifted a finger to his lips. 'Shh. We don't make loud noises in this house; Mother doesn't like it. Little girls should be seen and not heard. Haven't you ever been taught that?'

She stared at him, wide-eyed, shaking her head. He smiled at her and closed the door behind him. Turning off the bright light, he crossed to the other bedside table and put the lamp on.

'Do you like to play games? I adore playing games. My favourite is Cluedo. If you're a good girl we can play that one tomorrow. I thought we could have a nice, quiet game of Scrabble to pass the time. I'll untie your wrists so you can play, but if you do anything silly then I'm going to have to tie you back up again, and that would be such a shame to ruin what could be a pleasant way to get to know each other. Nod your head if you understand me and agree.'

Her head moved up and down fast.

'Good, that's very good. Have you ever played Scrabble?'

She looked at the green box in his hands and shrugged.

'That's okay, it's really easy. We both get some of the little cream squares with letters on and you have to make words up with them. For every word you get points. I'm sure you'll get the hang of it.'

He took the tray he'd brought her sandwiches up on. 'You didn't eat. Why? You'll make yourself ill if you don't.'

Then he looked at the gag in her mouth and let out a shrill giggle. 'I'm so silly, I forgot to take that off. No wonder you couldn't eat. You must be so hungry; can you ever forgive me for being such a bad host?' He leant forward and removed the silk scarf from her mouth. She began to sob. He patted the top of her head.

'It's okay, don't cry. I'm afraid the bread has gone a little bit hard, but you can still eat them, can't you? I can't waste them; it's a sin to throw away good food.'

He offered her a drink from the glass. The paper straw he'd put in had gone all soggy and he plucked it out and threw it into the bin. Lifting the glass to her lips, she took some huge gulps of the orange juice then smiled at him. He blotted the sides of her mouth with a piece of paper towel then lifted up a quarter of a sandwich for her to nibble on. She did, small bites at first then bigger mouthfuls until she'd eaten everything, even the stale crusts.

'My, you must have been very hungry.'

'Thank you, I was.'

'Oh, you have a voice. That's nice, I was beginning to think you might be mute. You have a very nice voice.'

Macy smiled at him. He smiled back.

'Good, that's very good. Should we play then? I'm afraid I'll have to gag you again. I really don't like to but we can't let Mother know that we're having fun. She would be furious if she thought that we were enjoying ourselves.'

A tear began to roll down the corner of her eye and down her cheek.

'Oh, don't be sad. This isn't for long; you won't have to stay like this forever. I'll untie your hands so you can play, and if we enjoy ourselves, next time I'll free your hands and mouth.'

He leant across her as he carefully placed the band of soft material inside her mouth. He didn't tie it quite as tight as earlier – she had red marks on the corner of her mouth where the material had bit into the soft flesh. They played the game, and a couple of times she smiled when he praised her and laughed. After an hour, he must have forgot all about his mother, he was so absorbed in having fun. He jumped up. Grabbing the box, he threw all the letter tiles in it and the board and, placing the lid on it, he scrambled to the bedroom door. Realising he hadn't tied her hands up, he rushed back, managing to tie one hand. Leaving one hand untied he rushed out of the door, closed it softly and locked it behind him.

Macy had watched, bewildered, as he'd jumped up so violently and tipped the game back into the box. She hadn't heard anything, but realised when he'd shouted he was coming that his mum must be home. She had been shaking and scared, at first, when he'd brought her here, but now she didn't feel so afraid. He hadn't hurt her like she'd thought he was going to; in fact, he'd been kind to her. She knew he wasn't right in the head; everyone knew this who lived around here. The older boys called him names and she used to feel bad for him. Well she did until he kidnapped her. At least she knew where he lived and it wasn't far from her house. She just needed to be able to get loose and then she'd climb out of the window and down the drainpipe in the middle of the night. Boy would she run home as fast as she could. Her mum was going to be raging with her for being away so long. She would be grounded until she left senior school but she didn't care. She'd never wanted her mum this badly in all her life, and then there was poor Max. She hoped he'd gone home when she'd fallen over and not run away. She would never be the same again if something happened to him because she'd been selfish and wanted a bar of chocolate.

She heard him outside on the landing then his footsteps as he ran downstairs. She lifted a hand to wipe the tears that were filling her eyes and wondered what was wrong, then she wiggled her fingers around and smiled. He'd forgotten to tie it back up: she had a free hand and if she had a free hand, she could untie herself. The first thing she did was tug the silk scarf from out of her mouth and suck in air. She opened her mouth to scream for help then stopped: if he was that scared of his mum, she didn't want her to be the one to see who was screaming for help in the bedroom. She might be horrible and hurt her or not let her go, so she decided to be a good girl like he asked. Her first plan was the better one: she would get loose then clamber out of the window as soon as it was dark and they had both gone to bed.

She looked around the bedroom; he'd left the small lamp on by the side of the bed. It was really old, like the kind of bedroom in one of her favourite films *The Haunted Mansion*. The furniture was all dark wood and had pictures of flowers carved into it. Everything was pink; she had never seen a kid or a girl leave this house only the funny man. Although if this belonged to his sister and she wasn't like him, how would she know who she was? – she might have moved away from them both. Macy wouldn't blame her if she had. If she had a brother like him and a mum even scarier than her own, she probably wouldn't stick around either. She began to use her left hand to try and pick at the knots in the material he'd used to tie her hands to the bed, but it was hard work and for once she wished she'd listened to her mum when she'd told her to stop nibbling her nails until they bled. Long nails would have been really useful. Realising she could drink, she picked up the glass of juice and drank the rest of it, grimacing at the chalky, bitter taste at the bottom which tasted like some awful medicine her mum would give her when she was poorly. After some time she began to yawn. She couldn't get the knot loosened at all and everything seemed like hard work; she was so tired. It didn't help that things kept going a bit blurry. She yawned again and after another ten minutes found her eyes closing. She couldn't keep them open. She decided that the best thing to do was to have a little sleep; at least when she woke up he might be asleep and hopefully his mother would be too. She would have more energy after a little rest, then she would bite the knots out if she had to. This time as her eyes closed, she lay her head on the soft pillows and fell asleep.

CHAPTER THIRTY-TWO

Morgan didn't think she'd ever seen Ben wearing such an open expression of despair. He'd turned up with Des and told them what the plan was. She and Amy hadn't bothered to question it: they were running out of options, she knew this, and who was to say that Vince didn't have somewhere in the woods he could have hidden the missing girl? She hadn't thought about the woods, and now that she was, though, her aunt Ettie's soft, kind face filled her mind. She hadn't spoken to her for a while, and she lived in those woods. As soon as they found Macy, she would pay her a visit. She would probably remember Eleanor Fleming's disappearance.

'I feel as if I've let Macy down. We haven't located her and, as positive as I'm trying to be, I have a despairing feeling in the pit of my stomach that we're too late, and he's getting braver.'

She patted his arm. 'What are we doing about searching the woods?'

'Us, personally? Nothing. There's a search team going in with Mountain Rescue. We're still focusing on this area. I think she's around here, I honestly do. This is just a smokescreen to make it look as if we're leaving no stone unturned, but I have a horrible feeling it's a bit of a wild goose chase. I understand that it needs to be done, but still.'

There was the loud slamming of doors as a large van pulled up further along the street and four uniformed officers got out. A small car parked behind them and two women got out. Ben smiled at them.

'Vince is going to be royally pissed off with the police. How are they justifying arresting him again? And who are they?'

'Vince's mother's rescuers, they'll take her to the day care centre. Claire and Tom agree that he's the most suitable suspect. This time the house is getting emptied and CSI are going in to do a full forensic search. Oh and I'm going back to interview him this time, along with Amy, because he doesn't like her and we're hoping she might ruffle his feathers enough for him to slip up.'

Morgan felt deflated. She would have liked the chance to interview him, but she was only a level two interviewer and Amy was level four.

'You can oversee the search if you want. Keep me updated if they find anything.'

'What about his mother?'

'Social care is taking her to spend a cosy evening at Bevan House whilst we turn the house over. If he's innocent and we find nothing then she can come home when he's released, although she might prefer it there. At least she'll have company from others the same age, instead of being stuck with him all the time.'

'Good luck with Vince.'

Ben smiled at her. There was a lot of shouting, and they both turned around to see Vince being dragged from his house kicking and fighting. It didn't make much difference to the two officers who were marching him to the van; they towered over him and had lifted him off his feet, so he was effectively being carried to the cage, his legs pedalling into the air as if he was riding an imaginary bike, until they reached the van where he was thrown inside. The heavy doors slammed shut – the noise so loud it echoed around the street.

'He's not a happy bunny.'

'No, he isn't and, to be honest, as much as I want it to be him, and Christ knows I want this over with, I just don't think he has the balls for it. He's more of a sneaky, porn-watching little creep.'

'I'll wait for CSI then, good luck.'

'Should I leave Des with you, Morgan? Are you desperate for company?'

'Not that desperate, thanks. I'm good. There's really no point if it's just a matter of waiting for them to finish. You can, however, leave me a car to sit in. I'm not standing around freezing in this for hours. It's forecast heavy rain later; I'd like somewhere dry to supervise from.'

Ben smiled at her and threw the car keys in her direction. She caught them and wondered if she should go in and take a look when everyone had left. Then decided against it; she didn't want to compromise anything that may be evidential if there was any there. Instead, she drove the car Ben had arrived in to Vince's house and waited for the van to drive off, then she pulled into the empty space right in front of the house. The two women came out with Vince's mum, who looked confused but happy enough to be going with them. Morgan waved at her and she smiled at her then got into the car. Morgan began to Google 'Eleanor Fleming', to see what the newspaper reports said. There was nothing, except 'Teenage Girl Suspected of Running Away'; underneath the caption were two photos, one of Eleanor, who looked like your average teenager, albeit a rather conservatively dressed one in a long black dress that went almost to her ankles, and another of Detective Sergeant Geoff Peterson, a rather sturdy man with a shock of white hair and a ruddy complexion. She carried on scrolling and found a small article about the funeral arrangements for Geoff Peterson. She let out a groan: she wasn't going to be talking to him this side of her life.

CHAPTER THIRTY-THREE

CSI came out of Vincent's house with a handful of evidence bags, and Morgan got out of the car and walked to meet Wendy, who was followed by Isla.

'That doesn't look very impressive.'

Wendy shrugged, passing the house key to Morgan. 'It isn't, there is nothing in there to suggest he hid Charlie in there or has hidden Macy. I've bagged up some muddy trainers in case he trampled through the woods in them – we can get the soil tested, but even that's not much because the woods are a popular place to go walking. A couple of empty cola cans and sweet wrappers, to check for fingerprints, but there is literally no evidence that is going to help us find Macy.'

'Damn, Ben is going to be devastated.'

'He's not the only one.'

Morgan watched as they loaded the bags into the van, stripped off their protective clothing and then drove back to the station. Clutching the key in her hand, she paused at the gate to Vince's house and wondered if she should go and take a look herself. Not that she was expecting to find her but she'd been in a similar situation with the Potters' case and was the one to find them dead in the cellar of their house. She didn't need gloves; the house had been forensically examined. Locking the car, she took a quick look up and down the street, to make sure Vince wasn't on his way back, and then she slipped inside, closing the front door behind her, and began to search the house. This wasn't some large, detached, secluded home with a hidden cellar and they'd checked the attic. Still, she wasn't giving up that easily. Satisfied there was no cupboard or hidden doors, she went upstairs. There was a ladder to the side of the loft hatch. She leant it against the wall and climbed up it, pushing the hatch open. She pulled herself up into the dusty space and turned on the torch on her phone. Shining it around, she saw it was definitely just the same as it had been when she'd checked with Ben for Charlie. *Where are you, Macy?* she whispered, then began to climb back down the ladders. She saw a man standing on the landing, who took one look at her and let out a strangled cry.

'Oh my God,' Morgan screeched; her heart was pounding. Vincent Jackson's complexion was paler than hers.

'Jesus Christ, will you people leave me alone? I've had enough of this now. Everyone in the whole street thinks I've taken those kids. I told you the other night I didn't, I haven't. I'm tired of this.'

'I'm sorry and yes, you did.'

'Get out.'

Morgan nodded. She smiled at him and walked past him downstairs and straight out of the front door, furious that no one had phoned her to tell her Vince had been released – that could have turned out disastrous. Her phone began to ring, and she tutted to see Ben's name.

'Yes.'

'*We had to release him. We have nothing on him and his solicitor was foaming at the mouth.*'

'Really, thanks for letting me know.'

'*Why, where are you?*'

'I was in his attic, just double-checking, when he tipped up. I almost had a heart attack, Ben.'

'*Jesus, Morgan, what were you doing in there on your own?*'

'I don't know, hoping that I'd find her like I found the Potters. Well not like that. I want Macy to be alive and full of life but…'

She couldn't find the words to continue and the silence between them hung in the air until Ben broke it.

'*The search of the woods and river has been called off; it's too dark now to continue safely. They'll be out again at first light. There's been a press release issued to warn parents and carers not to let children outside on their own without adult supervision under any circumstances.*'

'That's good?'

'*Why don't you go home? There is literally nothing else we can do.*'

'Are you?'

'*Yes, I am. At some point I need to catch some sleep. It's Emily's birthday and we're going out for a couple of drinks. Do you want to join us? I'm sure she'd love that. She asks about you all the time, Morgan, I think she'd like to be friends.*'

'No, I'm okay, thanks. Have a lovely evening and tell her Happy Birthday from me.'

'*You could tell her yourself.*'

She ended the call. If her stomach was churning before, it was in complete turmoil now. She was glad that he'd told her about going for drinks with Emily. It was nice, but it still made her feel this way and she wondered what was wrong with her. She was seeing Fin, so she shouldn't be remotely bothered by what Ben got up to – this was totally ridiculous – and what did he mean that Emily would like to be friends? That was a weird thing to say. She was nice to her and chatted whenever she saw her. What else did she want from her? She drove back to the station to take this car back and get her knackered old Corsa that had seen better days.

CHAPTER THIRTY-FOUR

Driving home, Morgan decided she was going to lie in bed and read. She didn't want to see anyone, but as she pulled into the drive and saw Fin's car parked up, she quickly forgot about those plans. This time she decided she was happy to see him: if Ben could enjoy himself whilst they were in the middle of a high-risk missing child case, then she could kick off her shoes and let down her hair a little too. Despite her initial reservations about Fin, she found that she liked him a little more every time she saw him. He jumped out of the car, and she smiled – he was the kind of good looking you saw in magazines; the sort of man who would model for Gucci or Armani – and she found herself staring at him. He exuded an air of elegance and charm that was the sort brought on by being brought up by wealthy parents, which was why his choice of flat puzzled her. She didn't know his financial standing but he always seemed to have a wallet bulging with cash and lots of credit cards, so how come he didn't want to stay in a much nicer place than the one he was in? Then again, who was she to judge? Her apartment was far more expensive than she'd like, but to her being able to live in such a beautiful place was worth every penny. She hadn't gone to university like some of her friends, so had no extortionate student loans to repay or lots of debt. She got out of the car, and Fin grinned at her. Leaning into the passenger side, he pulled out the biggest bouquet of the most exquisite roses and lilies she had ever seen. He passed them to her along with a bottle of rosé Bollinger and did a little bow. Taking hold of her hand he kissed it.

'Thank you, they're beautiful, but what's the occasion?'

'Beautiful flowers for a beautiful lady, and, to celebrate.'

Morgan smiled. Catching sight of her reflection in the window of his Porsche, she currently looked like she'd just come back from a day walking up the fells. Her bobble hat had flattened her hair, her lipstick had come off hours ago and the tip of her nose was bright red with the cold. She laughed, shaking her head at him, two tiny perfect circles of red appearing on her cheeks.

'Well in that case you better come inside and see if you can find the glasses you must have mislaid last time you were here.' An uncomfortable feeling inside her chest took away some of the surprise. They went inside, Fin following her. She shut the door behind him, bolting it. Shrugging off her coat and hat, she hung them in the cupboard and walked to the kitchen, where Fin was already uncorking the champagne.

'What are we celebrating?'

He smiled at her. 'My book deal.'

'Oh, I didn't know you were writing one. Congratulations, I mean what a fantastic achievement.'

He nodded. 'God, it's been so long and I've had so many rejections that I don't even talk about it any more. Why don't we have a drink and if you're ready to be bored, I can tell you all about it.'

Placing the flowers in some water, she opened a cupboard and took out the only two wine glasses she owned. 'Sorry, I've never bought champagne so I don't have any proper glasses.'

'These are fine, we can fill them up and it saves messing around. I have two more bottles in the car.'

'I'm just going to freshen up and change out of these damp jeans. I won't be long.'

She went into her bedroom, which was still an untidy mess from last night. Throwing the duvet back on the bed, she plumped up the pillows and grabbed a pair of shorts and a soft white silk shirt that she only buttoned halfway up, showing a good section of her cleavage. Stripping off the damp clothes, she quickly spritzed herself in deodorant and perfume and got dressed. Brushing her hair, she backcombed it a little and pouted her lips whilst dabbing on her favourite deep red lipstick. Feeling a bit less stuffy, she walked back into the lounge where Finn was waiting for her. He walked up to her, and wrapping his arms around her waist, squeezing tight, he bent down his lips, brushing her cheek.

'Mm, you always smell good enough to eat.'

She laughed, pulling away from him. 'Better than my cooking then? I burnt the pasta bake I made this morning.'

He smiled and began expertly unwrapping the wire from the cork. He did it with such ease it struck her that he had done this many times before, because she wouldn't have a clue where to start. Popping the cork, he held it under her nose. She sniffed and nodded, not quite sure what she was sniffing or what her reaction was supposed to be. The fizz began to leak over the side of the bottle, and he took a glass from the side to catch the fizzing pale pink liquid. When it was almost full he passed it to her. Filling the other, he raised it in the air, clinking it against hers.

'Cheers, Morgan, here's to hard work, never giving up and dreams coming true.'

'Cheers.' She took a sip. 'Oh, now this is nice, I could get used to drinking this.'

'Well if I sell plenty of books, we will drink it for breakfast every day.'

She laughed. 'Sounds good to me.'

CHAPTER THIRTY-FIVE

Ben was sitting in The Black Dog with Emily, who looked stunning, but he couldn't concentrate on her conversation because all he kept thinking about was finding Charlie's killer, Macy – and Morgan. He felt like he was watching a train wreck happen in slow motion and there was nothing he could do to stop it. He wished he'd never asked his friend to do some digging into Finley Palmer's business; if he was still oblivious, he wouldn't be feeling this responsible. How could he tell her without admitting that he'd been snooping around when he had no right to? Before he'd left home, he'd read the message and had been so overwhelmed by rage, he'd punched a hole into the new plasterboard wall in the lounge, and now his knuckles were swollen and painful. He'd wished the satisfying crunch as his fist went through it had been Fin's nose. How dare he come here and do this to her without any thought of the harm he was causing? He could feel a vein throbbing in the side of his temple and hoped he wasn't about to have a stroke. He was trying to keep calm for Emily's sake – this was so unfair on her.

'So, what do you think I should do? Would I make a good police officer or should I stick with teaching?'

'What?'

'Should I apply to join the police? They're advertising. Have you listened to anything I've said, Ben?'

'Yes, I'm sorry. You could try it, I suppose, if it's something you've always wanted to do. If you don't like it you could go back to teaching.'

'I suppose I could, yes. I'm just a bit worried about the dead bodies, you know. Would I manage with the smell and all that mess? I don't know how you and Morgan do it. I suppose you get used to it.'

He stared at her, realising they were on two completely different planets. 'Excuse me, I have to make a phone call. I won't be long.' He left her there at the table, staring after him, as he went outside and rang Morgan. It went to voicemail.

'Morgan, it's me, can you ring me back when you get a minute?'

As he went back inside the pub, he hoped his voice hadn't sounded desperate. Emily had been to the bar and this time there was a bottle of wine in the middle of table. She poured herself a large glass and offered him one, but he shook his head. He might get a call from work, so he was only having one or two lagers.

'Have you had a nice day? Did you get anything nice?'

He realised he knew very little about her; he didn't know if she had family to buy her gifts and was glad he'd remembered to pick up some flowers and a card on the way here from the Co-op.

'Yes, thanks. Have you been busy at work? Any sign of that poor girl?'

'Very busy, and unfortunately not.'

Emily nodded. Taking a huge mouthful of wine, she stared him in the eye. 'Did you ask Morgan to come?'

'Yes, I did. She was going home. She said "Happy Birthday" though, and she'll see you again.'

He had his fingers crossed under the table. He hated lying and Emily was so nice, but she wasn't Morgan and he knew this now. He was furious with Fin. He couldn't bear to see her hurt or treated this way; she deserved so much more. He'd spent many sleepless nights thinking about her and come up with lots of reasons why it wouldn't ever work between them: he had too much emotional baggage; she wouldn't understand; they were too alike. The crushing feeling in his chest, knowing that she was currently dating a liar, cheat and a fraud who didn't care about her, was such a betrayal of her trust. He needed her to phone him back so he could talk to her about it.

'You're a terrible liar, Ben. Your eyes go in every direction when you're not speaking the truth. Please, don't get me wrong, I don't mean it in a horrible way. I know you only do it to protect my feelings and that is very noble of you, but...'

Mortified, he took a gulp of lager. 'But, what?'

'If you like Morgan so much, why don't you tell her how you feel? You're both consenting adults. I think she likes you just as much as you like her.'

'Am I that transparent?'

She smiled at him, nodding her head. 'I think that you would make a great couple. I know you're her boss and she's younger than you, but at the end of the day it's what's inside here that counts.' She patted her heart. 'Life is too short not to be happy, Ben, and I like you a lot, but I know I don't make you happy like she does. I'm a bit forward and always have been. I asked you out, so you don't need to feel bad for me – it's not like we're in a serious relationship. I phoned my friend whilst you were outside, and she's on her way now; we can get drunk, sink shots and stagger home. You don't have to worry about leaving me here on my own.'

He reached out and took hold of her hand. 'Emily, you are such a lovely woman. I'm sorry for spoiling your birthday.'

'Bah, you haven't spoilt it. I'm a sucker for a good love story, go see her and tell her how you feel.'

He laughed. Standing up, he bent down and kissed her cheek. 'Happy Birthday, thank you.'

She waved him away, and he walked out of the pub.

Once he was in his car he wasn't sure what to do. He didn't want to ring her, but what choice did he have? She hadn't answered and he wondered what he should do. He needed to warn her. Was he causing trouble or looking out for her? He didn't know. What he did know was that he couldn't stay here and let her get hurt this way. He'd seen the headline for tomorrow's paper and knew she was going to be devastated. He took a screen shot of the photo he'd been sent and forwarded it on to Morgan. If she didn't answer his call, hopefully, she'd see the message and smack that smarmy bastard into next week herself.

CHAPTER THIRTY-SIX

Morgan sipped at the champagne as she took the burnt pasta bake out of the fridge and put it in the oven to reheat.

'Do you want to eat now or later?'

'Later is fine, I'm not hungry.'

She didn't want to say that she was, that she was in fact bloody ravenous, because she'd only eaten a slice of toast this morning and half of a sandwich Ben had shared with her this afternoon. Fin was leaning back on the oversized chair and he patted the space next to him.

'Come and sit down, you've had a long, busy day.'

She squeezed in next to him. The champagne was nice, too nice, and before she knew it she'd drunk the entire glass. He got up, took hold of the bottle and tipped the rest of it into her empty glass. She didn't argue with him. She felt drunk off the one glass, and her cheeks were flushed. She knew she should have eaten something before she started drinking, but she hadn't wanted to spoil the moment.

'I'll go grab the other bottles.' He went out to the car and came back moments later with two more bottles of champagne. Putting one in the fridge he opened the other. Sitting next to her again, they snuggled up. As she looked out of the picture window into the dark gardens outside, she could see their reflections staring back and felt as if she was living another life. Was that really her, sitting next to this gorgeous, extremely talented man who was about to become a published writer? Her phone began to ring in the bedroom where she'd left it charging. As she hurried to answer it the ringing stopped. She paused, deciding not to go and get it. She couldn't do anything now if it was work, as she was a little too drunk and she wasn't on call. Sitting back down, they talked about everything except the subject of Fin's book and her work. Ben had Fin all wrong: he wasn't like most journalists; in fact, he was the complete opposite.

After finishing another large glass she stood up, a little surprised at just how wobbly her legs were. 'I need the loo, be right back.' She stumbled off, leaving him there. As she went into the bathroom, she heard his phone vibrating.

As she walked back towards the chair, Fin was on his phone, texting, and he didn't hear her. She looked over his shoulder to see the words.

I can't wait to see you again darling, I miss you so much xx.

Before they disappeared off the screen, a wave of sickness filled the pit of Morgan's stomach and she felt hot bile rise up her throat. Her phone began ringing again in the bedroom. This time she went to answer it; she needed to buy herself some time to think about what she'd just seen. It could be his mum or his gran he was texting, it didn't mean it was another woman. For all she knew he could have a kid somewhere. She closed the bedroom door behind her as her phone rang again.

'Hello.'

'*It's me, did you get my message?*'

'No, I didn't. What's wrong, Ben?'

'*Look at my message then ring me back. Morgan, have you been drinking?*'

She let out a loud laugh. 'Yes, champagne actually, why?'

'*Are you drunk?*'

'Christ, Ben, you're not my parent. I'm old enough to get drunk if I feel like it. Why are you ringing me when you're out for birthday drinks with Emily anyway?'

'*Look at the message and whatever happens do not get in a car and drive.*'

'What the hell are you talking about?'

She ended the call and opened her messages to see a print screen of a newspaper headline. The words looked blurry but she recognised the clear picture of the man: it was Fin. There was also a small picture of her in the corner. The feeling of uneasiness intensified. Enlarging the photo she stared at Fin, his gleaming smile and the photo of her that had been taken when she'd been attacked a couple of months ago, looking half dead, on her way to the hospital. The headline didn't make sense and she had to reread it several times before it sank in.

WRITER OFFERED A SIX-FIGURE SUM FOR A TRUE-CRIME BOOK ABOUT THE SORDID STORY OF TAYLOR AND SKYE MARKS: GOOD COP, BAD COP FIGHTING GOOD AGAINST EVIL AND EACH OTHER.

The description read:

Fin Palmer, better known as Fin Holmes, the husband of daytime TV Queen Ellie Holmes, has landed himself a book deal worth celebrating. He has exclusive access to inside information about the case and has become friendly with Skye Marks, in a bid to write the story of this decade.

She felt the phone slip from her grasp as everything became clear. The unease became a burning rage inside her chest, so hot that it felt as if her lungs were on fire and made it hard to breathe. He had used her, he was married and now he was going to write a book about her sordid childhood. The whole world would know who her father and brother were. She grabbed her phone and marched into the lounge, where Fin had taken the food out of the oven and was eating burnt pasta bake out of the dish.

'This is not bad actually.' He took one look at her face. 'Morgan, what's wrong?'

'Get out.'

'What?'

'You heard me, how dare you. Get out of my home now before I arrest you for trespassing. How dare you use me this way?'

He nodded his head. 'I was going to tell you. I was waiting for the right time.'

She took a step closer to him. 'Tell me what? That you're married, that you only came here to get your story, that you don't give a shit about me.'

'Yes, I am married but it's not a wonderful marriage – we have our problems – and yes, I do want to write a book about your story. It's amazing, unbelievable, but it's not in any way disrespectful to you. I wanted to write it from your perspective; we would write it together.'

'Get out.' She screamed the words, blinking her eyes furiously at the tears that were pooling in the corner. She did not want to cry in front of him, she would not. He was backing towards the door, his hands in the air.

'Please let me explain it to you and then you might feel better about it.'

She looked for the nearest thing at hand to throw, which just happened to be the pasta bake, and before she could stop herself, it was flying through the air towards him. Meatballs and pasta sauce splattered all over his white shirt, the Pyrex dish landed on the wooden floor with a crash and the rest of the contents splattered up the walls and went everywhere.

'Are you nuts, this shirt was expensive!'

His shirt was a myriad of tomato passata, onion and garlic, which was quickly soaking into the white material and spreading like a flower that was blooming. Morgan began to laugh, tears streaming down her cheeks. She laughed even louder as Fin turned and marched out of her front door and, she hoped, out of her life. So angry, she ran after him. Picking up the empty champagne bottle – he was already in his car and backing out of the drive – she launched the bottle after him, but it was too heavy to go far and it ended up hitting the gravel with a loud thud. The rain, which had been falling on and off all day, turned into tiny ball bearings of hail as the temperature outside dropped. Morgan stood there watching the tail lights on Fin's car as it sped down the lane, and when the hot tears began to flow she couldn't stop them. She stood there in the dark, under a cloud of hail, and couldn't move despite the sharp balls pelting her skin and soaking her through. She had been attacked, almost died and it hadn't hurt this much. The pain in her chest made her double over as she cried loud, retching sobs that were drowned out by the hailstones. She sat down on the huge boulder to the side of the entrance step, unable to move, relishing the cold as it washed away the effects of the champagne, sobering her up. How could she have been so stupid, so bloody naïve? She should have known someone like him wouldn't be interested in her, that there was some ulterior motive.

Headlights turned into the drive and she felt her entire body tense: if that was him, she was phoning the police. She looked around, praying it wasn't Fin, or Emily – fancy having to explain what an idiot she'd been to anyone? The car stopped and for a second the beam of the lights highlighted what a complete mess she was. Then the door opened and she heard footsteps running towards her. She froze until she smelt Ben's aftershave, and then he was there, his arms wrapped around her. He helped her up and pulled her close to him; even though she was a dripping, sodden mess he didn't let go. He stood holding her whilst the hailstones gradually began to ease and her hitching breaths began to calm down. He didn't speak. He rocked her against him, and Morgan wished they could stay this way, his arms around her. He was rubbing her back and he kissed the top of her head gently. They stood that way, dripping wet, yet neither of them wanted to pull away. Eventually Ben did, and he took her by the hand.

'Come on, let's get you inside before you catch your death.'

She gripped his hand tight and let him lead her back inside, closing her front door behind him. He paused in the hallway to take in the mess.

'Blimey, Morgan, this looks like a violent crime scene, your cooking isn't that bad.'

She smiled at him, shaking her head.

'Come on, you need to get out of those wet clothes and have a hot shower. You go and drip in the bathroom whilst I clean this up.'

She whispered, 'You don't need to clean my mess up. I made it, I can sort it out myself.'

He looked at her, and she felt as if his eyes were searching for her soul, his gaze was so intense.

'I want to clean it up. I want to help you and to make sure that you're okay, Morgan. I want to be here for you.'

She felt a fresh stream of tears begin to roll down her cheeks, and she turned away before he could see. Nodding, she walked towards the bathroom and realised that Fin had been nothing more than a distraction whilst she'd tried to ignore her feelings for Ben. Her head was a mess and her heart was even worse. She had no idea where to even start sorting all this out, but she was grateful that Ben was her friend and here in her life, and even if that was all they ever had it would be enough.

CHAPTER THIRTY-SEVEN

After a hot shower Morgan cleaned her teeth. She had a thumping headache from the champagne and felt sick. By the time she came out of the bathroom Ben had cleaned up the pasta and sauce, tipping the lot into the bin, including the cracked Pyrex dish. He had taken some bacon out of the fridge and was now frying it. There was a large mug of coffee on the breakfast bar, and she sat on one of the stools watching him. She didn't speak. What was there to say? That she was an idiot, a gullible idiot who had thought that someone like Fin Palmer had been interested in someone like her: a rookie detective with a death wish and awful cooking skills. Ben passed a toasted bacon sandwich to her that he'd smothered in tomato sauce.

'Eat that, it will make you feel better, trust me, I know. I have a lot more experience of hangovers than you do.'

'Thank you for cleaning up and…' Her breath caught in the back of her throat. She couldn't say anything else, so she took a bite of the sandwich instead, which tasted amazing.

'Morgan, I'm sorry. I shouldn't have gone digging around, but when I saw that I had to tell you. I'm taking from the mess that you had no idea what he was up to?'

She shook her head.

'Oh, good because it struck me when I was driving here that you might have agreed to write the book with him.'

This time she did speak. 'Absolutely not. Do you think I want to be the subject of some crime book?'

'You like true-crime books.'

'Yes, but when they're about other people and not my shitshow of a life. Bloody hell, I'm a living Netflix series. It's a complete disaster. Will I get in trouble at work?'

'No, we'll tell Tom first thing in the morning. None of this is your fault.'

'I feel so ashamed, Ben. It's bad enough you and the team know about my past and know Gary Marks is my dad, without some stupid arsehole of a reporter telling the whole world – a stupid arsehole who is going to ruin my life.'

'The legal department might be able to do something about it and put a stop to it. You're a serving officer, so they can't let this go ahead.'

'Where's Emily?'

'She blew me off for her friend. I wasn't very good company.'

'Flipping heck, we both get a chance to date and have a bit of fun and look how it's ended up. Sorry, was that because you kept phoning me?'

He shrugged. 'I have to phone you; I work with you and we're mates, you said so yourself the other day.'

That made her laugh and she felt a lot better. 'What a pair we are. Don't tell Amy; we'll never live this down.'

Ben nodded. 'I can't stop thinking about them.'

'I know, I thought I'd switch off for a couple of hours. Try not to think about Charlie lying in the mortuary fridge all alone, and Macy on her own somewhere terrified, but it always comes back to them. What are we going to do, Ben? It's been too long.'

'Find the bastard who took them, that's what we're going to do.'

Morgan held up the palm of her right hand and Ben leant across and high fived her.

'Amen to that, boss, no more distractions. We can do it; we found the Potters' killer and Taylor Marks, although technically he found me. But that's a moot point.'

'First though, you, my star detective, are going to sleep off the rest of that alcohol, although I think your fury burnt it off. I had no idea you could get so angry. I like it, I'm glad you can stick up for yourself even more than I imagined.'

'What are you doing? You can stay here if you want.'

She saw the pained look on his face as he looked at the chair, then glanced at the bedroom door and away again.

'Sleepover, mates do that, you know, it's in the rules. You can top and tail in the bed. I won't make you sleep on the chair.'

'You're not going to make me put a face mask on are you, and wash my hair?'

Morgan chortled. 'Definitely not. You're too old for a face mask to make a difference, and I'm not wasting my expensive shampoo on your shaved head.'

'Kick a guy while he's down, why don't you. If you're going to leave me alone, I'm in.'

Morgan smiled at him. She would leave him alone – maybe another time and place and they might realise that they could be more than friends – at this moment in time, the girls were their priority.

CHAPTER THIRTY-EIGHT

Ben left Morgan sleeping. She'd climbed into the bed, curled up in a ball, whispered good night and within seconds was asleep. He'd guessed the combination of exhaustion, champagne, tears and sadness had helped her to fall into a deep sleep. He'd wanted to wrap his arms around her but didn't; for the time being they were still friends and nothing more, which he supposed was a good thing. He had to find Macy: she was his priority, and he knew instinctually that when he found her he'd also have Charlie's killer.

As he opened the front door, he was greeted by a blanket of torrential rain. Shielding his face from the rain, he dashed towards his car. The punch to the side of his head that came out of the darkness stunned him so much he stumbled forwards, falling onto the car. He had his fingers on the handle, which was what kept him from falling to his knees. Another hit with something hard to the side of his skull caused an explosion of blackness filled with silver stars that blurred his vision. He turned to see a dark figure coming towards him again. This time he lifted his hands to defend his face, and the man put his head down and ran at him. Ben threw a right hook at the man's head, returning the favour and then the man hit him in the stomach with his head, knocking the wind right out of him. Ben grunted as he fell to his knees. Looking up Ben wondered who the hell was attacking him and looked straight into a pair of black eyes. The man punched him in the nose, blinding him. Ben felt it explode as a warm rush of blood ran down his face. He knew he had to get up – if he got the better of him, he was a dead man – but his attacker lifted his leg and kicked him full force in the ribs with a pair of heavy-duty hiking boots, and Ben heard the sound of one of his ribs crack. Trying to protect his head with one hand, he felt in his pocket for his phone. All he could think before he was punched again in the side of his jaw full force was *Morgan*. Then he felt himself falling forwards, face down into a large puddle as he lost consciousness.

*

The front door opened, and Emily peered out into the front garden. She saw a guy dressed in black rushing as fast as he could to get away and she called, 'Hey, you. What are you doing? I've phoned the police.'

The man carried on and never turned around. She looked at the cars to see if they were okay and realised Ben's car was here. Then she saw the lifeless figure lying face down on the drive and let out a scream. She ran towards him, but she had no shoes on and her feet were frozen in seconds, giving her no choice but to turn around.

'Ouch, ouch. Morgan, Morgan.' Emily didn't think she'd ever raised her voice so loud. She ran to the front door and back into the flats and hammered on Morgan's door, screaming, 'Get an ambulance now, he's hurt.'

Morgan threw her door open and looked at Emily as if she'd gone insane. Her face was pale and she was shivering, pointing at the open door.

'Oh God, he's hurt. He's not moving.'

The fear in the pit of Morgan's stomach pushed her into action. She shoved her bare feet into a pair of tattered Converse, grabbed her phone and ran out of the door. She saw Ben's lifeless body, face down, and let out a scream even louder than Emily had. Running towards him she dialled 999.

'*Cumbria Constabulary, what's your emergency?*'

'Officer down, he's hurt, he's been attacked. Oh God, I don't know if he's breathing.'

'*Who is this?*'

'DC Morgan Brookes, I'm at Singleton Park Road with an injured DS Ben Matthews. Hurry, get an ambulance.'

She hung up. As she reached Ben, rain was pooling around him. Bending down she whispered, 'Ben, oh God, please be okay.' Pressing two fingers against the side of his neck, it was still warm; despite him lying on the wet gravel there was a pulse. Emily, who had helped herself to a pair of Morgan's boots, appeared beside her.

'Is he breathing?'

'Yes, but we need to get him out of the cold. He could get hypothermia lying here. Can you help me move him?'

Between them they managed to roll him onto his back, and he let out a groan. His face was a mess. Bending down they hooked their arms under his and tried to lift him. This time his eyelids fluttered open and he let out an even louder moan.

'Sorry, but we can't leave you here in this puddle. You'll freeze to death. We're going to try and get you to the front steps. Help is on the way, Ben, you're okay.'

Her voice quavered and she wished she felt as confident as she sounded. Who the hell had done this and why? They managed to half drag, half carry him to the front steps but couldn't get him up them: he was far too heavy. Morgan sat down and lay him between her legs the best she could. Emily disappeared inside and came back moments later with Morgan's duvet and some pillows.

'Should we lay him down?'

Morgan didn't want to let him go. She wanted to protect him and felt better with her arms holding him up.

'No, it's okay. I think he's better close to me so he can absorb my body heat. What the hell happened? Do you think he fell?'

Emily was shaking her head. 'No, I heard a racket and thought someone was trying to steal one of our cars. I opened the front door and saw a man, dressed in black, running away. I didn't even realise straight away Ben was there or was hurt.'

Morgan felt sick. Who had come here and attacked Ben? Did they know him? Or had they come to pay her a visit? The first person who came to mind was Fin: had he seen Ben leaving and attacked him? Or had it been the man responsible for killing Charlie and taking Macy? As she sat on the cold stone steps cradling Ben, she whispered to Emily, 'Keep your phone ready. If you so much as see a shadow out there, ring 999.'

Emily's face was pale, but she nodded and with a shaking hand she kept her phone in the air ready to dial 999 if she saw him again. The sound of sirens in the distance filled Morgan's heart with joy; never had she been so glad to hear them. As she cradled Ben, she realised how he must have felt when she had been unconscious and bleeding: despite everything, they were bonded on a level far deeper than most friendships could ever reach.

The ambulance seemed to be gliding through the puddles in slow motion, the blue lights illuminating the inky sky like some strange disco. Behind it was a police van, and Morgan breathed a sigh of relief. She knew Ben was breathing, but his breaths were shallow as if he was struggling to take air into his lungs, and she was terrified in case he was injured far worse than he looked. One of the paramedics jumped out of the van, trudging through the water to get to them whilst the other kept on driving to get as close as possible.

'What happened?'

'I don't know. He's been attacked; we found him face down unconscious.'

Two officers came rushing towards them. Cain she knew, but she had no idea who the other one was. Cain looked at them and muttered, 'Oh, shit, is he okay?'

'I don't know. Does he look it?'

Cain shook his head. 'Dog handler is on the way; do you know who it was?'

'No, but I have two possible suspects: Finley Palmer or…'

'Or?'

'Whoever killed the little girl and abducted the other is trying to stop him or us from getting too close.'

'Jesus, this is like some movie. Madds is on his way, so are CSI. Which way did he go, did you see the direction of travel?'

Morgan pointed to the road. 'He went that way?'

'Oh, still, the dog handler might pick up his scent.'

The two paramedics lifted Ben onto a stretcher, and he let out a groan but his eyes didn't open. They began to attach electrodes to his chest.

'What's his name?'

'Ben Matthews.'

'Ben, Ben, can you hear me?' He was holding his eyelid up and shining a light into it.

'Yeth.'

His speech was thick and slurred as if his tongue had grown twice its size, and Morgan wanted to high five the paramedic next to her.

'It looks as if you've been ten rounds in the boxing ring, mate, but you're okay now. Apart from the damage to your face is anything else hurting?'

'My ribs, hurts when I breathe in.'

Morgan pushed closer to see his face. She bent down and whispered, 'Did you see who it was?'

'I'm sorry, Morgan.' He began to cough and groaned, clutching his right side.

'Did you recognise him?'

Ben closed his eyes. 'No.'

The paramedics began to load him into the back of the ambulance.

'Sorry, we need to get him to A&E before the roads flood too much, they are a nightmare. Are you coming with him?'

'I'll follow on. I need to get dressed and speak to the police.'

'No worries, you know where to find us. We're going to West-morland General.'

She nodded. 'Thank you.'

Turning to Cain and his student officer she beckoned them to her. 'We can't rule out Charlie's killer. Whoever it is, he's attacked Sergeant Matthews. We can't rule out that he isn't armed or still in the area.'

The student looked from Morgan to Cain, his eyes wide, and she felt bad. He looked terrified, but this wasn't over. There was no way she was going to let him get away with this. Just what had he been doing here? Had he been looking for her? Did he want to hurt her but settled for Ben? Whatever it was she was going to do her best to find the bastard and put him where he belonged.

'We need to get as many people here as possible. I want the area flooded with patrols to flush him out. Give me your radio.'

Cain unclipped the radio from the body armour he was wearing, and Morgan relayed everything over the airwaves, so the control room inspector was aware of the situation they were dealing with.

'I'm going inside to get dressed. I won't be long. Do you want to get a first account from Emily over there? She heard it and came out to chase him away.'

Cain nodded. 'Jack, can you go and speak to the witness, please? Get her inside, it's cold out here.'

Jack didn't need to be told twice and headed towards Emily. Morgan didn't blame him. He was probably wondering what the hell he'd got himself into and whether this was the job he'd dreamt of; colleagues getting beaten senseless and water up to your ankles to freeze in whilst on scene guard for hours wasn't for the faint-hearted.

CHAPTER THIRTY-NINE

By the time Morgan left to go to the hospital, the area looked as if it was a scene from a disaster movie. Madds had arrived to take command of the scene. Thanks to the rain, which had now turned into a sleety sludge, any evidence had been watered down and washed away. The dog handler had followed his trail across a field then lost it on the other side, where it was a busy pavement that led into Rydal Falls – a path which had been well trodden by school kids waiting for the bus to Queen Anne's School, in Kendal. This wasn't her investigation; she was a witness of sorts and it was too close to home. On the way to the hospital, she phoned Amy on speakerphone.

'Ben has been attacked; he's on his way to A&E.'

Amy didn't speak for several moments.

'What, where and by who?'

Morgan realised the consequences of having Ben stay at hers last night: they would now be the talk of the whole station, and nothing had even happened – or at least nothing memorable had happened that would have been worth the weeks of gossip this incident had just incurred. Her head was pounding, and her mouth felt dry; she'd never had a champagne hangover but thought that this could be the one, which was exactly what she didn't need right now.

'It's a long story.'

'Well, you better spill it, kid, because I'm not hanging up until I know what's gone on.'

'Do you want the full story or the shorter version?'

'*Morgan, first of all, is he okay?*'

'Yes, well his face is a mess, and he was knocked out, and he may have a couple of broken ribs but he's as okay as he can be.'

Amy whistled down the phone.

'*This must be good then, full story, leave nothing out.*'

'He came to see me last night to tell me something, but I was drunk and had just thrown Fin out. I was in a bit of a state, so Ben came inside to calm me down.'

'*Oh, this is exactly the kind of phone call a woman wants this time in the morning before her morning caffeine. Hang on, I'm just going in the newsagents to get some milk. Do I need a bag of popcorn for the rest of it?*'

Morgan smiled. 'Probably.'

Amy let out a small squeak then the line went quiet. Morgan heard her thanking someone then her voice came on the phone once more.

'*Part two, you may continue but why had you thrown Fin the reporter out? Damn girl, you're a quiet one. They say quiet ones are the worst.*'

'The reporter who is also a major creep. Ben stayed over.'

'*Whoop, about time.*'

'Not like that, he slept on the sofa.' Morgan was trying to save him any further embarrassment.

'*He slept on that chair, he absolutely did not, but go on.*'

'I was a drunken mess. He made me clean myself up and go to bed, alone. He left early without telling me, and the first thing I know was Emily from upstairs was hammering on my door, screaming for help. I followed her outside and.'

'*And?*'

'Amy, it was horrific; I thought he was dead. He was face down not moving. I've never been so scared. Thankfully he came around and the paramedics arrived to sort him out.'

'*Holy shit, Morgan.*'

'I know.'

'*No, you don't know this. You're on the front page of* The Express *along with a photo of Fin, your posh lover boy.*'

Morgan had never wanted to scream and punch something, anything, so hard in her life, this was so unfair – all of it.

'*Did you know? I mean did you agree to it or is this the reason you threw him out?*'

'Yes, I mean no, I didn't know anything and yes, that's why. Ben found out and sent me a screenshot of the article. That was why he came to see me last night. It's why I was drunk and once again my life is a disaster being played out in full public view, for everyone to gossip and scrutinise. Ben is paying the price for being my friend, so if I were you, I wouldn't admit to being anything other than a colleague to me, because who knows what's going to happen next. It's so unfair and I'm tired of all this bullshit, Amy.'

She ended the call before her voice broke. She wasn't letting Amy hear her cry tears of frustration, or anyone else for that matter. She wanted her life back, the way it was before she'd joined Ben's team, when she was a fresh-faced copper who had no concept of just how evil humans could be. Back to the days when Stan was still alive and the only dad she knew, before she discovered her biological father was a rapist and a killer, before she'd almost died at the hands of another killer.

She abandoned her car at the hospital, scrubbed at her red eyes with the sleeve of her jumper, wiping away the tears, and grabbed the lanyard containing her warrant card out of the glove compartment. She needed to see Ben, make sure he was okay, and then she was going to find Macy. Once she knew Macy was safe, she was going after Charlie's killer, and she wouldn't tell a soul; this was her fight. She knew it was him, and they were getting close to finding him. He must be scared and he'd brought it to her. Now she had a score to settle, not only for her, but for Ben. She didn't even care about the consequences of what would happen when she found him, and she would find him – after all, she was the daughter of a killer; she must have a little bit of him inside her, she just had to drag it up from the depths she'd hidden it. He'd brought the fight to her; she was taking it back to him, and there would only be one survivor.

CHAPTER FORTY

Morgan took a seat in the waiting room; she wasn't there long before the double doors which led into the department opened and a nurse called her name. She stood up, desperate to see Ben. The curtains were drawn across most of the bays, but she knew which one he was in because Cain was leaning against the wall, looking out of place.

'Morgan.'

'Cain, have you taken a statement yet?'

He shook his head. 'Doctor is a right grump. She said I had to come back later and I wasn't sure what to do, as I felt bad leaving him on his own, even though she wouldn't let me go in with him. I don't think she realises he's one of us; she thinks I was bothering him.'

Morgan smiled. 'It's the uniform, some people love it, and for others it's like a red flag to a bull. Maybe you gave her a ticket and she hasn't forgotten your face.'

Cain's cheeks turned red. 'Oh, I hope not. She'd have to be a pretty rubbish driver for me to give her one. Only time I dish them out is when I have a pesky student.'

'Shh, there are seriously ill people here. And you are?'

Morgan turned slowly to face the stern voice behind her. The woman wearing a pair of green scrubs was standing there, staring at the pair of them.

'Sorry, I'm here to see Ben Matthews.'

'And you are?'

Cain was listening.

'His close friend; he was leaving my house when he was attacked.'

Morgan wasn't about to disclose to her she was also a police officer, in case she decided not to let her in either. Morgan glanced down and was glad to see her lanyard had flipped around so she couldn't read it.

'I'm Doctor White, I'm looking after Ben. He's had an X-ray and, apart from the cracked ribs and severe bruising around them, there's no internal bleeding or damage.'

Morgan let out a sigh. 'Thank you. Can I see him?'

'On your own, yes, with him' – she pointed a finger at Cain – 'absolutely not. He's a bit concussed and has vomited a couple of times. He's in no fit state to give a statement at the moment, so I'm not sure why you're still here to be honest.'

'What's your name?' she asked Morgan.

'Morgan.'

Cain added. 'My boss said I was to keep an eye on him and make sure he was okay.'

'Well, you can tell your boss he will be better without worrying about giving a statement. Give the man a break. Come back in a couple of hours and we'll review the situation.'

Cain nodded. 'Yes, doctor.' He glanced at Morgan, who shrugged, then began to walk towards the exit. The doctor pulled a curtain to the side and stepped into the cubicle.

'Mr Matthews, you have a visitor: Morgan. Do you want to see her?'

'Yes.'

She turned to Morgan and waved her in, then shut the curtain behind her. The blood had been cleaned from Ben's face, but it was a myriad of purple and black bruises. His eyes were swollen and he was going to have two cracking black eyes, but he smiled at her and she felt a whole lot better.

'You look.' She didn't know what to say, *awful, a mess, wonderful.*

He laughed at her. 'Ouch, my ribs hurt the most, don't say it, I can imagine how I look judging by how I feel, although the shot of morphine they gave me before has taken the edge off it.'

She pulled a plastic chair over to the bed. 'I'm so sorry, Ben, I didn't know or even hear.'

He reached out, grabbing her hand. 'Stop it, Morgan, sorry for what exactly? This isn't your fault.'

She lowered her head and swallowed the lump that had formed in the base of her throat.

'It is. You were at my house because I was in a drunken state. Whoever it was is my problem, he was at my house, so he wasn't even looking for you; he was looking for me. You just happened to be in the wrong place at the wrong time, and he could have killed you.'

'I could have taken him, you know. He caught me unaware, the sneaky bastard. He came at me from out of the shadows. I didn't even hear him because the rain cushioned his footsteps. As soon as I can go, will you pick me up and take me to work? I can't hang around here all day, we have to find Macy.'

'You can't go to work like this.'

'I can't drive, but I can sit in an office and supervise you lot, which is what I'm supposed to do anyway, only I don't because I like being out and about, helping with investigations and spending time with you all. Can you find out what's happening with the investigation? Have they started searching for Macy again?'

'Yes, everyone is searching for your attacker. I think it might have been the person who took Charlie and Macy; either that or Brett Mosely. If it was Charlie's killer, there must be a reason why. He must be feeling threatened. I think we're closer to finding him than we realise.'

'Good, I want every resource put into finding Macy. I think we have to face the possibility that she might not make it out of wherever she is alive, as it's been much longer than the time he had

Charlie. I don't think she's in the woods either, not unless they're looking for a body, but he didn't hide Charlie, did he? So why do they think he'll change his MO and hide Macy?'

'Maybe because there are so many people out searching, he might think they're looking for him and won't feel as brave; but I think he's getting scared that we're closer than we realise.'

'If everyone is out searching the woods then it's the perfect opportunity for him to dispose of her body. I was thinking about it all night. If he's a creature of habit, he's going to repeat what worked for him the first time. I want you, Amy, Des and whoever else you can grab to concentrate on the immediate area surrounding both girls' addresses and have a plain-clothed patrol parked up near to Piggy Lane just in case.'

Morgan nodded; this she could deal with. She liked that he was still up to organising them all and telling them what to do. She had a sneaky feeling he was trying to keep her busy and out of trouble, but she didn't mind. She was grateful she could do what he asked and that his injuries weren't any worse. 'Got it, anything else you can think of?'

'Not at the moment, Morgan, be careful. I don't think he will have the courage to come after you again now he knows we are onto him. Now stop wasting time here and go and sort Amy and Des out. You might have to avoid Tom and Claire or they'll draft you in to the search of the woods.'

'Don't worry, I will.' She stood up, bent down and brushed her lips against the top of his shaved head.

'Don't go getting all soft on me, Brookes, you have a killer to apprehend and a missing girl to return to her mum.'

Morgan saluted him and slipped out through the curtain; thankfully, Doctor White was nowhere to be seen and she left the department, walking briskly out to her car. She had a plan, it was a bit crazy but it could just work; but if it didn't, at least they had done everything they could.

CHAPTER FORTY-ONE

Morgan felt like a criminal sneaking into the station. She used the door that the office staff tended to use, which wouldn't take her past the parade room, duty sergeant and inspectors' office. She slipped up the fire escape staircase to the third floor, where the CID office was located – on the second floor the major enquiry room was now being utilised, and she saw the back of Claire's head and heard Tom's voice as she passed. Keeping her head down, she carried on upstairs to their office. Amy and Des were the only ones in there. They both looked up at her.

'How's Ben?'

'Okay, broken ribs and bruised but he's in good spirits. He wants us to concentrate on the area where Charlie and Macy lived. He doesn't think that Macy, or her body, is in the woods and neither do I.'

Des blew a long breath out. 'It's supposed to be all hands on deck downstairs. They have their knickers in a twist about Ben, and the girl still being missing.'

Amy looked at him. 'Tough, they have enough officers. We're doing what Ben, who is our superior, has asked us to do. Morgan, I know this is a bit of a sore point but how well do you actually know that Fin guy?'

'Why?' Morgan didn't know where Amy was going with this, but already she felt defensive.

'Well he's not from around here, is he? He made a beeline for you, and it's a bit funny how he turned up and we had a dead girl turn up and another missing. Has anyone checked him out on the system? For all we know he could be an RSO.'

'He's a journalist and an arsehole, Amy, but I don't think he's a registered sex offender, if he's all over the front page of the newspapers celebrating his crappy book deal. Don't you think they'd bring it up?'

'Not if they didn't know that he was. Maybe he's left a string of dead kids around the country and he's clever.'

'Oh God, I hope not, please let this be way off the mark. I can't do anything. If I look him up or were to speak to him, he'd put a complaint in before I'd left his street. We didn't part on the best of terms last night.'

Amy giggled. 'Jesus, you did have a busy night. No, you better not look him up, cos if he makes a complaint they'll suspend you without a second thought, but I can, or Des can. We'll do some digging and go speak to him. When was the last time you were actually in his flat? Could he be hiding Macy there?'

The room was starting to spin and Morgan felt as if she was going to pass out. This wasn't the time for her hangover from hell to kick in. 'A couple of days ago.'

'Did you go there after Macy went missing?'

'I don't think so. No, I didn't but I was with him when Ben rang about her, although not for long.'

Amy looked over at Des. 'What do you say, Desmond? It can't hurt to go and pay him a visit, can it? We can ask him what he was doing last night as well, and where he was when Ben got attacked.'

Des shrugged.

Morgan began to log on to her computer and brought up a map of the area where Charlie had gone missing from; the alleyway where Macy disappeared from was on the same street. She crossed the room and plucked the printout from the tray and walked to the whiteboard, where she Blu-Tacked the zoomed-in map.

'I agree it wouldn't hurt to check him out. After all he is a newcomer, but I think whoever took Charlie and currently has Macy lives locally and knew both girls. Both girls come from similar backgrounds: single mothers, absent fathers, no close family or friends keeping an eye on them. Charlie we know spent a lot of her time out in the front street; Macy went to the shop. She walked the long way around on the way there but chanced it through the alley on the way back, which is dark and has broken street lights. Someone managed to take Macy without her kicking up a fuss and causing a disturbance. I don't think that they would have been able to take her far without being caught. Killers quite often kill close to home the first time they actually choose a victim. We have Cloisters Lane, Bay Fell Grove and Peel Street all within close proximity to each other, all of them connect to each other. I think we need to focus our attention on Cloisters and then spread out from there. We need to physically go inside each house and check them from top to bottom. I know we checked some of the outbuildings and garages when Charlie went missing, but I'm saying that we need to actually have officers, PCSOs, us, special constables – whoever we can draft in – to go in and search every single house.'

She drew red lines along each of the streets to show them where they needed to begin, then looked around at Amy and Des.

'What other option do we have? We all know that Macy is on borrowed time. We have to do something before it's too late.'

Des answered. 'But every house? That will take some manpower and time, and everyone is tied up with the search of the woods.'

'So, we can make a start until Madds can free up officers from the next shift.'

'We can't possibly get search warrants for all those addresses; it would take forever,' Des muttered.

'We don't need them; we're relying on people's good nature and willingness to help find a missing girl. If they won't let us in to search, then what are they hiding? Those are the ones we'll get a search warrant for. Look, time is running out, Des. I don't see that we have much choice.'

'I suppose not, but we better run this by the DCI and see if it needs to go higher.'

'Can we not make a start right now, after you've paid a visit to Fin?'

'Morgan, whilst I fully appreciate your input and this is an excellent idea, there are certain rules and regulations we have to abide by. I'm not sure demanding to be let in by everyone who lives in the areas you've marked out is going to be the most productive use of our time.'

Morgan sighed, and Amy smiled at her.

'Well, I think it's a great idea. I don't see why we can't do this. Have you got a better idea, Des?'

Des shrugged. 'Christ knows, someone needs to run it by Tom though.'

Both Morgan and Amy said, 'No,' at the same time.

'Don't say anything to them. They won't let us. Come on, Des, let's get this visit to Fin Palmer out of the way. Who knows, we might find Macy there and arrest his arse without the need for knocking on all these doors.'

Des stood up. 'I don't know why I'm such a pushover and let you talk me into these things, Amy.'

She shook her head at him. 'It's called using your initiative. Ben isn't here to give us the okay so we're taking it on ourselves. What can go wrong? It's just good, old-fashioned police work.'

'What could go wrong? We could all get suspended for sneaking around.'

'When did you turn into such a fanny, Des? Why don't you go downstairs to the incident room and go offer to help them, if you're that worried about it?'

'I don't want to; this is our team for what it's worth.'

'Yeah, so there you go, take it or leave it.'

'Come on, the sooner we get this over with the better.'

They headed for the door and the same fire escape that Morgan had come in via. Amy turned to Morgan. 'What's his address then and what are you going to do? Why don't you take a car and park up, wait for us to get back then all three of us will start door knocking. Grab yourself something to eat and some paracetamol. By the time we get back, you'll feel a lot better than you look right now.'

'He lives in a house on Steel Street near to the Co-op, number fifteen; it's been converted into flats and he lives on the top floor and yeah, thanks. That's a good idea, I will.'

She watched them go and then grabbed the map and a set of keys from the whiteboard. She was happy to head to Cloisters and start door knocking on her own. There was no way she was sitting in the car for however long it took them to speak to Fin and search his flat. She could have been inside and searched half of the houses by then. Opening the desk drawers, she found a packet of ibuprofen and popped two out, dry swallowing the small pink tablets. She hoped they wouldn't make her throw up. She wasn't wasting time going to get something to eat though, she was itching to start checking houses. Just knowing that she was doing something useful had already made her feel a little better. Hopefully, the tablets would kick in soon and before she knew it she'd be back on top form.

CHAPTER FORTY-TWO

Des never spoke a word to Amy all the way to Steel Street. She kept glancing at him but he was staring straight ahead at the road, his hands gripping the steering wheel so tight they looked as if the circulation had stopped.

'What's wrong?'

'This, all of this, we should have run it by the boss first and got his permission. I like Morgan, she's a good kid but she's a walking disaster magnet. Look at Ben, he could have been killed last night. Everything that goes wrong always links back to her; she's bad luck, Amy.'

'Are you for real? Tell me you didn't just say that crap and actually mean it, Des. Things have been a bit intense since she joined the team but you can hardly blame it all on her. Do you think she likes that her entire family are psychopaths? She didn't ask for any of this. I feel sorry for her.'

'You feel sorry for her? You don't feel sorry for anyone.'

'I do, I felt bad about you getting strangled. Did I not save your arse?'

'I suppose so. I'm still blind in one eye though, because you're a rubbish aim with the CS.'

'God, you really are ungrateful.'

He parked the car outside number fifteen. 'Did you see this morning's paper?'

'Yes, I did, and she was horrified when I told her about the story that reporter wrote about her.'

'What if it's her, Amy? What if Morgan's the one kidnapping and killing kids?'

'Why the hell would she do that, Des? Give me one good reason why you even just spoke such bollocks.'

'You just said her entire family are psychopaths. Who's to say she isn't but is good at hiding it? I mean, did the killer attack Ben, or was it her?'

Amy held her hands up. 'Stop it now, you are talking absolute rubbish. The girl who lives above Morgan witnessed it. She saw a man running away, and she had to knock Morgan up because she was sleeping off a hangover. For the love of God, if you say anything else so stupid I'll strangle you myself.'

She got out of the car, slamming the door so loud it echoed around the deserted street. Des scrambled out after her.

'Amy, it was just a thought.'

She held up her hand, and he didn't speak again. She didn't bother ringing the doorbell of Fin's flat, instead she rang the one on the bottom and middle, not wanting to warn him they were there. After a few moments, a voice came through the intercom.

'*Yes, who's there?*'

'Police, can you let us in, please? We're making some enquiries.'

'*Hold on, I'll buzz the door open.*'

The door did buzz and she pushed it off the latch, walking inside with Des following behind her. The door opened on the ground floor and an elderly man poked his head out.

Des asked, 'Thank you for letting us in. We're trying to find a missing child. Does anyone here have children?'

'Oh, that poor girl, her mother must be beside herself. No, not that I know of. My children are all adults with kids of their own. The middle flat is a young woman who works at the hospital, and the top flat has a posh bloke from down south in it; he doesn't speak much.'

'Does he have kids?'

'No, I've never heard any. These flats aren't really big enough for kids, although I suppose there are worse places.'

'Thank you.'

Amy was already hammering on Fin's door, and Des had to take the stairs two at a time to reach her. The door opened and standing on the other side was a semi-naked man.

'What's going on?'

'Police, we're looking for a missing girl. Can we come inside and take a look?'

He shook his head. 'Yes, you can, but why would you think she's here?' He crossed his arms. 'Did Morgan send you?'

'Who? No, we're here because you're new to the area, and since you arrived we have a dead girl and one that's been missing for over forty-eight hours. You can let us in now or we can come back with a warrant, either way we will be searching your flat, Mr Palmer.'

He opened the door wide and stepped to one side. 'Help yourself.'

Amy walked in, tugging on a pair of nitrile gloves. Des followed her inside, apologising to Fin who was standing watching them both with a bemused expression on his face, but he said nothing. Amy opened every cupboard, drawer, wardrobe; she checked under the bed and in the bathroom.

'Do you have an attic space, with access to it?'

He shrugged. 'I've no idea, it's not something I've thought about.'

Des glared at Amy, who was enjoying making Fin uncomfortable. She ignored him and carried on searching for any clues that might give them something they could use to drag him to the station for further questioning. After a thorough search of every single square inch of the small flat she had to concede.

Des smiled at him. 'Thank you, Mr Palmer, for your cooperation, it's very much appreciated. One last thing, where were you the early hours of this morning?'

Fin shrugged. 'I was here, on my own. I'm not a bad person. I'm a journalist; it's my job to write stories.'

Amy shrugged. 'That's your opinion, Mr Palmer.'

She walked out of the flat, annoyed that it had been clean and she hadn't found Macy tied up in the bedroom. Neither of them spoke until they were back inside the car and Des asked, 'What was that? Did you really think we were going to find her in there?'

'No, but I wanted to. I wanted it to be him. Aren't you not the least bit sick to the teeth that we haven't found that little girl?'

'Of course I am. It makes me feel like shit.'

'Good, I'm glad it does.'

Amy's phone had been ringing the whole time they had been inside Fin's flat, but it was on silent and she'd ignored it; now Des's was ringing. He pulled it out of his pocket.

'It's Tom.'

'Don't answer.'

'Morning, boss.' There was a pause. 'Where are we?'

Amy was shaking her head at him. He shrugged.

'In town following up on a lead; yes, I know about Ben. Oh, okay that's fine. We were on our way back anyway.'

He slipped the phone back inside his jacket pocket. 'Don't glare at me, we have to go back. Tom is fuming we missed the briefing, and he said if we knew where Morgan was we are to get hold of her and tell her the same.'

'I'll text her. You drive back. I can't believe you answered him.'

'I like my job, Amy, and I want to keep doing it for a good few years yet. It's the only thing I have in my life that makes me want to get up in a morning. If you want to throw it all away that's down to you, but don't drag me down with you, please.'

Realising she'd been a bit harsh, she elbowed him in the side. 'Sorry, I like my job too. I got a bit carried away. I just wanted to find her, you know, and put an end to it all. He seemed like such a good lead, and after what he did to Morgan, writing that story about her for the papers.'

'The man is an arse, no doubt about it, but we can't let that distract us from doing the right thing, Amy. Claire is in charge and Tom is her second in command; they're both experienced and have families, and I'm pretty sure they want to find Macy as much as we do. We're on the same side so we have to work together.'

'Yes, we do. You're right, take us back to face the music.'

She waited for Des to start driving then sent a message to Morgan.

Nothing at Palmer's flat. We've been summoned back to the nick for a briefing and Tom is on the warpath looking for you to go back as well. You have been warned, but if you want to keep watch I'll be there as soon as I can.

She sent it not expecting for one moment that Morgan would abandon her lookout and return for another briefing, but at least she'd warned her, and they could cross Palmer off the list.

CHAPTER FORTY-THREE

Morgan drove along Cloisters looking for a place to park. She had made up her mind to start close to Charlie's house. Ben thought she hadn't wandered far and neither did she. She parked the car and took out her work phone. Had anyone been and revisited the houses where there had been no reply? She scrolled through her emails on the subject and realised that there were nine houses that still hadn't been accounted for. How had they missed this? She was furious: this had been such a simple oversight. It was a huge investigation for a relatively small police station and finding Charlie's body had thrown them all for six, but still, what if it could all have been avoided by following up on one of these houses? Her phone was almost out of battery, so she wrote the house numbers she needed down on the back of her hand and plugged her phone into the charger and hid it in the glove compartment. She had no idea whether it would still charge or not when the engine wasn't running but hoped that it might do something. She got out of the car. The slush around here had turned into a dishwater grey sludge and she was glad she'd worn her boots, otherwise her feet would be sodden in minutes and there was nothing she hated more than wet, soggy feet.

Pulling her lanyard out of her coat and tugging her hat down, Morgan walked to the first house on her list and knocked on the door. The occupant was an elderly woman who shuffled to the door with her hair in rollers and a big smile on her face.

'Hello, sorry to bother you, I'm Detective Constable Morgan Brookes. We're looking for a missing girl called Macy. Do you know anything or have you seen her?'

'Hang on let me turn my hearing aid up. Ah, that's better. A missing girl? Oh yes.'

Morgan held her breath in anticipation of what she might say, crossing her fingers she was going to say yes, she's here.

'I read about that in the paper, such a dreadful carry-on and that poor girl Charlie too; she was always out on the street, bless her.'

'Did you know either of them?'

'I knew Charlie to say hello to. She liked my cat – would sit and talk to it.'

Morgan felt her heart begin to beat faster; the scratch on Charlie's arm could have been a cat scratch, so that would have put her here just before she died.

'Can I come in and see your cat?'

'You can come in but I'm afraid you won't be able to see him. I had to have him put to sleep in the summer. He was too old, and his back legs went from under him. Broke my heart. I can't imagine how those girls' mums are feeling.'

The adrenalin that had begun to pump around her body stopped. She smiled at the woman.

'Are there many cats in this street?'

She was waiting for her to say hundreds.

'The house three doors down has a horrible one, it's always hissing and fighting. Big ginger thing it is, never stops miaowing either. I've had to come down and throw water at it before to chase it away. Most people around here have dogs. You see them out walking them, but not so many cats. There's also a big white one that comes around but I don't think it's from this end of the street.'

Morgan looked at the house three doors down: that would be number thirteen, Elliot Fleming's house, where Eleanor disappeared from. She looked at the numbers on the palm of her hand: it wasn't there, so they had been spoken to on the initial investigations and she'd been back to speak to Elliot. But she suddenly had a terrible feeling that she had missed something.

'Thank you so much.'

'You're welcome, lovey.'

The door closed, and Morgan walked along the path and along the street to number thirteen. She stared at the gate; it had seen better days and the house was badly lacking a coat of paint. The wooden windows must be the originals from when the house was built, all the other houses had double glazing, but these had once been painted green and yellow, at least what was left was. The paint had chipped and flaked off, leaving the wood rotting and weathered. She looked around for a cat but didn't see one. As she turned, she could see Charlie's house on the opposite side, just a few doors up. *Did you come here, Charlie, to see the cat and it scratched you? Or am I looking for a miracle? And did you really run away, Eleanor, or are you still here?* She knocked on the door and waited and waited but no one answered. She pressed her ear to the door. She couldn't hear anything from inside.

Instead of wasting time, she went to the next house on her list, deciding to keep an eye on the front garden of number thirteen. She would try again later. The other houses on her list all opened the door and invited her inside to look around. By the time she'd finished at the last house, she was feeling more than a little deflated. As she said goodbye to the woman with three children at number twenty-six, she spied a figure scurrying through the gate of thirteen with their head down.

'Hello, hello.'

Whoever it was never turned around, and Morgan splashed her way along the pavement back to the house. The front door was already shut but at least she knew someone was home. If they didn't answer she would come back with a warrant. She hammered on the door a little too loud, not giving them the excuse that they didn't hear her knocking. This time she heard footsteps inside the hall. There was the sound of a heavy bolt being drawn back and the door opened wide.

'Hello again, Elliot.'

He beamed at her, the smile friendly. He was dressed in an old-fashioned purple and yellow shell suit with a pair of purple and pink Nikes on his feet, a pair of purple gloves on his hands: he could have given Prince a run for his money any day.

'Hello again, you seem to be spending a lot of time around here.' He leant towards her and whispered, 'I've been baking this morning, would you like a cake?'

'Can I come in?'

He paused, his eyes flicking behind him then back at her.

'I just need to have a chat with you if that's okay. Nothing to worry about; we're still making enquiries into a missing girl.'

He lifted a finger to his lips. 'You can as long as you're quiet. Mother doesn't like noise or strangers, so we better not wake her up.'

Morgan smiled at him, thinking what a funny thing to say. She whispered back, 'Of course, I'll be quiet.'

'Good, you can come inside then.'

He stepped to one side to let her in, shutting the door behind her. He led her along a long hall to the kitchen, where the sight of a large plate of cakes sitting on the worktop made her stomach groan.

'What have you been baking? It smells lovely in here and they look amazing.'

'Thank you, I adore baking. Earlier this morning I made salted caramel and white chocolate cupcakes. I haven't iced them yet; well, I prefer buttercream to icing – it's a much nicer texture – but you're welcome to try one with a cup of tea. I had to nip out to the shop to buy more butter. Mother complains about the money and time I spend baking, but she doesn't complain when she's eating them.'

Morgan stifled a laugh, so it ended up coming out as a snort. Not wanting to wake his mother up, she clapped her hand across her mouth. Although the house was run-down from the outside and inside was a floral tribute to the seventies, it was clean and tidy, but she still wouldn't eat anything because how was she to know if Elliot's hand hygiene was as bad as his dress sense?

'I'm okay, thank you, though. That's very kind of you.'

Something nudged her leg with quite a shove, and she looked down to see a huge ginger cat that was the size of a small dog. It began to rub against her trouser leg then it let out a loud meow.

Elliot turned around, his eyes wide. 'Shh, you stupid cat.' As cats do, it took no notice of him and meowed even louder. 'Oh God it wants you to stroke it, or it won't shut up. Would you mind?'

'Of course not, I like animals although I don't have any myself.' She bent down and began to stroke it behind its ears, which resulted in a purring so loud it sounded like lawnmower.

'Oh, he likes you. He's a pain, always hungry, always wanting attention.'

Morgan stroked it's back and let out a yelp. 'Ouch.' She lifted her hand to examine it and saw a long, thin line of blood on the back of her hand. Every hair on the back of her neck began to prickle. She looked at Elliot who was shooing the cat out of the door. He turned around to her.

'I'm so sorry, I don't know why it does that. You'd think it was happy to get some attention then it goes and does a nasty thing like that.'

'Does he scratch a lot?'

He nodded. 'Come on, let me get you cleaned up. I have a first aid kit under the sink.'

Morgan felt her skin crawl as fear snaked along the base of her spine. Her stomach lurched: he still hadn't taken off the gloves. 'It's okay, I'm allergic to plasters. Please could I use your toilet though? I'm desperate for a wee, and I'll wash it under the tap.'

Elliot glanced at the staircase, then back at her.

'I suppose so, but you mustn't wake my mother. She won't be happy I've let a stranger in the house. It's the third door on the right.'

'Thank you, I won't wake her, I promise.' Morgan stood up, trying to stay calm and not let him know that she knew what he was. Her legs felt as if they were going to give way. She was in this house alone with a potential killer. Charlie must have stroked the cat and got scratched. Was that how she ended up in here? She smiled at him and began to walk to the stairs, wishing she'd brought her phone inside with her. She looked around to see that there was an old-fashioned rotary dial house phone on a table at the foot of the stairs. She could phone for help off that if she had to. The thought that she might be so close to Macy wasn't lost on her, and she listened intently as she walked up the stairs. This house was much bigger inside than it looked. She paused, counting the doors; there were six altogether, although one of them looked like a built-in cupboard.

Elliot whispered from the bottom of the stairs, 'Third door on the right.'

She nodded and walked towards it, trying to work out how long it would take her to open the other doors and check in each room. They all had old-fashioned locks on them, with keys in the locks, on the outside, except for one at the front of the house, where the lock had no key. Morgan went in the bathroom and began running the cold water tap, holding her stinging hand underneath it. The pulse in her hand was throbbing in time to the racing of her heart. She took care to wipe it on a clean towel, so if anything happened to her there would hopefully be some traces of her blood and DNA left on it.

She left the tap running and opened the door slowly. Peering out into the landing, she couldn't see Elliot and stepped out, creeping towards the door which had no key in the lock. As she reached the door, she bent down to peer through the lock and whispered, 'Macy', before she felt an almighty thump on the side of her head and she collapsed to her knees.

CHAPTER FORTY-FOUR

Amy glared at Des the entire way through the briefing and he purposely didn't look her way. She was fuming with him for having no backbone and turning around to come back. Tom, who was standing at the front of the packed room with Claire, kept looking at the pair of them, but she didn't care.

'Thanks for coming, we have a busy day today, there's a lot going on – the search for Macy Wallace being the top priority. We also think that her abductor attacked DS Matthews early this morning, and he is currently in hospital with two cracked ribs, a broken nose and multiple injuries to his face and head. This is a dangerous man, as he has clearly demonstrated. Whilst you are out there you must be vigilant. I do not want anyone on their own, everyone is to be double crewed.'

Amy finally took her eyes off Des and took her phone out to message Morgan.

Hey, wait in the car. Inspector has ordered us all to be doubled up, wait for me and Des to get to you.

Tom was pointing at a map of the woods that were covered yesterday, and the riverside.

'We pretty much covered three quarters of the woods yesterday, thanks to the help from Mountain Rescue. I want the rest of them boxed off. I also want the area around Piggy Lane searched just in case.'

Amy held up her hand. 'We'll take Piggy Lane.'

He nodded.

'Claire will tell the rest of you what to do about Macy.'

He walked towards the door, bent down and whispered in Amy's ear, 'A word.'

She stood up and followed him outside, everyone watching them. He didn't stop. He carried on upstairs to his office and she followed him. He didn't speak until they were inside with the door shut.

'Where exactly is Morgan? If you tell me she's at the hospital with Ben that's fine, but anywhere else isn't. And what's the deal with you and Des? You keep staring at him like Christine does to me whenever I've royally pissed her off. Spill the beans, Amy. I know you're all a close-knit team and I appreciate your loyalty to each other, but we know what happens when we let Morgan loose. I'm concerned for her safety. A potential killer was waiting outside her address, and he may be after her next. I'm not going to see her get hurt again, not when I'm in charge.'

He wasn't shouting, he hadn't even raised his voice, he genuinely looked worried and she decided to come clean.

'With all due respect, sir, when Morgan gets loose she usually uncovers a murderer. She's out looking for Macy. All three of us were supposed to be, but Des chickened out and came back for the briefing. Morgan thinks that whoever took her lives in the same area. We were going to knock on all the doors and ask to search the houses. We only took people at face value when they were initially asked on the nights both girls went missing.'

He began to rub his hand across his chin, scrubbing the stubble which Amy noticed for the first time. Tom was always clean-shaven and impeccably dressed, but his shirt was rumpled and his tie was loosened. Seeing how distraught he looked brought it all home to her, exactly what they were dealing with: the enormity of it was weighing heavy on his shoulders.

'Without warrants?'

'How are we supposed to get warrants for that many houses, in so short a time, sir? We're relying on people's good will, for now. Anyone who declines gets put on the list to look closer at. I know it's crazy, but it's the best we have, and I think it's a pretty good idea. He didn't leave Charlie's body in the woods. So why do you think he is going to be holding Macy there?'

Tom nodded. 'Find Morgan and carry on with that line of enquiry. Anyone who is less than helpful let me know. I'll get Tracy in Intel to run in depth checks on them. And be careful.'

'What about Piggy Lane?'

'I'll go there myself. Amy, please be careful, and don't let her out of your sight.'

She nodded, thinking, *it's a bit late for that, boss* but she didn't say it out loud.

'Thanks, boss.'

CHAPTER FORTY-FIVE

Macy was sitting up on the bed, her knees drawn to her chest. She was sure she'd heard a woman's voice call her name. Terror that his mother had found her filled her insides with ice. She had a free hand and the scissors, but she didn't know what he kept doing to her – she was sleepy all the time. She thought maybe he was giving her some kind of medicine. The door opened and Macy sucked in her breath. He had his back to her and was dragging something heavy. He bumped and pulled the body into the room, dragging it by the ankles, muttering, 'How dare you come here, asking questions then sneak around in my house like that? What if you'd woken Mother? Then we'd all be in so much trouble, and why are you so damn heavy?' His voice was raised in anger.

Macy's eyes were wide open and there was a mewling sound coming from inside of her that she couldn't stop, the terror was so real. She'd never seen a dead body before and didn't want to now. He carried on dragging the woman towards the radiator.

'She's asleep; she fell and hit her head. Shut up making that racket. I'm just putting her here until she wakes up and then you can both go home okay, because I never asked for this to happen.'

Macy nodded.

'Good. Christ, she's heavy.'

He dropped her feet and disappeared. Coming back moments later with some rope, he began to tie her hands, wrapping it around her wrists, knotting and knotting it, hoping she wouldn't be able to escape. The woman let out a soft moan, and Macy realised she was still alive and felt a spark of hope that maybe she could help her escape. He then took a scarf and used it to gag the woman like he'd done to her. He pulled it tight then knotted that as well. He stood up and nodded his head. Macy couldn't stop staring.

'What would you like for breakfast? I bet you're starving. Do you need to go pee? I've been baking, and I was just going to bring you something to eat when I was rudely interrupted.'

She looked at the woman on the floor, then at him and shook her head.

'Are you sure? It would be much easier now whilst Mother is still asleep if you want the toilet. After, you'll have to use the bucket and that's not very nice, is it?'

She carried on shaking her head; she didn't want to be separated from this woman.

'Suit yourself, I'll bring you something up anyway.'

He left them to it, locking the door behind him, and Macy continued staring at the woman, who had blood trickling down the side of her head. She heard the man running down the stairs and the radio turned on somewhere. Macy knew they didn't have much time before he came back with her breakfast and began to work furiously at the binding on her wrist.

CHAPTER FORTY-SIX

Ben had just been told he was being moved to Ward Five for a twenty-four hour stay, to monitor him because of his head injuries. He nodded, too scared of Doctor White to argue with her. As soon as she left, though, he took out his phone and rang Morgan. It didn't even ring before going to voicemail.

'Hi, come rescue me, please, as soon as you pick this up. I can go home. Thanks.'

Even the simple movement of reaching for his phone off the table had caused immense pain in his side, despite the morphine. He breathed out; he didn't care, there was no way he was staying in here any longer than he needed to.

A voice on the other side of the curtain said, 'Knock, knock,' and Cain popped his head through.

'Where is she?'

'Who?'

'That scary doctor.'

'Looking for a porter to take me to Ward Five. Help me up, Cain, I need to get out of here.'

Cain looked at him, horrified. 'No, boss, I'm not that brave.'

'Do it, I'll take the blame. It's a direct order.'

Cain sighed. 'I don't want to burst your bubble but you're wearing a hospital gown, boss. We took your clothes earlier for CSI to examine.'

'I don't care, cuff me and pretend you've arrested me.'

'Boss, this is crazy.'

'Just do it, but you'll have to help me off the bed.'

Cain grabbed Ben's legs and swung them off the side of the bed, then slipping an arm underneath his he pulled him to his feet. The pain was so intense Ben gritted his teeth to stop himself from groaning out loud. He held out his hands in front of him.

'Cuff me and walk me out of the nearest exit, but make sure you hold this gown at the back. I'm not flashing my arse to the whole of the A&E waiting room. Cain, that is definitely a direct order.'

Cain did as he was told, leading Ben out of the exit, through the waiting room and out to the van that was parked in the police bay.

'Can you climb in?' He opened the door and stood behind Ben, ready to shove him in the back of the van in case the doctor came looking for him. Ben lifted a leg up and groaned, but he grabbed onto the back of the seat and dragged himself inside, where he fell onto the seat clutching at his side, colds beads of perspiration forming on his forehead. Cain slammed the door shut, rushed around to the driver's side and drove away as if he was going to an emergency call.

'Are you okay back there, boss?'

Through gritted teeth he answered, 'Yes, take me to my house, please.'

He phoned Amy, who answered straight away.

'I tried Morgan but her phone's off, what's happening? I'm coming home.'

'*What do you mean her phone's off? And are you sure, boss? I'd have thought they'd want to keep you in for observations.*'

'It went to voicemail. Nah, I'm fine, Amy. Why were you surprised Morgan didn't answer her phone?' There it was, a cold, familiar fear chilling him to the bone.

'*She's out looking for Macy; me and Des were going to help but we got called back to the nick. Morgan didn't come with us. Her phone probably died. I'll come get you.*'

'Is she out looking for Macy alone?'

He didn't even need to ask, what a stupid question: who else would she be out with, if Amy was with Des? They normally paired up and he was here.

'Yeah, but she's in the Cloisters Lane area. We'll go find her, she can't be far.'

'Okay, thanks.'

Cain drove to Ben's; he'd dropped him off a couple of times so knew where it was. The whole time Ben kept ringing Morgan's number – it was still voicemail and he was doing his very best to quell the panic rising inside his chest. The van stopped outside, and he realised he didn't have his front door key.

'I'm going around the back, as I might have to break a window to get in. Can you climb through and open the back door for me?'

Ben thought that Cain's face looked more pained than his own and he smiled.

'I'll sign your pocket notebook to say this was under my orders, Cain. I'm not going to expect you to get a joiner to board it up or to scene guard it until one comes. I need to get to Cloisters Lane now.'

He was aware of the desperation in his voice, but he didn't care. Cain helped him out of the van.

'What a shit shift this is turning into. I don't know whether to help you or 136 you and get you sectioned at the nearest mental health unit.'

'After this is over, Macy Wallace is safe and Morgan is not in any danger, trust me you might have to section me, but for now let's just pretend I know what I'm doing, okay?'

Cain shrugged as he uncuffed Ben's wrists and helped him out of the van. 'You know Madds is going to have a meltdown over all of this, don't you? He'll probably need sectioning with you.'

Ben smiled and hobbled around to the back of his house through the gate at the side of the garden, glad he hadn't locked it when he'd put the bins out yesterday morning. He tried the back door, which was locked; it was a solid wood door. Pointing to Cain's body armour, he asked, 'Baton?'

Cain undid it and passed it to him. Ben smacked it as hard as he could against the kitchen window and let out a groan at the sharp pain in his ribs. The glass had cracked but hadn't gone through. Taking the baton from him, Cain bent down and picked up a rockery stone, launching it through the window. The sound of breaking glass filled the air. Ben smiled, thinking about the first time Morgan called at his and broke the window to get inside. 'Where did you learn that: the Morgan Brookes school of policing?'

Cain had no idea what he was talking about and shrugged. Using the baton he smashed the rest of the glass out of the frame and climbed through, opening the back door for Ben.

'Thanks, you can wait in the van if you want.'

'Can you manage?'

'Yes.'

Cain left him, and the first thing he did was open the drawer and take out the painkillers he kept inside it. He took two paracetamol and two ibuprofen for good measure and went upstairs to find some clothes. By the time he'd pulled on some joggers and a thick jumper, he'd plucked up the courage to glance in the mirror. He shook his head at his reflection, thinking, *what a bloody state*, then went back out to the van where Cain was waiting for him. He handed Cain a pair of socks.

'Last favour.'

'Bloody hell, this is above and beyond the call of duty, Ben.' But he took them from him and put them on Ben's feet. Ben slipped his trainers back on.

'Thank you.'

As Cain began to drive in the direction of Cloisters Lane, Ben hoped that Morgan was fine and her phone had died, that he was panicking for no good reason.

CHAPTER FORTY-SEVEN

Morgan didn't know where she was or what had happened. Her head felt as if it had been run over by a truck, and then she felt small hands shaking her shoulders and she opened her eyes to see a blurry figure leaning over her.

'Wake up, wake up, he's coming back with breakfast.'

She had no idea who this was and wondered if she was still in bed, hung-over to shit and dreaming. Closing her eyes, she felt those hands again shaking her, the voice urgent, almost at the verge of panic.

'Please, lady, you have to wake up, we need to get out of here.'

This time she opened her eyes and saw a girl staring at her, opened her mouth to speak and realised she couldn't: there was a tight band of material gagging her. Then the girl began untying it and she felt it loosen and fall from her mouth.

'Macy?' the relief in her voice was palpable.

'Yes, I'm going to try and untie your hands.'

Morgan realised that she was on the floor in a bedroom tied to an old-fashioned radiator and tried to pull her hands away from it. She couldn't think straight; her head was a pounding mess of jumbled thoughts. She closed her eyes and let the relief wash over her. Macy was alive and here with her, thank God for that.

'I can't do it; he's done it too tight.'

'Can you look around in the drawers and see if there's anything in them to cut them with? How did you get out?'

'We played Scrabble last night and he forgot to tie my hand back up when he heard his mother come back. I was going to climb out of the window, but he gave me a drink that was disgusting, and I fell asleep. I have some scissors I stole out of the bathroom.' She pulled a small pair out that were better than nothing.

Morgan smiled; she liked this kid a lot. 'Good, that's good. Well, you're safe now. I'm a police officer, I won't let him hurt you and pretty soon my friends are going to be here looking for us both. We've been looking all over for you, Macy.'

'Is my dog okay? Did he go home?'

'Yes, he did.'

Macy's eyes filled with tears then she stood up and began to try and cut through the rope. As she moved to the side, Morgan saw a figure lying perfectly still under the big four-poster bed and she let out a yelp. Macy turned around shushing her. Morgan nodded. There was someone under the bed staring at her, and she wondered if he'd not even left the room and was watching them both, enjoying giving them a few minutes of hope before he killed them, but the figure never moved, it didn't even take a breath. It looked as if it was wearing a black shroud.

She whispered, 'Eleanor?'

Heavy footsteps on the stairs made Macy turn around in panic, and she began sawing, trying to cut the rope.

'His mother, I don't know her but she's scary. He's terrified of her.'

Morgan whispered, 'It's no good, they're not strong enough to cut the rope. Can you use them to loosen the knots? Poke them inside if you can.'

Macy nodded and began pushing and poking at the knots until they were loose enough to use her fingers. Morgan slipped her hands out of the bindings and whispered, 'Get back on the bed, pretend you're still tied up and whatever you do don't open your eyes. I'm taking you home.'

Macy held her little finger up. 'Promise.'

Morgan hooked hers around it and whispered, 'Pinkie promise.' She watched as the girl clambered back on the bed and slipped her wrists back through the material he'd used to tie her up with. Morgan closed her eyes. Macy nodded, lay back and squeezed her eyes shut.

The footsteps stopped outside the bedroom, and Morgan pulled the gag back into her mouth. Hiding her hands behind her back, she sat up with her back against the cold radiator, clutching the small scissors in her right hand. She glanced under the bed and realised that if it was Eleanor, she had been there for some time because the room didn't smell of death or decomposition.

A gentle knock on the door and a voice whispered, 'I'm coming in to see you.'

Morgan swallowed the lump in her throat as the door opened slowly. Elliot was standing there, his right hand, hanging down by his thigh, was gripping a solid wooden rounders bat. Morgan thought how easily she had been deceived by this small, harmless-looking man who was far stronger and more powerful than she could have ever imagined. He'd killed Charlie with a single blow to her head and rendered Morgan herself unconscious just now.

She glanced at the bed to make sure Macy wasn't looking. No matter what happened she had to protect her and keep her safe. She wouldn't let him hurt her any more than he already had. He stood there taking in the scene in front of him and she knew he was trying to figure out what was different. The tension was unbearable as she tried to gauge what he was about to do. Where were Amy and Des? Why was no one looking for her? She realised that the scissors Macy gave her were little protection against Elliot. Her head was pounding, but she had to distract him so that he wouldn't realise Macy was unbound.

'Where's your mother, Elliot? Aren't you afraid you're going to wake her up?'

'Shut up, she's sleeping.'

'If I scream loud, will she come looking to see what you're doing?'

He took a step closer to her; the bat, small but deadly, was swinging against his thigh, making a dull thwacking sound.

'If you scream then I'll have no choice but to hurt you, Morgan, like I did the man outside your flat, and we don't want to do that, do we?'

Morgan glanced at the body under the bed. 'Where's Eleanor, Elliot? Is this her bedroom?'

His eyes flickered to the bed, telling her everything she suspected was true.

'I told you we don't know.'

'I think you do. I don't think she ever left this house, did she? But how did your mother not discover her body?'

And then it hit Morgan: his mother was dead too. And probably had been for a long time. She whispered, 'It doesn't matter how loud I shout, Elliot, your mother isn't going to come and see what you're doing, is she? I know that you killed her too.'

'I never meant to hurt her, you know, but she was horrid; a selfish, stubborn girl. She packed her case and told Mother she was leaving to go and live with her boyfriend, that she wasn't ever coming back. I've never seen Mother so upset, it wasn't fair. All I did was stop her from leaving. Mother never got over it. Then when she was gone I realised I was all alone. It's been so long since I had someone to talk to. I thought it would be nice to have a friend and that kid was always on her own; she reminded me so much of myself.'

'Why did you come to my house and attack my friend?'

'You were asking too many questions, Morgan. I was angry. I wanted to stop you but I didn't know who it was until it was too late. I only wanted to stop you from coming around here again. I wouldn't have hurt you too much. But he fought back and I had no choice.'

He glared at her, black eyes filled with fury and something else. He stepped inside the room lifting the bat high, and Morgan gathered her strength. She clambered to her feet and ran at him. All hell broke loose. Elliot let out a scream and ran for her at the same time as she ran for Elliot. He swung the bat towards, her but she ducked in time and it swooshed through the empty air where her head had been seconds ago. Throwing him off balance she managed to barge him out of the room away from Macy, who clambered off the bed and began hammering at the window. A police van and several cars had just turned into the street. Morgan heard a loud crash as she was grappling with Elliot, who was much stronger than she had anticipated. She could hear Macy screaming 'Help!' out of the broken window.

Morgan lunged for Elliot. She stabbed the small scissors into the soft flesh of his neck, plunging them in as far as she could: it wasn't deep but it was enough for Elliot to lose his concentration. She got behind him and caught him in a secure hold, dragging him further away from Macy before he could do any more damage.

Elliot was screaming, 'Mother, Mother, come help me! Look what you've done.' He shook off Morgan's grip. He lifted the bat again. Morgan drew back her fist and punched him square in the nose, and hot blood sprayed out of it as the bone crunched. He fell to his knees crying.

Cain reached the top of the stairs, his taser drawn. He pointed it at Elliot.

Ben stepped out from behind Cain and couldn't quite believe what he was seeing. There was a small guy in a purple shell suit with a broken nose and a pair of scissors sticking out of his neck and Morgan, who apart from a line of dried blood on the side of her head, looked relatively unharmed. Macy ran to Morgan, wrapping her arms around her tight and Morgan hugged her back, turning her face away from the blood and carnage in front of them. Amy appeared behind Ben, took one look at the mess and spoke.

'Brookes does it again.'

Morgan led Macy to Amy. 'Please take her home.'

Amy reached out for the girl's hand and took hold of it gently, leading her away, her other hand clamped over her eyes so she didn't see the blood. Cain and Des cuffed Elliot and took a step back, leaving Ben, Morgan and a heavily bleeding Elliot behind. Morgan knelt next to the man who had ruined so many lives.

'The ambulance is on its way.'

He stared at Morgan, opening his mouth to speak but he couldn't; blood was flowing freely from the wound in his neck now. This man, who had attacked Ben without so much as a second thought, thinking it was her, and had killed a little girl and stolen another, looked as far away from the boogey man as she could imagine. She heard sirens in the street outside.

'Paramedics are here.'

Two paramedics ran up the stairs, and Ben moved back out of their way.

'Morgan, let them take it from here. Cain and Des will accompany him to the hospital.'

She nodded. She turned away to face Ben, who was looking out of the landing window down onto the front street.

'Why are you here? Shouldn't you be in hospital?'

He smiled, turning back to look at her. 'I was about to ask you the same question. But you can tell me later. I think there's someone outside who wants to see you.'

She raised an eyebrow and stepped closer to the window to look outside. Macy was there waving frantically with one hand at her, the other cradling Max to her chest. Her sobbing mum was behind her, her arms wrapped around her, and Morgan couldn't stop the tears this time, nor did she want to.

More footsteps on the stairs and she heard Tom's voice.

'What in the name of God is going on here? I let you loose for two hours and it's carnage, complete carnage.'

Morgan lowered her head. 'Sorry, boss.'

'Well done, Brookes, good job.'

He clapped her on the back and stepped to one side as the paramedic working on Elliot glanced at them. She began to walk down the stairs to go and see Macy then turned to Ben.

'You might want to check under the bed, as there's a body underneath it that I think might be his missing sister. God knows how many he's got hidden around this place.'

And then she was outside on the street where residents and people were congregating everywhere watching the house. Macy broke free of her mum's grip and ran towards Morgan at full pelt with Max still under one arm. She hugged her fiercely, and Morgan dropped to her knees on the wet, slushy path and hugged her back, holding her tight. A round of applause began to echo around the street, and she looked up to a sea of smiling faces and clapping hands. Despite having a hangover from hell, she grinned at Macy and ruffled the fur behind Max's ears. She stood up and walked Macy to the gate, back to her mum who was standing with Amy.

'Mum, this is…'

'Morgan, I know who she is, she came to see me when I couldn't find you. Thank you, Morgan, I asked you to find my baby girl and you did.'

Amy intervened. 'What do you say we go to your house and get warmed up? It's freezing out here.'

'Can I have hot chocolate?'

'You can have cream, marshmallows, the lot,' said her mum.

Amy led them to the car and opened the rear door for them. When she'd closed it she turned to Morgan.

'Is he?'

'Dead? No, there's a body under the bed as well.'

'Shit, no way.'

Morgan smiled. 'God knows, but he has some serious issues.'

Amy nodded. 'Have you seen the state of Ben? And why is your head bleeding?'

'Elliot hit me with something. I'm okay though, just have a really awful headache.'

'Well, here's a little tip from me, get Ben out of that house and get Des to drive you both to Ben's house, where the pair of you can get cleaned up and take it easy. Cain said he's not going anywhere near the hospital or Ben because he's a nightmare. Claire is on her way; she and Tom can take over this one, but I will tell you one thing for sure.'

'What?'

'Wendy is going to be pissed at the state of that crime scene. How many bodies and cross-contamination can you get at one scene? I'd get out of here before she arrives.'

Morgan smiled, thinking that Amy had a point. She turned to see Ben standing at the front door watching. He slowly began to walk towards her. Des held out his hands to Morgan.

'Car keys, I've had it from the top that you two are to be driven somewhere safe and away from prying eyes. Seeing as how the whole world knows where you live, Morgan, I'd suggest Ben's house.'

They didn't argue but got into the back of the car, both of them battered, bruised but never happier because Macy was safe, back with her mum where she belonged and a dangerous killer was off the streets.

TWO DAYS LATER

Morgan heard the knocking on Ben's door and got up to answer it, slipping out of his spare bed that she had done nothing but sleep in since she'd got here. Glad to be safe and alive; it was all they needed now. She went downstairs, her hair a mess, and opened the door to see Amy and Des standing there with four coffees and a bag of fresh donuts.

'Oh, is this a bad time?'

'You have coffee, never a bad time.'

They came in, and Ben appeared at the top of the stairs. Amy looked up at him.

'Bloody hell, whatever you do you better not leave the house without a balaclava on, you look monstrous.'

'Cheers, Amy.'

He shuffled down the stairs, spurred on by the smell of coffee and donuts. Morgan led them into the kitchen, where they all sat down.

'So, what's happened? Was that a body under the bed and who was it?'

'Hold your horses.' Amy passed the paper coffee cups out and opened the bag of donuts, taking a huge bite out of one.

'Some of us have been working non-stop while you two were skiving.'

Des spoke. 'It was a body, Morgan; it was his sister, and the pathologist thinks she'd been there at least fifteen years give or take. Apparently, she was mummified because of the condition of the room, something to do with the air flow and the dry heat.'

'Were there any more?'

'No, but we haven't been able to locate his mother, so we're thinking that he might have killed her and hidden her body.'

Amy finished her donut. 'Sick or what? He's been taken to a secure psychiatric hospital to be evaluated.'

'I knew he'd killed them both. I'm pretty sure you'll find his mother's body somewhere. How's Macy?'

'She's doing great. She went to visit Charlie's mum and took her some flowers. She keeps asking about you. She wants to be a copper when she's old enough, just like Morgan.'

'Oh God.'

'Yep, you certainly made a lasting impression on her.' Amy laughed. 'Oh, and I have some good news for you: a certain journalist has left to go back to London. He was slapped with an injunction to stop him writing about any of this, and you, for the time being because it's an open investigation. Tom really enjoyed himself passing on the good news to him.'

'That's amazing, tell him thanks.'

'You can tell him yourself. He said he wants you back at work tomorrow; there's too much to do with all the mess you've caused. Ben, you're not allowed back until you won't scare innocent members of the public, and I kind of agree with him.'

'Cheers, Amy, you sure know how to flatter a guy.'

She winked at him. 'Right, well before we go I have some not so good news to pass on to you, Morgan.'

'What is it?'

'Gary Marks escaped from prison in the early hours of the morning. He was taken to hospital with suspected appendicitis and made a run for it.'

All the colour drained from her face. 'Have they caught him?'

'Not yet, but Tom said to tell you before you saw it on the news. It's okay, he won't come anywhere near here, not if he's got any sense. He must know that if anyone is going to find him and throw his sorry arse back inside it's going to be you. Anyway, we better get going, we only nipped in to check you were both okay. Are you both okay?'

They both nodded.

'Good, we'll see ourselves out.'

They left Morgan and Ben still drinking their coffee. Ben reached out and patted Morgan's hand.

'She's right, if he's made a great escape he's not going to ruin it all by coming back here.'

'I really hope so, Ben.'

Ben stood up and looked at his face in the small mirror on the wall. 'I suppose she's right; it is a mess.'

'I don't know, I think you look kind of handsome in a Frankenstein way.'

He laughed.

'I have just the thing to help with those bruises you know.'

'Really, what?'

'A face mask.'

Morgan laughed, dodging the tea towel he threw in her direction. This was all she needed: friends like Ben, Amy, Des and her job – it was the perfect combination.

A LETTER FROM HELEN

Dear reader,

I want to say a huge thank you for choosing to read *The Hiding Place*. If you did enjoy it and want to keep up to date with all my latest releases, just sign up at the following link. Your email address will never be shared and you can unsubscribe at any time.

www.bookouture.com/helen-phifer

I hope you loved *The Hiding Place* and if you did I would be very grateful if you could write a review. I'd love to hear what you think, and it makes such a difference helping new readers to discover one of my books for the first time.

I love hearing from my readers – you can get in touch on my Facebook page, through Twitter, Instagram or my website.

Thanks,
Helen Phifer xx

Helenphifer1

@helenphifer1

helenphifer

www.helenphifer.com

www.unleashyourcreativemagic.com

ACKNOWLEDGEMENTS

Thank you so much for taking Morgan Brookes into your heart and loving her adventures. Rydal Falls is indeed a real place, it's a beautiful waterfall a short walk away from Rydal Mount, which was the place that poet William Wordsworth called home. The Rydal Falls where Morgan Brookes and Ben Matthews live and work is a fictitious town, half the size of Kendal and Barrow. Many Cumbrians, especially Barrovians, will recognise street names and places which I beg, borrow and steal. I hope you don't mind, it's so much easier writing about the places that I know and have visited.

A huge thank you goes to my fabulous editor, Emily Gowers, she is amazing and such a dream to work with. Thank you, Emily, for taking the first drafts of my books with open arms and not flinging them straight back at me or throwing them in the bin. It takes a brave person to read a first draft of a book and not cry at the work ahead. Emily, in the words of Tina Turner, 'You're Simply the Best'.

The hugest of thanks goes to the amazing publicity team at Bookouture, who work above and beyond to get our books out there. I'm so privileged to work with Noelle Holten; thank you, Noelle, for always having my back on cover reveal and publication days when I seem to always end up at work, another rendition from Tina for you because you're also 'Simply the Best'. Huge thanks also to Kim Nash for taking such good care of her writers, and the lovely Sarah Hardy.

A huge debt of gratitude goes to the rest of the team at Bookouture, who make all of this a reality. So much work goes on behind the scenes to make a book sparkle and shine, from the hugely talented design team to the copy editors and proofreaders. I'm so thankful that I get to work with you all, it really is a dream come true. I'd also like to say a huge thank you to the team at Audio Factory who turn my stories into the audio books that you can listen to. A special thank you to Alison Campbell for always bringing my characters and stories to life. You're extremely talented not to mention fabulous.

Another special thank you goes to all the wonderful book bloggers and advance readers who are absolutely amazing. That you take the time to read my books and champion them makes my heart swell with gratitude. There are far too many of you to name, and I would hate to miss someone off because I have such a terrible memory (most days I don't remember what my kids are called). But please know that I thank each and every one of you from the bottom of my heart.

As always, a special thank you goes to my family for providing me with entertainment and lots of love. I'm amazed I find the time to write these books because you all keep me so busy. I love you all very much; keep being the wonderful, crazy, loving humans that you are.

Can I thank coffee? I feel as if I should because without it my brain wouldn't function. So, a special shoutout to the wonderful baristas who provide my brain fuel with such smiles on your faces and gentle words of encouragement.

Where would we be without friends? It doesn't bear thinking about. So, thank you to my wing gals Sam Thomas and Tina Sykes for always being there for our group chats on Messenger. Hopefully, it won't be long before we can get back to our weekly coffee shop staff meetings.

I'd also like to thank my writing friends who have seen me through thick and thin, answered my really stupid questions and supported me from day one. Jo Bartlett, Jessica Redland, Sharon

Booth, Jackie Ladbury, Rachel Thomas, Alex Weston, Deirdre Palmer, Helen J. Rolfe and Lynne Davies. Look how far we've come, ladies, from dreaming about being published writers to bestselling writers. We are proof that if you follow your dreams, never give up and keep on going you can achieve anything you want with a lot of hard work in between.

This last year has been incredibly tough for everyone. The world and our lives changed beyond our wildest dreams and fears but we've managed to hang on, there's light at the end of the tunnel and we're almost there. Keep smiling, keep taking care of yourself and each other, be kind to yourself and know that you are loved.

Love Helen xx

Printed in Great Britain
by Amazon